ETERNAL
WHITE

ISBN-13: 978-0-692-15810-4

ISBN-10: 0-692-15810-3

First printing edition 2018

To those we leave behind

ETERNAL WHITE

T. FURUYAMA

∞

SOME SAY WE are born with endless possibilities. Has anyone tried to count them? More than Graham's number? More than a googolplex? More than the number of atoms in our visible universe? A billion? A million?

Regardless of how many we started with, it does feel like life's possibilities dwindle as we age, doesn't it?

… 100, 99, 98, 97, …

$$49\,\frac{364}{365}$$

BY THE TIME I began college, the endless possibilities at birth had been replaced with a long list of things I could never be, like a professional ballplayer, an astronaut, a concert pianist, or the President of the United States. At the end of my freshman year, faced with the pressure to decide on a major, I picked mathematics. Aside from having some AP credits and fondness for it, I had no real reason or firm determination to become the best. My grades were average—not A-grade. Luckily, minoring in philosophy and religious studies kept my grade point average afloat, and I graduated *cum laude*. I struggled through basic linear algebra in my college sophomore year, while a young kid sitting next to me, who probably skipped high school entirely, solved all the problems like they were two plus three. I came to the conclusion that the brains of professional mathematicians are wired differently from the rest of us, and I wasn't going to make it as a professional mathematician. Yet, I found something surreal about math, like it was the gateway to the secrets of the world. Thinking about equations, like Euler's identity ($e^{i\pi} + 1 = 0$), 0.999999...

forever equals 1, or even the good o' Pythagorean theorem, gives me goosebumps. I figured if making a living as a math professor wasn't an option for me, at least I could help somebody else on the path to becoming one. I couldn't imagine teaching young ones their multiplication table year after year, so I became a high school math teacher.

A lot happened since then. Faye and I have two daughters Abigail and Nina, born a year apart. The universal law of time perception is inescapable—the happier we feel, the faster the time flies. The kids are seventeen and sixteen now, and the dizzying time compression now seems unfair. For years, I counted time by their birthdays, not my own, but the upcoming one felt a little different somehow.

50-50

WHEN YOU'RE TEN, birthdays are all about the presents—I suppose the same applies to some people in their twenties. At thirty, many think their prime is already past; some even jokingly count their age as the anniversary of their twenty-ninth birthday. At forty, the body starts to feel the toll of abuse from younger years. At fifty—well, that's a nice round number, isn't it? I know it's just because we happen to use the decimal number system, but still, there are fewer days ahead than behind. It's the time when people check to see if their life insurance is still in effect—what seemed like an unnecessary expense when they signed up now feels like a lifeline on a rock wall at the half-century mark.

Today, I was no longer forty-nine—I turned the big five-O. Like the jug of milk that just crossed the expiration date, the same but different.

I woke up without an alarm, as it was Saturday. Faye was already up, but her side of the bed still felt warm, and her pillows hadn't bounced back to their full height. I stared at the ceiling fan that hadn't been dusted off in over a year until the blurriness of my morning sight sharpened. I reached for a tablet on the nightstand, a weekend ritual of mine for a few years now, and lifted the cover off the screen. A frying pan banged on the stove in the kitchen. My girls were arguing over something. I cleared my throat and hoisted my head up against the headboard, stacking Faye's share of pillows behind my back. I tapped on a news icon on the screen, and the national news headlines populated. Nothing particularly interesting, just some actor whose face seemed familiar had died at the young age of twenty-five, exactly half my age. "Unknown cause of death," said the headline.

Drug overdose, what else? I flipped to the local news.

The top banner read, "Amber alert— eleven-year-old girl abducted from her home."

I opened up the article. It happened not too far from my home, five or so miles, maybe. *How sad*, I thought. That's when Faye and the girls came into the bedroom, singing *Happy Birthday*. They hopped on the bed and finished the song.

"Thanks, guys," I said as I held my hand over my mouth to hide my morning breath.

They kissed me on my cheeks anyway.

Oh, each of us feels like the happiest person on earth from time to time. I know it's a cliché, but it's a cliché for a reason. How could I not? A Saturday morning, lying in a warm bed, with sunshine bursting into the room through the gap in the curtains, and the three girls of my life giggling around me.

"How are you feeling today?" said Faye.

"I'm alright," I answered, not really thinking about the question.

"Your back?" Faye rubbed my back as I sat up straight. Abby readjusted the pillows before I leaned back down.

"It's not too bad." I cracked a smile.

My lower back had been bothering me quite a bit for the last couple of months—that's what I told Faye; actually, it had been closer to a year. I only went to the doctor when there was something wrong with me, like a cold that lasted two weeks, or a cough lasting over a month, but the backache had to be just an age thing. I know the point of a wellness check is just that—to make sure nothing's wrong. But I had grown to dislike going only to be told I was fine.

"Old man, you gotta take care of yourself," said Nina.

"Who are you calling old?" I reached over and tickled her off the bed.

My back hurt. *I am old.*

"Ok, Dad,"—she got up laughing—"your breakfast is ready, come and eat."

I slid into a pair of well-worn slippers, the kind that's fluffy when you buy them but becomes an unsightly tatty mess in a week or so. As soon as I got up, my head throbbed, so I stopped in the bathroom to take a couple of pills before joining them in the kitchen. I wasn't going to let a headache ruin my birthday.

"Wow, are you trying to kill me with this?" I said jokingly as I sat in front of a plate of sausage, bacon, hashed browns, and a neatly cut pile of toast with butter on the side.

"Oh no," said Faye, and then placed a pile of parsley on top of the sausage patties. A small plate of smiley-cut oranges was a nice addition to cut through the grease. She gave me her signature smile as she tucked her hair behind her ears. She looked as beautiful as the day we first met:

It was a year or two after I graduated from college. I was in a corner of the kitchen at a friend's house party. She came over to introduce herself—okay, she was getting her wine refilled, and I was in her way. She was gorgeous, and her laugh turned the heads of most men. She was way out of my league, and the thought of asking her out, let alone holding a conversation with her for more than a minute, didn't even cross my mind. But somehow, we ended up talking for hours until the last beer in the refrigerator was gone. It turned out we went to the same college and she was only one year junior to me, but our paths had never crossed. "Let's get together again," she said before she left, moving her hair behind her ear just like now. I was in shock, but I said *sure*. Six months later, I asked her to marry me. I never considered myself a lucky guy until she said *yes*.

As I reminisced the past, Abby poured me a cup of coffee in my favorite mug. It was the biggest in the house, a subconscious display of human greed perhaps. She placed the coffee on the right side of the plate and my tablet on the left. She knew just how I liked things.

"Thanks, guys. What service."

The tablet still showed the article about the abducted girl. I swiped to return to the front page in search of something less depressing.

"I thought we could all go see a movie today. What do you think, Dad?" Abby asked me.

My headache returned momentarily, so I moved my neck side to side, trying to hide my grimace. "We haven't done that in a while, that sounds good. As long as it's not a chick flick," I warned.

"Oh, come on. I know you want to see 'Jasmine Bloom,'" Nina said.

Coincidently, the movie title was under the dead actor on my tablet's screen.

"You mean Bruce Reese?" I said. "He just died, you know."

"What are you talking about?" said Nina.

I showed the news article to her. She couldn't believe it.

"It's my birthday. I want the most mindless, action, action, action."

The girls rolled their eyes, but I knew they didn't mind what I liked.

"You guys go and enjoy," said Faye, "I need to help my mom at her house."

"With what?" I asked.

"Oh, she needs some help…around the house."

I knew then; they were planning a surprise party. The girls were getting me out of the house for a few hours so she could get the house ready. This was not the first time, so I decided to play along.

"I'm driving today," said Nina, who had just gotten her driver's license. She dangled the keychain on the hook of her finger.

"I can't believe you already have the key. Do you sleep with that thing?" said Abby. "You're gonna get us all killed."

Nina stuck out her tongue at Abby. "You only got a year on me, sis. I parallel park better than you."

Not a single day has gone by that they didn't argue. I still remember when Nina was learning how to count. We were reading one of those "advanced" counting books that went beyond ten, which interestingly didn't have zero in them. It soon devolved into a contest of who can name the biggest number. Nina said a million because it was in the book, even though she didn't know how big that was. Then a million million, and million billion. When they got tired of saying random combinations of hundred, thousand, million, and billion, Abby said infinity—she didn't know it's not a number. Nina countered with infinity and one, and Abby infinity plus infinity. I told the girls that infinity plus anything is still infinity, and called the contest a tie before their imminent quarrel. Despite always being at each other's throat, they were best friends. I couldn't have asked for better kids.

My headache was gone by the time we left the house, which was a good thing as the drive to the theater was a bit unnerving. I don't think Nina's skills were that bad. It was just my perception as a father. I insisted on full stop, which even I don't do most of the time. I gave a lecture about not texting and eating behind the wheel. "Do as I say, not as I do" is a great parental tool against the generational downward spiral. We all use it, knowing it can bite us back.

Abby derided Nina for every little thing, like not signaling early enough or slamming on the brake too hard. Abby was not that much better, sometimes worse; but I kept my mouth shut. No reason to fuel the flame.

The tub of popcorn was half gone by the time the previews ended. I couldn't say the movie was great, but it was entertaining enough for two and a half hours, and I was in between my two girls. What more could I have asked for? We got out of the movie theater and stretched in the Pacific Northwest summer sun.

"Just a sec." Abby took out her phone and moved to a spot near the concrete steps, away from me.

Nina took hers out, too.

I always told them to refrain from using their phones when we were together, but I suspected that they were checking in with Faye to coordinate the surprise party. Their skills at being inconspicuous still needed work. I thought it would look strange if I didn't say anything, so I cleared my throat and gave Nina the *Dad* stare.

"Oh, and it's okay for Abby?" She pointed at her sister with her chin.

"Hey, Abby." A teenage boy approached her at the top of the stairs.

"Who's that?" I said to Nina.

"That's Robert. Abby's…friend from school."

"Friend, like *a boy*friend?"

"Ah, well…I don't know. You ask her."

He wore a ridiculous flat-brimmed baseball cap backward, talking to Abby with his arms spread wide as if he thought he was a hip-hop star. Abby glanced at me with the corner of her mouth raised and crossed her arms.

"This is Robert," she said as I approached them. "He's a friend from school."

"Nice to meet you, Mr. Byne." He reached out his hand.

"Nice to meet you, Robert." I shook his hand. "Nice boxers," I added.

He pulled up his jeans over the plaid boxers, but it was hopeless. As soon as he let go, the jeans dropped back down.

"Dad." Abby gave me a look with bulging eyes and pursed lips.

"I should get going," he said. "I just wanted to say *hi*. See you later, Abby" He gave a peace sign salute and went down the steps backward before scurrying into the parking lot.

This time, Abby got the *Dad* look.

"Ok, I went out with him. Like twice."

"Three times," said Nina.

"Shut up, Nina. The first one doesn't count."

"I don't care, Abby. Just no secrets." I put my arms around my girls and headed down the steps.

"You don't like him," Abby said.

"I just met him, exchanged a couple of words. I can't judge him on that. Plus, I was distracted by his pants." Okay, the first impression sucked. I didn't like him. But I didn't say that. "Does he know they sell this thing called a belt? It's been around for centuries."

"Ha, Ha, Dad."

"Maybe suspenders?" I said.

"Please stop," Abby said.

"Oh come on, suspenders with a rainbow strap? It'd pull all the colors from his boxers."

She didn't respond. She was almost eighteen, but her disgusted look was the same as when she was eight, and I loved it.

Nina suggested getting some coffee. I figured Faye needed more time, so I splurged on a tall latté, which for some odd reason meant the small size.

My headache was coming back, and I rubbed my temple.

"You okay, Dad?" said Abby.

"Oh, it's nothing." I checked the time and counted backward, and sure enough, it's been about five hours.

Abby dug out a travel size bottle of acetaminophen from her purse, rattled it, and put it in front of me. It was a little difficult to take pills with hot coffee, but I managed.

Since Nina drove to the theater, Abby drove us home. It's a habit of mine to make things equal for the girls. Thankfully, we zipped through most of the lights, keeping the drive, and Nina's running commentary, to a minimum. Abby did drive faster than she should have, and I had to tell her not to focus on finding a song she liked on the media control screen—another case of Do-as-I-say. Overall, I thought Nina drove better. But it was just a matter of time for Nina to catch up with Abby's recklessness.

Unlike my "surprise" fortieth birthday, there were no cars in front of our house this time around. *Nice touch.* I walked into the house, fully expecting to act surprised, but it was just Faye and her mom, Jane.

"I thought you were going to her house."

"She reminded me that it's your birthday today," said Jane.

"How was the movie?" Faye said.

"Oh, it was good… you know, guns and explosions. We got some coffee afterward," I said, trying not to act strange or seem disappointed that there was no surprise party.

"Great," said Faye and took a sip of whatever she had in her glass. As she went to set down the glass, she missed the coaster and spilled the rest of her drink all over the table.

"Shit. Hersh, can you grab me some paper towels from downstairs?"

I glanced over at the empty paper towel holder on the kitchen counter and answered, "Yep."

I went downstairs and flicked the switch to turn on the lights.

"Surprise!"

They got me. Everyone was there, friends, co-workers, and neighbors, all crammed in the basement.

I turned the lights off and pretended to head upstairs.

"Hershel!" they all yelled in amused disgust.

I laughed and turned the lights back on.

"Happy Birthday, Hersh," Faye said as she came down the stairs.

I asked her if she practiced spilling her drink. She smiled.

We all came up from the cramped basement and spread out upstairs and into our backyard. It was a gorgeous day filled with abundant sunshine, a little hot in the sun but perfect in the shade. It's hard to beat summer in the Northwest. Abby poured me a pint of my favorite IPA and Nina handed me a plate of chips, guacamole, and salsa.

I walked over to Duncan Drew, a good friend of almost twenty years in the neighborhood.

"Hey Hersh, welcome to the fifties," said Duncan. "You thought you were heading downhill when you turned forty. You got another thing coming, buddy."

"What are you talking about? It's been downhill since I turned twenty-five!" I replied, shaking his hand. "How was the doctor's visit yesterday?"

"Same as always, man. Drink less soda, lose weight," said Duncan, patting his gut and reaching for a buffalo wing.

With Duncan, being overweight was a bit of an understatement, and it came with a whole lot of health issues. I loved the guy. He had been the go-to guy for just about anything. We shared a love for beer, getting together almost every weekend for an after dinner drink to bitch about life and reset our lives for the next week.

"The doctor's right, you know?" I said to him, looking at the tubes running into his nostrils.

"Yeah, I know. I just joined the gym across from the Asian mart. My doc said maybe in a couple of months I can get rid of these if I worked at it." He adjusted his oxygen line.

"That's great, man. How about brewing a batch of stout when the tubes come out?"

"That sounds good," Duncan said, taking a small bite of the buffalo wing. "Hey, I see you all the time. Go around and you know, *talk* to others."

"Right." I tapped him on his shoulder and walked away.

I knew Duncan too well, and something didn't seem right. I looked back and saw him put the buffalo wing into a napkin and pick up a stick of celery. Only green I ever saw him eat was a Skittle.

Faye was in the other corner of the yard, welcoming Reverend Reed who came through the side gate. I avoided eye contact with him and found Jessica Dublin by the picnic table that Abby and Nina just covered with a checkered tablecloth.

"Hi, Jessica, how are you? Gosh, it's been a while, thanks for coming."

"Happy Birthday, Hershel," she said and gave me a hug.

Faye told me she ran into her a week prior. She told me Jessica still wasn't doing too well. "How've you been?" I asked her in a cheerful tone, taking another sip from my cup.

"Oh, you know." She paused. "I'm good." Her empty hand wandered around the table in search of something to grab.

"Keeping busy?" I asked. She lost her husband James about a year ago.

"Oh yeah." She waved her hands and put on a smile. "He left a mess in the garage. I'm hoping to park my car in there soon."

"That's great," I said and paused. I should've just left it at that, but words just rolled out. "I miss him, too. I wish he was here."

"Oh, Hershel, it's your birthday. Don't be so depressing." She tried to lighten up the mood. "Here, have another one." She reached into the cooler at the foot of the picnic table and handed me a beer.

I did miss James. He was one of the smartest guys I knew. He was a scientist, quite well respected, judging from his memorial service full of scientists from all over the world. He told me a gazillion times what he studied, something about how genes are regulated by proteins that bind DNA. But considering my understanding of proteins didn't go much beyond steaks and chickens and DNA was something a forensic expert talked about in a crime drama, there was no chance that I would ever fully appreciate what he did.

"He told me once that the taste of beer changes depending on how it's poured," I said.

"He was very particular about that," she said. "He always poured it slowly; he said he liked his bitter and full-flavored." She grabbed a beer for herself.

James was always right, and I liked my crisp, refreshing gulp of pilsner with a thick head on top.

"You pour it his way, and I'll pour mine fast."

We poured together and clanged the plastic cup.

"I'm gonna go talk to your kids now, enjoy," Jessica said with a smile, gently patting my arm.

I looked back and knew why she hurried away. Reverend Reed was heading my way.

"Thanks, Jessica," I said to her, rolling my eyes like James would've done. She waved as she walked away.

Faye's father passed away a couple of years after we got married. Reverend Reed had taken over the church after his father retired and offered a lot of comfort to Faye as she grieved the loss of her father. She became more devoted as time went by. She invited me to come to church a couple of times, but I never went. It's not that I was completely against religion. My father was an atheist, but my mother was a Catholic, and I went to church a handful of times. Then I went to college and learned how evolution and physics explain our world better than the story of Noah's ark and the firmament. But since my philosophy and religion classes said we couldn't disprove the existence of God, I just stayed agnostic—a cop-out position, I know, but it never gave me a problem.

"Hershel, it's good to see you," said the Reverend. He was always cheerful—a little over the top for my taste.

He looked sharp in his suit. A gold watch gleamed through the pressed white cuff of his sleeve.

"Hi, Reverend, I didn't expect you here. Thanks for coming."

"Faye invited me. Happy Birthday, I hear it's the big five-O."

"Thank you. How's the business nowadays?"

"The church is doing well," he said.

"That's great," I said chugging half of my beer.

"We're having a summer party next week. You should come."

"Hmm, that sounds great." I looked for Faye.

"Faye said she'll come," he added.

I nodded and looked around, hoping someone would come to rescue me. "So," I said, but I had nothing to say. I just hated the awkward silence.

He adjusted his collar and smiled.

"Ah, did you see the news? About the little girl?" I picked a topic. My brain went into overdrive, looking for anything to fill the silence, and that was what came out.

"You mean Isabel Remming? That is really terrible."

I didn't remember her name at the time, but I guessed we were talking about the same girl. "Have they found her?"

"No, I pray for her and her family," he said.

"I just saw the headline this morning. Do they know what happened?"

"She was abducted from her house when her mom went into the backyard. They think it's someone she knew or someone who lives close by. There are just too many of these senseless crimes these days."

I nodded. "Why do you think these things happen?" I regretted as soon as I said it.

The Reverend chuckled. "You mean why God...I get that a lot."

"Sorry, I'm not trying to mock you."

"Oh, no, no. It's my job to spread the teachings of God. Hershel, do you remember taking Abby and Nina to the doctor to get them vaccinated?"

"Oh, how time flies. Yeah, they both cried like hell. Sorry, Reverend." I was never sure why *hell* was a bad word.

"No worries," he said with a smile. "Do you think they understood your intention at the time? That you were making them suffer so that they'll stay healthier and have better lives?"

"Of course, not," I replied.

"I think it's a bit like that with these tragic events. We are all the children of God, and he knows what's best for us in the long run. Now, I don't pretend to know his grand plan, but a tragedy is nothing but a blink of an eye in the eternal life with God, just like the poke of the needle was to your kids lives."

He's good, I thought. I didn't quite buy it, but I played along. "That kind of makes sense...but I still don't get how anybody can do these things."

"God's not blind. Whoever did this will face his judgment," he replied.

Faye passed by, and I wasn't going to let her get away. "The Reverend tells me that you're going to his summer party next week?"

"Yeah, it'll be fun. You should come, Hersh."

"Maybe." I gulped the rest of my beer and glanced into the cooler full of red ales. "No pils," I said loud enough for him to hear. "Thanks for the enlightenment, Reverend." I was probably being a little rude for leaving, but I hurried away.

I made it across the backyard to another table. It didn't even have a tablecloth, but below it was a cooler with pilsners. I was looking for a bottle opener when Nina came toward me carrying a monitor.

"Coming through. Give me a hand, Dad."

"What's this for?" I grabbed one side of the monitor and helped her put it down on the table.

"You'll see," said Abby, carrying a laptop computer right behind Nina.

They hooked the two together, and a slideshow began on both screens. The guests started to gather around the monitors displaying both old and recent photos of me. There has not been a day in my life when I didn't see myself in the mirror, but I doubted that I was the man in a few of the pictures. *Did I really look like that?*

Then came a series of pictures from our wedding. One was taken right after the ceremony—a snapshot of Faye and me in the dressing room before walking out to the car. I remembered the conversation as I held her in my arms: I asked her why she stuck around talking to me at that party when we first met. She said that all the guys were trying to impress her with their fancy jobs and luxury vacation trips, but I was talking about π being a *transcendental* number. She didn't remember that exact word, but she remembered it was trans–something. She said she found the way I talked about numbers charming. She said, "I didn't care so much if π had random digits, but I thought I'd bake you a pie someday." When the photographer captured that moment, I said, "So it wasn't my fabulous looks that got you to marry me, but the numbers?" She kissed me and said, "I remember you talking about the Golden ratio or something, but all I thought was that you had a nice smile."

Faye hit the spacebar on the computer, and the slideshow paused. She took the beer out of my hand and set it on the table next to the monitor. She took off her shoes and posed like the picture, looking up at me. She was the one with a golden smile, and holding her felt unreal—just as I felt on our wedding day. And just like how imaginary numbers are as real as real numbers and the world is incomplete without them, she was still real, and we were complete. She gave me one big smooch.

"Okay, guys. That's enough." Abby hit the spacebar, and the slideshow continued.

Everyone laughed.

Next was a picture of the girls and me at the beach—it must've been when they were five and six. Even with my embarrassingly scrawny biceps, I could lift them both in my arms. I was planting my lips on Abby in the picture. I remembered that day; I wished for the moment to last forever, but it was gone in a flash—yet the memory still lives on.

"Thanks, girls," I said to them, hugging them close.

"Love you, Dad," they both said.

There must have been thirty or so people gathered around the screen, shifting their heads to see the pictures through the sun glare. It was a mix of joy and embarrassment, but I just turned fifty, so I embraced being uncomfortable. We all watched the slideshow until it began repeating.

"Let's do cake," Faye said. She went into the house and returned with a giant square cake.

"We had to bake a second cake to fit all the candles," Jane said with a smile.

"Remind me to bake you three cakes for your birthday." I returned the jab and gave her a hug.

The cake looked like it was made by a pastry chef, with perfectly piped shell borders and "Happy 50th Birthday, Hershel" written in stylish cursive letters. I did get a kick out of the candles, arranged in the shape of a walking cane.

It must've been after I had my second serving of cake—and maybe one too many drinks—that I felt dizzy. My lower back ached, with alternating sharp and heavy dull pains. I slammed the beer bottle on the edge of the picnic table, and the beer shot up like a geyser with bubbles spraying everywhere. I grabbed my lower back and collapsed on the spot. My shirt and pants were getting soaked, but I couldn't move. My head throbbed like never before.

Visiting the emergency room on a Saturday—on my birthday—was not what I had in mind when I woke up this morning. You know how you instantly feel better when you get to the doctor's office after days of being sick? Yeah, this visit was just like that. I walked into the reception area with a daughter on each arm, even though I could've walked fine by myself. By the time we signed in, I wasn't feeling that bad, which made me feel horrible for ruining my own party. The triple dose of ibuprofen began to kick in, and my headache was under control, so being stable meant hours of waiting. For a split second, I considered faking a convulsion or something, but a glance at the expression on Faye's face nipped that idea faster than I could snap my fingers. I took my phone out of my pocket, but Faye pointed to a sign that read: No Cell Phones.

"Hey, I'm ok now," I said to Faye.

"Just stay put." She stood up and walked to the receptionist.

The room was busy. Abby and Nina ended up offering their seats to a couple escorting a boy who fell from the top of a slide and broke his arm. The young man sitting across from me had his head against an armrest, his sleeve nasty from throw up. Behind him was an old man rocking back and forth with a woman next to him rubbing his shoulder trying to soothe him.

"She said they're swamped." Faye returned to my side.

"Let's just go. I'm really ok now."

She looked at Abby and Nina, standing with their backs against a wall, taking their phones in and out of their pockets.

"I'm going to get sick sitting here," I whispered in her ear.

The young man with the soiled shirt rushed to the trashcan at the end of the row of chairs and threw up.

I thought, *Happy Birthday to me.*

Faye rolled her eyes. "Let me call Dr. Beckman." She took her phone from her purse and headed outside. Nina followed her.

Abby took Faye's seat. "I think I'm going to get sick. What's mom doing?"

"Calling our family doctor."

"Are you okay, Dad? How's your headache?"

"I'm fine. Sorry to ruin the day. Did you have anything planned for tonight?"

"Nothing important. My girlfriends wanted to hang out."

"Really? Not a date with this Robert guy?"

"Dad!"

"Is he nice? Do you like him?"

She looked around, obviously looking for Faye to return and rescue her from talking to me about her boyfriend. "He's ok. I like him."

"He's the popular type, I bet."

"When are they going to see you?" She stood up and looked at the receptionist.

"Hey, Hersh." Faye returned. "Dr. Beckman said he's on call at the hospital and if no emergency comes up, he can see you tomorrow. Are you sure you'll be alright until tomorrow?"

"Yeah, I'll be fine. If not, I'll be wheeled back in here and be the first to be seen."

"You aren't funny." She started to slap my head and stopped—probably remembering I had a headache.

So we told the receptionist to take my name off the list and went home. Faye made me go to bed at eight o'clock. But it was late June in the Pacific Northwest, the sun was up past 9 o'clock, and that's not counting twilight. So I lay there quietly as the light leaked through the curtain. The clock advanced by only three or four minutes every time I glanced at it.

What's happening to me?

The ceiling fan remained stationary, but my mind pinballed between positive thoughts and the worst of the worst. But the exhaustion eventually took over me, and I didn't even hear Faye come to bed.

Schrödinger's Cat

THE NEXT DAY, Faye and I went to see Dr. Beckman. We spent forty-five minutes between a magazine rack and a fish tank, "reading" stuff like *Wine and Fine Dining*, *Golf Digest*, and *Cosmopolitan,* which were all seventy percent ads. I thought, *at least I'm not the fool who paid to read the advertisement.* But then I realized I was wearing a shirt with a Nike logo, shelling out extra for the privilege to walk around advertising for them. When I began flipping through the same magazines for the second time, a nurse came to take me to the exam room.

"Can she come with me?" I asked the nurse. I figured Faye would have a heart attack just waiting there.

"She should wait." She turned to Faye. "I can come get you after the physical exam."

"Thank you," said Faye. She returned to watching the pair of clownfish playing hide and seek around the treasure chest.

Maybe we are entertainment for the fish—a relief for their intolerable boredom.

The exam room looked the same as I remembered from

a checkup two or three years ago. There was the same small tear in the wallpaper near the sink, and the same old generic landscape poster in a faded frame.

I sat on the exam table with fresh paper rolled out, and the nurse took my temperature and blood pressure.

"Dr. Beckman will be right with you." She handed me the gown that opens in the back. "You can leave your underwear on," she said on her way out of the room.

The room was a little on the chilly side, and I didn't want to get undressed. The exam room always seemed to double as a second waiting room for at least ten minutes anyway. The gown felt too short, and I couldn't reach the top set of strings to close the back. I hoisted myself up on the exam table and tucked the gown under my thighs to avoid feeling like sitting on a public toilet with a wax paper cover. I looked back and forth between the clock and a magazine rack.

Dr. Beckman knocked on the door and came in seven minutes later.

"How are you, Mr. Byne?"

"Not great, that's why I'm here."

"Faye told me that you went to the emergency room yesterday. How's your head today?" He slathered hand sanitizer and worked it in between his fingers.

"You know how it goes, one look at a doctor, and I feel better."

"I know it felt silly to go to the emergency room, but it was the right thing to do. Better safe than sorry, right?" He felt around my neck in a choking position. He took a tongue depressor and told me to go *Aah*. "How are the kids?"

Why do doctors always ask me a question when I can't

talk? As soon as the flat wooden piece left my mouth, I said, "Fine."

"Pretty girls like yours. They must give you heartaches."

"Yeah, you got that right." I went along with the obligatory small talk.

Then he asked me whether there had been any changes in my family history, like whether anyone in my family had cancer and whatnots. I answered all those and then told him about the backache that I had for nearly a year.

"You really should have come sooner," he said.

I knew he was going to say that.

He had me lie on the exam table on my stomach and pressed here and there on my back. He hit a spot on my left side, and I told him that was where it hurt. I rolled back and looked at him. He had a thinking look, not a good sign when you get that from a doctor.

"What is it? My kidney?"

"Around there, but it's hard to say anything yet." He must have heard me sigh, he quickly added, "Don't overthink it. It's pretty common. It doesn't mean anything."

"Yeah, sure," I said.

"It doesn't matter what I say; you'll be anxious. I'll order an x-ray now. You'll just have to go downstairs for it. Go have lunch, and come back for the results."

"Today?"

"Unless you want to come back tomorrow. If things get hairy around here, I may have to reschedule you though."

I thanked the doctor. He was always nice to us.

"The nurse will come in and do a blood draw and collect a urine sample." He winked and left.

Of course, things got busy at the hospital. I got my

x-ray, but they rescheduled my appointment with Dr. Beckman for Tuesday. Forty-eight hours, when each hour felt like a whole day, was mental torture. We told the kids that it was probably nothing. I managed to keep a poker face, and they didn't ask any questions; maybe they didn't want to know, or maybe they were more interested in going out with their friends—probably the latter.

We went back to the hospital on Tuesday. Faye held my hand in the waiting room, rubbing her thigh with her other hand. She said she slept okay, but she had bags under her eyes. We were led into a larger exam room with a computer desk sitting in the corner. Dr. Beckman came in. After a short greeting, he sat at the desk and typed in his login and password.

"I looked at the x-rays this morning." He clicked the mouse several times to find my records. "If I can find it…"

We were hoping for *everything-looks-normal*, but that wasn't it. I took a deep breath and waited.

"Here it is." He pulled up an image that even an amateur would recognize as an X-ray image of a body. But I couldn't locate my kidneys on it. "Now don't get too worried just yet, but there is a small lump on your left kidney." He moved the cursor to a small white dot on the screen. Now I knew which blobs were my kidneys.

"Oh my god." Faye leaned into me with her hands over her face. Her body trembled against mine.

"We don't know anything yet," he said. "We need a biopsy to see if it's benign or not." He paused and brought up a spreadsheet on the computer screen. "These are the results of your blood work and urine test."

We scooted our chairs closer to see the screen. The

numbers didn't mean much to us, but the color-coding was obvious.

"There is blood in the urine, probably too small of an amount to notice in the toilet. But it's there."

Faye couldn't hold back the tears and grabbed a tissue.

"So it's cancer?" I said.

"Let's not jump to any conclusion. Benign tumors can cause blood in urine, too. You said you went to the emergency room because of a headache. Maybe we should get a brain MRI, just to be sure."

"You think it's spread?" I said.

"No, let's not jump the gun. I know it's hard, but at this point, we want to know as much as we can before making a diagnosis. We should get a better image of your kidney too."

"When can he get the scan?" said Faye.

"I have a friend in the imaging department, and I've already called to see if they have an opening. It's early, but he'll squeeze you in tomorrow if you can make it."

"We'll be there," Faye said before I could even think.

"Great. Let's set up a time to meet back here at the end of the day tomorrow. I should have the results by then."

"Thank you, Dr. Beckman," she said.

This was the start of my medical leave from teaching summer math classes.

It wasn't clear what the doctor thought the odds of my tumor being malignant were. I spent an hour that night looking for the answer on the Internet, but never got a clear number. In the absence of concrete probabilistic data, people often resort to saying *50-50*, even if the true value is 99 to 1. I too settled on 50-50, at least in part so I could sleep.

We arrived at the imaging center just as the door opened. Even though we were the first, we still had to wait. I read about MRI on my phone to distract myself from the anxiety. It apparently stands for magnetic resonance imaging. It was originally called nuclear magnetic resonance, but people feared the word *nuclear*, so they changed it. It is one of those things I usually laugh at, like how people panicked over the dihydrogen monoxide (water) hoax. But as I waited for an MRI scan, I understood how a small thing like the word *nuclear* could push some patients over the cliff. In fact, as I closed the MRI tab on my browser, another tab filled the screen; I lost my cool at the mere sight of the words "renal cancer" on its title bar. My body started to tremble, and my breathing got uneven. I didn't want to cry in front of Faye, so the bathroom became my only escape. Just as I closed the door, I started to hyperventilate. I rested my head against the mirror and cupped my hands over my mouth to restrict my oxygen intake. The sound of running water in the sink eventually calmed me. I tried my best to fix my face, but Faye knew—no amount of cold water could tame my puffy red eyes.

"You okay?" She rubbed my neckline with the back of her hand.

I answered *yes*, but I knew it wasn't convincing.

"Dr. Beckman said we don't know anything. It's just a test."

"I know." I gave my best effort to smile, and so did Faye. We held hands and didn't look at each other until a nurse came to escort me to the MRI machine.

This was my Schrödinger's cat moment. I had to know, but I didn't want to know. Just like looking at the cat inside the box collapses the quantum superposition in the famous thought experiment, this scan would reveal the cause of my headache.

The room was not inviting. She told me to lie down, but I just kept looking at the instrument. She hid her sigh with a smile when I finally lay down, and offered me a blanket.

The big circular scanner seemed very small when my head was inside of it. I'm not a claustrophobic, but it made me anxious, and I wanted to get out of it. Not to mention, it was loud.

Well, the box was opened, and the cat was dead. The MRI scan showed a small lump on my brain, which Dr. Beckman told us later that day could explain my headache and collapse. He insisted that he still didn't know if the tumors on my kidney and brain are benign or malignant until I got a biopsy.

I was barely digesting what he said. Faye held my hand the whole time, biting her lips so as not to cry. I nodded a lot, but I was more concerned about how we were going to pay for the treatment, than whether I was going to live. I held Faye's hand as if *I* was consoling her. By the end of the appointment, we had decided on doing a biopsy on my kidney first.

When doctors think you may have cancer, it's like you're on a conveyer belt. I was put through test after test. Take this, swallow that. Blood draws became so routine that my arm was sore from being poked. It was dizzying being pushed from one place to another. But it was good in a way, as it kept me away from thinking about the *what-ifs*. The kidney biopsy was easier than I expected, just local sedation and a poke with a large needle that burrowed down to the tumor— another cat in a box.

The hardest thing was thinking about how I should tell the girls if the results were bad. We told them that the doctor found *something* suspicious, but we avoided using words like *tumor*. When the girls pressed, we told them that Dr. Beckman found a white dot on my x-rays, but he said not to worry about it.

I was getting tired of trying to act cool by the time I got the dreaded call from Dr. Talman, the surgeon who did the biopsy. Faye had decided to work from home, saying she wasn't feeling the best. I think she knew the phone call was coming. She had her laptop open, but she wasn't doing much typing. It was probably business as usual for him, but there was a slight hesitation in his voice when he said *hello*. I knew then the second cat was dead too.

A rare form of kidney cancer, for Christ's sake. He didn't answer my question about whether the tumor on my brain and the one on kidney were related; instead, he told me to talk to an oncologist. He was nice, but I knew I wasn't his problem anymore. We made an appointment with Dr. Lamant. Did I know him? Of course not. It wasn't like I had the luxury to go through all the doctors in the country and pick the one I wanted. We went with Dr. Beckman's referral and moved down the flowchart: yes to kidney cancer, next up: has it spread?

It was hard, but we decided not to tell Abby and Nina about the biopsy result just yet. After the girls went to bed, we searched the Internet well past midnight. My brain went numb from trying to understand medical terms that I was reading for the first time. Clicking away at her laptop with a box of tissues by her side, Faye rubbed her eyes a lot. After hours of searching, the consensus was that if the two tumors were related, the prognosis was—short. We found all kind of shit, some who miraculously recovered and lots of other sob stories—completely unproductive hours of my life. All the half-digested information that swirled in my head made falling asleep impossible. After tossing and turning on the bed, I snuck out and downed two shots of whiskey. That helped.

Uncertainty Principle

TWO DEAD CATS, and now I was the one in Schröding-er's box.

We met Dr. Lamant, the oncologist. He said he was sorry about the news, but insisted on staying positive and taking things day by day. For five minutes or so, he made a lot of small talk. It felt like an eternity, to be honest.

Eventually, he typed his password into the computer to log in and pull up my records. "You do have a unilateral kidney tumor, but it is still small. Your kidney is still functioning well, which is good news. But as you heard from Dr. Talman, the pathologist found that the tumor is cancerous." He pulled out a printout from a manila envelope. He moved the mouse around and clicked on an image of my head.

"We can't be sure if the tumor on your brain is related to the one on your kidney."

"But you think it is," I said, afraid of his answer.

"I...I don't know. There's a possibility, but we need more tests."

More? Just dig it out, then we'll talk.

"The pathology report says the cellular morphology is consistent with the type that metastasizes." He paused. I knew then it was bad. He added, "In that case, your cancer is what we call stage IV. We should schedule a biopsy on the brain tumor."

Apparently, the prognosis is not on a one-to-ten scale. It's on a one-to-four, and mine was the worst. Stage V must mean dead. Dr. Lamant continued to talk about the disease. I only heard his every other word, maybe every third word. My mind was racing—our mortgage payment, morphine drips on my death bed, the picture of my girls at the beach, James' funeral, seeing my family gathered around my grave… I extrapolated his words to fill in the words I didn't hear in my background processes. It was not the most efficient use of my diseased brain, but my emotions were running amok. That was the best I could do.

"Hershel," he said my name slowly and made solid eye contact with me. He must have known that I wasn't really listening.

He continued on to discuss possible outcomes, from the best to the worst. He said the surgical removal of my kidney might not be a good option, considering it might have metastasized. He said radiation was an option. He thought the tumor on my brain should be removed because of where it was—even if it wasn't malignant, as it would probably cause issues if it got bigger. Faye responded as if I should be on the operating table in the next hour to get it removed, but it turned out he was just giving us his opinion. He said we needed to consult a neurosurgeon for proper assessment. When he got to the worst-case scenario of managing symptoms and hospice care, Faye just lost it. My lower eyelids were the levee that held back the flood. I thought I might lose my lower lip from biting it so hard. Faye asked about the odds, so he threw out some numbers with an optimistic look on his face: 80% success for this, 75% for that, and pretty good chance for something else. But I know how to multiply probabilities. The odds for a complete remission quickly dipped below fifty percent, which didn't sound that great to me—ignorance can be bliss indeed.

Ironically, knowing more about my condition seemed to make my future less certain, which made me think of Heisenberg's uncertainty principle. *Even the fabric of the universe was against me*, I thought.

I held Faye's hand over the armrest as I drove home. The first five minutes of our car ride was quiet. We both wanted to say something, but we didn't know how to say it right.

We came to a stop at a red light, and I finally said, "You know honey, I don't want hospice care."

"Of course, you'll beat this thing."

"No. I mean, if I can't beat it. You know, if…IF it becomes obvious that I can't beat it—"

"What do you mean?"

"We live in Washington. You know, doctor-assisted… you know, the dignity thing?" I wasn't ready to say some words.

"No. I can't… I can't let you go." She squeezed my hand tight and banged it on the armrest.

"Come on, Faye. I'm just talking about *ifs*."

"Are you gonna give up? Just like that?" She started raising her voice, so I had to pull over into a parking lot as soon as we crossed the intersection.

"What about the girls, Hersh? Abby and Nina, they need you."

"They don't need to see me shitting in my pants!" I realized I yelled way too loud, so I took a deep breath. "Faye, I love you. But you have to understand. I can't stand the thought of…you know."

"I don't mind."

"But I do."

She wept but calmed down.

"We don't have to decide now. I'll do my best to beat this thing." I handed her a tissue. "I was just talking about *what-if*. Okay?" I held her cheek with my hand, and she leaned her face into it.

To tell the truth, taking the doctor-assisted-suicide route wasn't my rational decision. It was more of a declaration of defiance against nature or God—a show of strength when I had none. I was scared shitless.

When we pulled into our driveway, neither of us wanted to get out of the car. There was no way to hide it from the girls any longer. When we opened the front door, Abby and Nina were at the top of the stairs. Faye was a mess, shoulders heaving from crying. She hugged the tissue box she had grabbed from the car, throwing the dirty ones randomly on the floor. They knew it wasn't good news. Somehow, I, the one with cancer, had to take on the consoling role. It was kind of good that way. I still had something to hold onto—being a husband and a father. Being tough. And strangely, it kept me from crumbling to the floor in front of my daughters. "It'll be okay," I said repeatedly as if I was trying to hypnotize everyone—myself included.

It took a little while for things to start calming down. Internally, I moved from denial to anger. I questioned everything I did in my fifty years: drinking, smoking at college parties, and eating one too many fast foods. Beating myself up for every little thing seemed pointless, but I did it anyway. Accepting that I was just unlucky was harder than it needed to be.

We look for the cause, the source of faults. My dad died of a heart attack, but maybe he would've died of cancer if it wasn't for that. Did I inherit bad genes? Who should I blame then? My father? My mother? Their parents? Or my ancestors before that? Was it the chemical in our foods or not eating enough antioxidants? But in the end, it was hard not to feel that the world had singled me out to be the bearer of misfortune for no reason. Was God ordering me to die? Was I the immunization shot for a better world? Maybe *He* deserved to be the target of my anger.

Over the next few days, I realized I was going through the five steps of grief—even though I skipped bargaining. It wasn't like I could trade stage IV cancer for stage II with a bottle of single malt whiskey as a sacred offering to God. My body was still doing okay. Beer still tasted good and eased my anxiety, so I had more than I should. Faye was worried about the impact on my kidney, but she didn't push too hard. I sat on the couch and watched TV. Actually, I did a lot of that.

Every channel was still covering the abduction of Isabel Remming, an adorable girl. She had been missing for a couple of weeks now.

"This just in, the police have identified a suspect," said an anchorman. "His name is Jon Nadson, a thirty-four-year-old white male. He has been missing from his apartment for at least a week. The police are on a massive manhunt, trying to locate the suspect."

The pleas from her parents were all over the news. Her mom held a prepared speech in one hand and a recent photo of Isabel in the other. The paper she was reading from was too crinkled to be of much use. The picture showed her daughter hugging a stuffed animal dog with an awkward "say-cheese" smile.

"Her name is Isabel Mae Remming. Everyone calls her Bella. She is four feet seven. Long, light brown hair, and hazel eyes. She was last seen wearing a blue shirt with flower beads, dark jeans, and pink tennis shoes." She paused to dab her eyes and nose. "She is full of light. She is a good student—always kind. She doesn't deserve this. We don't want…anything from you. We…just want our baby back. Please." She stuttered every other word with sobs.

Isabel's Dad took over, straightening out the paper he took from her hand. "We don't have a lot of money, but anything we have…it's yours. We just want our Bella back. Please." He crinkled the paper he just straightened. He took a moment before he spoke again. "Bella, if you are watching this…" He swallowed a lump in his throat. "We love you very much. Your little brother Nicky loves you. We… we…" He dug his fists into the podium. He probably had less than ten words to say, but he couldn't get any more words out. Someone had to escort him from the podium.

That moment was a turning point for me. In the tears Bella's family shed on the screen, I saw the tears of Faye, Abby, and Nina. I stared at the picture of Isabel Remming in the corner of the screen. "Hang in there, Bella," I said aloud.

My life isn't as bad as theirs. How can I mope and sit on the couch until my last day comes? I felt the sudden urge to make my days count. I got up and searched for things to do, things that would fulfill me even for a moment.

I went out to our backyard, where the lush greens of our garden invited me to step between a row of tomatoes and green beans. The tomatoes were starting to gain color; I rubbed my fingers on the immature fruit and caught a whiff of the distinct aroma of a tomato plant, the smell of summer. I harvested some green beans, which seemed to double in size in a matter of a day.

"How are the green beans?" Faye came home and joined me in the garden.

I showed her the strainer full of green beans that were still fuzzy to the touch. "Where have you been?"

She hesitated for a moment. "I was at church."

"With Reed?" I asked.

"Yes, Reverend Reed. I was talking to him…about… you know."

"Oh, you told him?" I wasn't irritated.

"He asked me if you've been baptized," she said.

"Come to think of it, I don't think I was. I don't think my dad was that into it," I replied, kneeling back down to collect the last few green beans for the day.

"He was a little concerned that, you know." She couldn't say it. She hadn't used the word *death* or *dying* since I was diagnosed.

"You mean I'm not going to make it to Heaven?" I said

with a smile, glancing back at her. She didn't look entertained, not even a bit.

"I think you should get baptized. The Reverend said he'd do it," she said.

"Oh, I don't know. I hadn't thought about it."

"Can you think about it? I...would feel better if you did." She tucked her hair behind her ear and tilted her head in a pleading look.

"I'll think about it."

Pascal's Wager

I FELT REASONABLY well, and I wanted to focus on something other than my health issues, so I went back to teaching.

I taught calculus for the summer. It's a subject that makes most adults proudly admit they are bad in math like a badge of honor, an intellectual equivalent of being a proud illiterate in my opinion. The kids who were taking my course weren't at the top of their class, and they were more interested in what they would do after class. But standing in front of this group of kids was a reminder of why I got into this job: if I could make one of them have an "Aha" moment and catch a small glimpse of the beauty in math, I would've succeeded in making the world just a little bit better. Insignificant? Maybe? But significantly better than none.

Today's class was about limits and infinity, and I started with a simple but counterintuitive example. "Ruby," I called on the most attentive one in the class, "which is bigger, 1 or 0.9999… forever?"

She answered, "One."

Jake, slouching in his chair, said, "It's probably the same."

I asked him why, and his answer was, "It's obviously 1, but it sounds like you are trying to trick us. That must mean the answer is *they-are-the-same*."

"Why does it seem obvious that 1 is bigger than 0.9999?" I drew dots in the air.

Ruby answered, "Because it's never going to get to one. It's always short of one by you know, zero point zero zero zero…"—she moved her hand to the right as she said each additional *zero*—"*one*. However small a difference there is, it's that much smaller than *one*."

"But it never ends," I replied. "You say it's zero point zero zero zero,"—I moved my hand like she did—"but you never get to the end of it. There is no *one* at the end."

"So they are the same?" said Ruby.

"I told you so," said Jake. "Why does this matter? In real life, they are close enough, and that's good enough. Am I right?"

"In some cases, yes," I told him. "But in many cases, things don't work out without the concept of infinity. For example, a perfect circle can't exist if π doesn't have infinite digits. Calculus works thanks to infinity, but it took mathematicians a very long time to accept it." I looked around the room and got the sense that I was losing their interest. Sometimes using an unrelated but wackier example was needed to get their attention back. What's the point of "teaching" if they don't listen? So I gave them a thought experiment.

"Do you think the universe is really really big, but finite, or do you think it's infinitely large?"

Half of the class raised their hands for finite, some for infinite, and some didn't participate. I assured them that no one knows for sure, but added as I looked to Jake, "*If it's infinite, then there are an infinite number of you somewhere in the universe, tapping his pencil on the desk, just like you are doing right now, Jake.*"

"Is this the multiverse thing?" said Jake.

"No, not necessarily. Inside, say a one-cubic-meter of space around Jake,"—I pretended to draw a box around him—"someone calculated that there are 10 to the 10 to the 70 possible quantum states of subatomic particles." I wrote on the board. "It's a huge number, but it's finite."

"So like 1 followed by seventy zeros," said Jake.

"No, ten to that number," I said. "10^{10^2} is 10 to the hundred, that means 1 followed by one hundred zeros, also known as a googol. $10^{10^{70}}$ is 1 followed by 10^{70} zeros." I wrote a bunch of zeros, ellipsis, then more zeros. "To put that number in perspective, imagine you are standing with a big sign that has the number *one* on it, and every atom that makes up the Earth assembles into a straight line behind you holding a sign with a *zero* printed on it. That number is only $10^{10^{50}}$."

I looked around the room, and many were engaged in actually trying to imagine the vast number. That put a smile on my face. "But since there is only"—I put an air-quote around the word *only*—"$10^{10^{70}}$ possible arrangements of quantum states inside one cubic meter of space, if the universe is infinite, things are going to repeat itself if you go out far enough. In fact, there has to be infinitely many Jakes."

"Wicked," said Jake.

"We already have one too many, dude," another student said to Jake.

Jake turned back and raised his middle finger behind his palm.

A chime ended the class, and they were quick to get out of their seats. I didn't get to cover the curriculum that I had planned for the day, but it was a good class. "What do I always say, guys?" I said.

As they packed their bags, they replied asynchronously, "Math can save your life." They always found it corny, but I loved their faces when they said it.

It was great to be in front of the class again, but when I came home, it was back to reality. No matter how much I tried, the negative thoughts over the worst-case scenario brewed in my head and flushed out everything else. Faye asked me how work was, and I said *great*. She cooked me a nice dinner and avoided *the conversation*, even though it was obvious she wanted to know if I had given more thought to being baptized.

I stayed up after everyone else had turned in for the night. With the movie left running on the television, I took out my laptop and searched for *baptism*, *agnostic*, *Heaven and Hell*, and whatnots. It's bad enough to be at the mercy of the search engine to dictate what I read, but having cancer-related sites and hospital popping up in the ad space was worse and creepy.

Would I start seeing advertisements for funeral homes? Discount caskets?

My surfing eventually led me to *Pascal's Wager*.

Pascal was a seventeenth-century mathematician, and

apparently, a Christian philosopher as well. His famous wager said: If you believe in God and he doesn't exist, you lose nothing. But if you don't believe in God and he does exist, then you go to Hell. So it's better to believe in God to be safe.

On the surface, it made sense, pretty straightforward. But a couple of search hits down was a link to "the fallacy of Pascal's Wager," so I clicked on it and read on.

The website had various explanations of the flaws in Pascal's argument, some easy to understand and others that were written with complicated mathematics or logic symbols. But after an hour or so, I got the gist of it. If God doesn't exist, it's a moot point. If God does exist, the chance of worshiping the correct one, out of the thousands of other gods, is slim. If God is benevolent, it doesn't matter what you believed; he'll let you in heaven anyway. So basically, believing is a waste of time and energy. If God is malevolent and you believed in the wrong one, then you are doomed as if you were a non-believer, maybe worse—who knows. Even if you picked the correct God but believed in him only to get into Heaven, the malevolent God would punish you for it. I have never read the Bible cover to cover, but Jesus sounded benevolent. The one from the Old Testament—definitely malevolent. *But aren't they the same? Father, Son, and the Holy Spirit? Do we need the Holy Spirit to break the tie?*

It was getting late, so I closed my computer. I sighed, squeezing out the last bit of air from my lungs. It's like buying a lottery ticket. The chance of winning is slim, but you can't shake the thought of winning.

And why can't we shake that feeling?

On my way to charge the computer on the desk, I peeked at Faye. She was sleeping on her side peacefully. *I may not have long to go. It is stage IV. Worst case, I have six months, maybe a year. It isn't about me anymore. It is about her and the girls.*

There was a row of picture frames on my desk, some new and some really old. In one simple black frame was a picture of my dog Lyla, tilting her head with a ball at her feet. It had been three years since she passed, but I still missed her. She was a happy dog, and her illness came quickly. In retrospect, maybe she was good at hiding her pain. I heard dogs do that by instinct. Faye didn't like it, but I used to sneak pieces of steak to her under the table. A wet pant leg was always a dead giveaway, and Faye would roll her eyes at me. Toward the end of Lyla's life, her appetite declined. The night before her last day, Lyla didn't want to eat the steak that I cooked just for her. We knew then it was time. I stayed up late, running my hands through her coat. We took her to the vet the next day to be euthanized. She was calm. She lay on a steel table with a catheter in her forearm. I got down on my knees, facing her nose to nose, and squeezed her paws for the last time. I didn't wish her to go to Heaven or anything like that. She was in pain, and it needed to end. Her tongue was hanging out, being drowsy from the sedation. As the vet delivered the last injection, I looked into her eyes until the sparkle of life extinguished behind the lens. I remembered thinking that was a good way to go. She didn't know that the death was coming. To her, it was another day with us, with one last sleep. Why do we wish anything different for ourselves? We are cursed by our ability to think of the day we die. Lyla never thought of having an all-she-can-eat steak buffet in Heaven or being sent to Hell for "accidentally" peeling off the wallpaper with her teeth when she was a puppy. For her, dying was unanticipated and came with a peaceful shot in the leg.

For me, the thought of dying would last many months, uncomforted by pain meds. And death would come with this baggage of uncertainty—*This-is-the-end* or *Welcome-to-the-afterlife*.

Who was the first human who became self-aware and contemplated his or her own death? How frightened was that person? Did he invent the idea of the afterlife? Or was it a gift from gods? Whatever the case, it must've happened a long time ago, and perhaps many times over, because the idea of afterlife pervades every culture we know. Lyla lived her life without the idea with genuine happiness.

But me?

What is this afterlife anyway? Is it really a world filled with happiness for all eternity? Maybe it's worse than life on Earth, and all the tragedies are preparing us for it. Or maybe there's nothing at all like atheists claim: no sound of laughter or sweet weep of a guitar, no aroma of spring flowers or winter citrus, no taste of a perfectly done steak with complimenting sip of burgundy wine that dries the palate, no warmth of sunshine on wind-chilled skin, or Faye's gentle touch on my aching shoulders.

I turned the lights off, and the afterglow of the light bulbs lingered in my eyes. I stood there until even that faded into total darkness. I tried to imagine nothingness, but my finger was still touching the light switch. I let go of it, and my hand fell to the side of my jeans. Darkness was not *nothing*—just a result of losing one sense—the world was still there. I heard a car go by. It was a small car. Even without sight, I knew it wasn't a truck or a stampeding elephant. Suddenly, I became aware of the lingering smell and taste of roasted garlic from dinner.

How are we to imagine nothingness when our consciousness is a culmination of our senses? And all of this would be gone—soon.

The primal fear of death, the refusal to face nonexistence, made me clench my hand into a fist. I let my nails dig into my skin until the pain convinced me that I was still there. In the darkness, the wall of the hallway offered a texture that was rougher than my recollection. The scent of air fresher from the bathroom slammed against the back of my skull, and the car's headlight that beamed through the shower curtain brought me back into the light. I got into bed and felt the warmth from Faye's body. I touched her hair and kissed her on the shoulder. I didn't want to wake her, but I wished she would kiss me back.

The next morning, Faye made waffles and bacon for all of us. No one said a single word after saying "Good morning" to each other. It had been like that for a while now. My cancer was on everyone's mind all the time, but no one wanted to cry anymore.

"I was thinking about what you said yesterday," I said to Faye, who was making the last waffle for herself.

"About what?" she said as she flipped the electric grill upside down.

"You know, Reverend Reed." I picked up a piece of bacon with my fingers. "Growing up, I didn't go to church like you guys, and you are right, I don't think I ever got baptized," I said as I chewed on the bacon. "I may be dying and —"

"Hersh," Faye interrupted, "Do you want another waffle or is one enough?"

I shook my head *no* to an extra waffle, regretting using the D word. "I was reading last night...I've not been a Christian, and I'm not sure if I should be one."

"You should, Dad," said Nina.

"I...if you were to...you know, we want you to rest in Heaven, Daddy," said Abby, shifting her jaw to resist tearing up.

"Abby, I didn't mean to...hey do you want my bacon?" I didn't know what else to say.

"What's the harm? A half an hour and you are set. Even if you are skeptical, you should just get it done," said Nina.

I didn't tell them about Pascal's Wager. "So you all think I should do it?"

"Yes, you should totally do it, Daddy," said Abby. She had a way of shifting her use of *Dad* and *Daddy* depending on how badly she wanted things.

After Abby and Nina left the house for the day, I insisted on cleaning up the kitchen. Faye had been doing too much around the house.

"To tell you the truth, I don't care one way or the other, but since all of you want me to do it, I'll do it. Call the Reverend."

"Thanks, Hersh." Faye gave me a long hug as the water ran in the kitchen sink. "But don't think even for a second we've given up. You'll beat this thing."

"Of course," I replied as I shut off the water. "But remember the thing we talked about in the car?" The question wasn't very specific, but she knew what I was talking about. She had been avoiding it ever since.

She let out a heavy sigh.

"I don't know what to do. I was thinking about Lyla last night and…"

"Oh, Hersh." She rubbed my shoulders and broke into tears. "I know you're scared," she said the words I didn't want to say. "You have to stay strong."

I tried, I really did. Not a day passed that I didn't search for miracle cures, the Amazonian medicine, and such. I held onto a glimmer of hope that I'd be miraculously cured, and end up on the news for beating the disease. But all hopes evaporated by the next morning, starting fresh with reality.

"If you get baptized, I'll think about it," Faye said and paused. "This isn't fair." She banged her head against my chest.

Faye already had everything planned. It was just a matter of me saying *yes*. We all got ready to go to the church early the next day, which happened to be a Sunday. I took out a pair of dress pants that I hadn't worn in years. I had to suck in my stomach a bit to button them. A belt wasn't necessary to hold my pants up, but I looked better with it, so I left it on. It took me five tries to put on a tie. Even though there was enough space between my neck and the collar to stick my fingers in, I still felt being choked. It probably wasn't the tie, but the thought of facing the Reverend, the man who would hand me the ticket to Heaven.

Reverend shook my hand. "Faye told me, I'm very sorry, Hershel. I pray for you. God willing, you will beat this thing."

If you think about it, that's a funny thing to say. Would God wish for some to live or die? God must already know the outcome, right? He is God. He isn't making stuff up as he goes, is he?

"Thank you," I said, "so where's the pool? It's hot out. I wouldn't mind a swim today."

"Dad!" Nina elbowed me.

The Reverend laughed and tapped my shoulder. "Not today, Hershel."

I figured he wasn't so fond of me, and he probably knew the feeling was mutual. I reminded myself that this baptism was for Faye and the girls. Perhaps naively, I always thought that baptism was just about getting dunked in water while a priest says this and that from the Bible. Well, apparently, being accepted into the church was not that simple. Although I was fully prepared to be wet that day, the first day was more of an orientation.

The Reverend began explaining the process, "Aside from an emergency, we don't baptize an adult until he has fulfilled the spiritual requirements, proving his commitment to Catholicism. After you pronounce your interest in joining the church, you will become a catechumen."

"A what-chumen?" I said, embarrassed for not knowing what that was.

"You'll be a student of the church," he said, "Faye will be your sponsor."

Faye nodded.

"What did you mean by 'aside from an emergency'?" I asked.

"We don't need to talk about that," the Reverend said.

But I insisted on knowing. He pulled me aside and

whispered to me that if someone is facing imminent death, baptism can be performed with a promise in earnest that he will commit to the Lord in Heaven.

That one hit me hard. If I was healthy and heard that, I wouldn't think much of it—kind of like buying life insurance when you are thirty—but the scenario wasn't so far-fetched for me anymore. *Things could go bad fast. What if the brain tumor caused me to have a stroke?*

"Reverend, I don't mean to cut in line, so to speak, but I may not have a lot of time left, and Faye wants me to do this." I regretted mentioning her name immediately after I said it.

"I understand that Hershel, but—"

"I meant *I* want this. Yes, Faye wants me to get baptized, but *I* also want this." There was a part of me that wanted to act tough—to try to convince myself that I didn't need this and that I'm doing this for a selfless reason—to appease my family. But faced with a fifty-fifty chance of life or death, I began to see the emotional side of Pascal's Wager a little more.

"If that's the case, you should begin your journey with us," the Reverend said.

We all stayed for Sunday service and made small talk with members of the church afterward. I already knew many of them through Faye, and they seemed to know why I was joining the church. Faye denied that she told them, and there was no reason to doubt her; it only takes one loudmouth to spread gossip—most attending the service probably came for the social aspects anyway. I was skeptical at first, but it did feel good to be there, out of the house. The people at the church were nice, but...

One guy said, "Nice to meet you. I heard, *um*, that your daughter is going to college in the fall."

That *um*—I knew he was going to say something about my cancer, but decided at the last second to say something else. I struggled to say anything back to him.

Duncan came over to greet me, saving me from the awkwardness. The guy must have felt the same way; he said *hi* to Duncan and then left.

"How've you been?" Duncan said, breathing heavy despite the oxygen tubes in his nostrils.

"Alright, considering… How are you doing?"

"Pretty crappy. I thought I was getting better, but the past couple of days, I can't walk half a block without stopping. Maybe the tube's clogged or something."

"Hey man, you need to go see the doctor. Tomorrow's Monday, you should go." I pounded on his back.

"Yeah, I know. So what are you going to do about Abby?" he asked.

"I don't know."

Entanglement

I WAS EXHAUSTED by the time we got back from the church. For the first time, having cancer felt real. There had been plenty of times when I was tired—I raised two kids. But this was different. It was like a nasty cold without the fever or stuffy nose; my joints ached, and the muscles all over my body felt sore. I popped three maximum strength ibuprofen in my mouth and planted myself on the couch in front of the TV, trying not to let everyone know that I was too tired to do anything else. Talking to Abby was on my mind, but I had to get some rest first. I turned on the TV only to hear about that Isabel Remming girl.

"...It's been three weeks since she disappeared. The authorities were losing hope until a few days ago when they identified the suspect. Now, the police are on a massive manhunt in the area, tracing the footsteps of Jon Nadson, a white male, age 34, who lived in the apartment a couple of blocks from Bella's house..."

I didn't know why this story captivated me. It could be as shallow a reason as the proximity of the crime to my neighborhood. Maybe it was because Bella reminded me of my daughters at that age. The night before, I even visited the social media site her parents set up to counterbalance the sensationalized news cycle with real stories of Bella, including pictures of her growing up, her bedroom, her art projects from school, and even a video of her playing the violin at a school concert. A picture of Bella with long straight hair and a pretty smile was on the TV screen now, with her name "Isabel Remming (11)" underneath. The image stayed with me even after it disappeared from the screen. I dozed off as the coverage continued.

When I awoke, the TV was still on, but a blanket had been put on me. Everyone knew turning off the TV would've woken me up. I tugged the blanket to my chin and took a deep breath.

"Hey, Dad. Are you alright?" said Abby, flopping on the couch next to me.

"Yeah, I'm alright," I replied, yawning.

"Do you want me to put a movie on or something?" she said, grabbing the remote.

"No," I said, reaching for her hand. "Abby, I want you to go to college this fall."

She told me a week ago that she wants to postpone college for a year to stay with me, but I didn't know what to say.

"It's just a year. I called the University, and they said it would be okay to defer for a year. I want to stay here with you." Her voice trembled on the last few words.

"What are you gonna do? All your friends will be gone."

"I already talked to my boss. He said that he'd hire me full time. I'll get a raise, too. It'll be for college, all of it. It'll be good, you know, with the medical bills and such."

"You don't have to worry about that, Abby."

"We are family, Dad."

When did she grow up? Her words should have made me happy, but the thought of being taken cared of didn't sit well with me. *I'm your father, and I take care of you.*

"Abby, you know I would like having you here, but it's not fair for you to waste a whole year."

"It's not a waste, Dad!" She slapped my leg, probably a bit harder than she intended.

I couldn't say a thing. I just bit my lower lip.

"I can't …I just…" Abby turned and sank her head into me.

I used the blanket to soak up the tear building in the corner of my eye in a futile effort to hide it from her. "Do you remember when you were, I don't know, maybe seven or eight? You wanted to be an astronaut and ran around all day to 'train'?"

"Yeah, I just wanted to be fit. Then you told me I had to learn a lot to be an astronaut—math, science, engineering."

"You wanted to go to college the next day," I said looking down at Abby's face on my chest.

"Okay, but I don't want to be an astronaut anymore."

"But ever since that day, I thought of dropping you off at a college dormitory somewhere. You need to get out there."

"But it can wait."

"I don't know, Abby. I could, you know, be gone in six months, then what?"

"It's just a year, Dad. And don't talk like that."

"What if I make it a past a year? Are you going to take two years off?"

"I don't know, Daddy." She sat up and looked into my eyes. "I just can't do it, okay?"

I didn't know what was best.

"We'll wait for the other biopsy." I squeezed her in my arm.

We sat on the couch, listening to another cycle of the news. Abby was usually on the go, especially with her new boyfriend. It was nice to sit with her for a change. She tucked her knees into the fetal position with her head on my belly. She was taller than me now, but cupping her shoulder with my hand made me feel like I had traveled ten years into the past.

The news anchors had nothing new on Bella's case, so they filled the time with one uninformative interview after another.

"Do you think she's still alive?" Abby asked.

"I don't know. If she was when the media started to cover her case non-stop, then maybe the guy is keeping her alive while trying to find a way out."

The news was now showing several pictures of Jon Nadson, who had a tattoo of chained stars on his neck. He had associated with people convicted of human trafficking in the past and police were investigating his current connections to them.

A media pundit speculated, "Because the Amber alert was issued within a day of her disappearance, Bella's face has been on all major networks. This coverage may deter any potential buyers because of the increased risk of being exposed. But on the flip side, it could mean bad news for her safety because he may simply get rid of her to cover his tracks."

"There are lots of bad and crazy people out there, you need to be careful," I told Abby.

"I know," she said. "I'm almost legally an adult, you know."

"So what time are you leaving tomorrow?" I said. She was going to one last summer party with her friends before some of them head out early to college.

"Zoe's picking me up at seven-thirty tomorrow morning to catch the ferry."

"Abby, I'm not stupid. I have a pretty good idea as to what you'll be doing at this party," I said lifting up one eyebrow.

"I'll behave, Dad. Don't worry."

"Look, I'm sure there will be alcohol there, but no hard drugs, I hope."

"Dad, it's not like that." She rose from my chest and sat up.

"Abby, I may not have a lot of time, and I want to make sure that you make good decisions. Not good all the time, but good ones when it counts."

"Dad, you are doing it again," she said with a whimper.

"Doing what?"

"You don't know what's gonna happen. There's surgery, chemotherapy, radiation, and… Lots of people get better these days. I don't want to think that way, okay?"

"Sorry, Abby, but I need to tell you things as they come. I was young too, you know, and I bet there will be booze there."

"Dad, it's not like that," she repeated.

"Abby." I gave her the *dad* look.

"Okay, I heard there'll be some beer," Abby said with caution in her voice.

"I can't say it's okay to drink. But there is one thing that will get me mad. Don't drive or get in a car with someone who had a drink. Never. You got that? No matter what," I told her.

She nodded.

"I mean it, Abby."

She tilted her head backward, rolling her eyes into her skull. "Okay, okay, I promise." She crossed her heart.

I had this urge to go on and on about life lessons, but I knew I couldn't possibly cover everything, let alone expect her to retain even a fraction of what I said. But I wanted this moment with Abby to last, so I wrapped my arm around her, and we continued to watch the news coverage.

Nina came home from the mall and sat next to me.

"Did you have fun? What were you shopping for?" I asked.

"Oh, just stuff," she said. There is very low information content when talking to a teenager.

"Who's coming to the sleepover tomorrow at Kelly's house?" I asked Nina.

"Just three or four girls, you know, Jacqueline, Gina, and maybe Lilith."

"No boys?" I said.

"No, Dad. Have you met Kelly's parents?" She put her fingers to her temple and pretended like a bomb went off. "There's no way boys would be allowed."

"Aren't you sneaking out in the middle of the night?" Abby said to Nina.

"Oh, shut up, Abigail. Where are you going tomorrow again? And who are you going to be with?" Nina tapped on her chin, pretending to recall something.

"Am I missing something?" I said.

"No, Dad, she's just being a butt wipe," Abby said.

"Girls, I'm not really against you spending time with, you know, boys. Just, um, use condoms, okay?"

Abby and Nina pulled away from me and yelled, "Dad," at the same time.

I grabbed their hands, not letting them walk away. They slapped my hands, begging me to let go. "It'll bind you for life. That's all I'm saying." That was awkward, and I knew it.

"Okay, that's enough," said Abby. As I let go, they both threw their hands in the air with pure disgust.

A little disrespectful? Yes. But, I deserved it.

The girls settled back down beside me, and Abby changed the channel on the TV. It went from same old news to a commercial that we had seen too many times. Luckily, Faye came home to rescue us from the uncomfortable air of silence.

"Oh Hershel, aren't you a happy camper sitting between your two cute girls?" Faye took her phone out of her pocket. "Stay still, let me take a picture."

A means one, but she always took at least three. Today, I didn't mind one bit.

"So I hear we are going to have the house all to ourselves tomorrow night," I said to Faye.

"Yep. I bought a rack of lamb and some nice wine for tomorrow," said Faye, winking.

"Oh, guys," Abby got up from the couch and left the living room, shaking her head.

"What?" Nina said, then realized what Abby figured out a second earlier. "Oh, gross." She stood up and walked away, too. Faye and I looked at each other and laughed.

Abby's friend Maya came early the next morning to pick her up. I waved her goodbye from the living room window as I sipped coffee from my favorite mug.

"Did Robert come get her already?" Nina said, yawning with bad morning hair.

"No, Maya did," I said. "I thought this was a girls' party?"

"Oh, yeah, that's right," said Nina. "I got confused with the one next week."

"There's another one next week?"

"It's summer, and we are busy girls." She winked jokingly.

Don't remind me.

"Oh, speaking of that, can I take the car today?" She rattled the keys that she had grabbed before asking.

"Sorry, but I need the car today. I have a blood draw this morning."

"Oh, it's fine, I'll call Gina." She put down the keys, got her phone from her back pocket and walked away.

My plan was to go into town to catch a movie after the blood draw. Faye decided to stay home to prepare the lamb dinner using the rosemary from our garden; the house was filled with the smell of chopped garlic when I left.

For a guy like me, who hardly ever drives into the city, driving through downtown was not pleasant. The traffic signs seemed awkwardly placed, and the intersections looked like they were designed as an afterthought. Bikers and pedestrians seemed to follow their own rules, and the traffic jams caused by uncoordinated traffic lights drove me insane.

I got stuck in a construction zone after the blood draw. My phone that was mounted on the dashboard updated the expected travel time to the theater—it looked like I was going to miss my show. The road had turned into a parking lot. Many drivers banged on their steering wheels, honked their horns, cursed through the windshield, or pointed their palms up in disbelief.

A reporter on the news radio I was listening to said the police had located Jon Nadson, the suspected kidnapper of Isabel Remming. I turned on a live video broadcast on my cell phone. I remembered recently telling Nina not to use her cell phone while driving.

But I'm an adult. I know when to turn it off, just until the traffic starts to move.

The live video stream showed an aerial view of a stand-off. A swarm of police cars surrounded an abandoned building with fully armed officers hiding behind their vehicles. Instantly, I had one eye glued to my phone on the dashboard and the other on traffic. Being on an uphill slope, I couldn't see what was going on at the intersection ahead—the big SUV with tinted windows in front of me did not help. But judging from how traffic moved, no more than two or three cars made it through each light.

I moved my car several feet forward and returned to the screen.

"...it appears that there is a negotiator on site." The reporter was probably less than a block away from the actual building. She had one hand on the microphone and the other pressed against the headset over her ear in an attempt to hear through the chaotic noise around her. "Wait, I'm learning that the police saw a girl at gunpoint through a window." She waved her hand in circles, obviously asking somebody to hand her something.

Holly shit, she's still alive.

The reporter was given a tablet and stopped speaking as she swiped at the screen. "Looks like…there's some activity at the front door."

The broadcast switched to the aerial view. The rusty door popped out of the abandoned building and hit the dusty soil.

"The suspect has kicked the door down. I can see the door on the ground."

Tough job saying what she sees.

"The suspect is screaming something… We can't hear what he's saying from here." The broadcast switched back to the reporter looking at her screen.

Come on. Go back to the aerial view.

"Can we get sound?" she said toward the camera.

The guy in the car behind me honked his horn loud and long and brought my attention back to traffic. I raised my hand to apologize, but said, "What the hell?" through the rearview mirror. There was only half a car space in front of me.

My right eye was back on the screen, which had returned to the aerial view.

The helicopter found the best angle of the doorway. The camera zoomed in. "We have sound from the scene," the reporter said. "Wait… He is holding a gun to her head, and she is crying. Oh my god. Oh my god."

"Just shoot him," I said to the small screen on the dashboard.

I got honked at again. This time it was my fault, two

car lengths in front of me. I made it over the hill, and could now see the intersection. *I get to cross the intersection with the next light.*

The broadcast constantly switched between the reporter and the view from the sky. I didn't need to see the reporter.

"The suspect fired his gun! No one is hurt, it appears to be a warning shot," the reporter said as the video from the chopper swayed a bit.

The light turned green, and the car in front of me began to move, but it yielded to another car making a left turn. I thought he was being too nice, so I honked in irritation. The guy flipped his middle finger at me and then crossed the intersection. The light turned yellow; there was not enough room for my car on the other side, so I stopped. I was over the crosswalk, but it was better than blocking the intersection. I got honked at again from behind. I raised my hand over the middle armrest. "Where am I gonna go, asshole."

The guy behind me was irritating, but I didn't want to get honked again. So I kept one eye on the light as I followed the news. There was another warning shot, and the helicopter shifted. I tapped my finger on the wheel until the aerial view returned to the previous position.

"The suspect is coming out with the girl," the reporter said.

The light turned green. I saw enough space across the intersection, so I stepped on the gas.

"The suspect is screaming. Oh my god, oh my god, he shot her. He shot her in the head!"

In the middle of the intersection, I saw a car approaching me from my left—fast. At the moment of impact, I squeezed the steering wheel hard. I felt my head move toward the door; my head bounced off the side airbag. I felt a crushing momentum in my gut. The phone on the dashboard was no longer there. I watched the view out the shattered windshield turn upside down. The sound was deafening, and the world was spinning.

Then I was gone.

Duality

PEOPLE SAY LIGHT flashes before your eyes when you take your last breath. It was bright alright. When my self-awareness returned, I found myself standing—not by the scene of the accident, not in a hospital—just in white light. The cuffs of my shirt were neatly pressed as if I dressed for a job interview. I took a step, then another, but without any sensation in my legs. A subtle swirl of white mist under my shoes was the only indication that I was moving. I spun around, looking for something other than white.

Where is this place? Why am I here? The car. The intersection.

I should've been in a panic, but there was certain calmness in the white mist—the exact opposite of being in a dark basement, which invokes the fear of walking into a spider web or a goblin grabbing my foot. It was clear this wasn't any place on Earth that I knew. Even a snowfield in Antarctica has more features; this place had no sky.

Am I dead? Is this where I think it is?

After a while, the never-ending expanse of white lights around me flickered; there were shades of red and blue.

Sirens blared, and my head throbbed. But in an instant, the whiteness and silence returned.

I kept moving, then suddenly I fell, like dropping from the top of a skyscraper in a dream; dark streaks appeared all around me. Then everything was black; I couldn't see a thing.

My body vibrated with the sound of rattling cart casters. My head throbbed. My abdomen felt like someone used me as a punching bag.

I heard Faye's voice, and maybe Reed's? Nina was calling to me in a panicked voice.

Faye screamed, "Where's Abby?"

My head throbbed harder with every heartbeat. I couldn't endure it any longer.

Then all the pain stopped, and I was back where I started: nothing but white before my eyes. The air was neither cold nor hot. I wasn't uncomfortable—or comfortable for that matter. I rubbed my left arm with my right hand. I could see my hand moving, but the sensation didn't register on my skin.

"Hello? Anybody here?" With nothing to bounce the sound, my voice vanished as soon as it left me. I was alone. In every direction, there was nothing but endless white light. "Faye," I shouted. There was no reply. I stopped and focused intensely on remembering what had happened:

I was in the middle of that intersection. I got hit. The car flipped over; there was intense pain. But now, the pain is gone… after a crash like that? What was I thinking? "Never use your phone when driving," I used to say. And there I was, watching a video of that poor little girl. Stupid. I could be having a nice lamb dinner right now. But now…where the hell am I?

Staring at the whiteness, I began to accept that I was

dead. This was not what I pictured of an afterlife. *Is this all there is? Eternal silence and loneliness?* It seemed no different from being in solitary confinement, except for the fact that there were no walls. Then the thought crossed my mind—*Maybe I'm in Hell; I've lost the wager.*

Sadness suddenly overwhelmed me when I realized I didn't get to say goodbye to my family. I had wondered what I'd say to them on my last day. Would I have said, "forget about me and move on?" Would I have left Abby and Nina a list of life lessons? Ever since my diagnosis, I had feared to die alone when my family was away, begging God for one last chance to hold their hands. My nightmare had come true, and there was no God to beg.

What are they going to do? How are Abby and Nina going to pay for college? Faye, I'm sorry. I looked behind me, hoping she would be there. It's been said there are no tears in Heaven—that people had cried all the tears in their mortal lives—but I cried. I had a fight that I promised my family. I had an ocean of tears ready to be shed over the misery of chemotherapy and the love for my family. I forfeited all of that by driving distracted.

"Where is this place? Why am I here?" I screamed. "Am I being punished? Am I in Hell?"

"No," a voice replied, but not from any particular direction. I looked all around but saw nothing.

"Just keep moving," the voice said.

Then the white became black again. The senselessness was replaced by pain and the silence by voices and a rhythmic beep that echoed my heartbeat. I could not move. I could not see. I had no voice. I could only hear.

"Hersh, I love you." Faye's voice whimpered. I felt my hand being squeezed.

"He'll make it, Faye. God will not do this to us… to take two of the best men——in a single day."

"—Mr. Drew — a nice man."

"—Reverend, please. Just in case."

The pain became overwhelming.

"He seems stable. Oh, wait——get the doctor!"

The rhythmic beeping in the background became erratic.

"Hersh! Hersh! Can you hear me?"

"—You need to get out. Now!"

The heart monitor flat-lined into a prolonged beep. The voices in the darkness faded, and so did the pain.

White light flashed and bleached the black around me.

"I can hear you. Where are you?" I spun around but didn't see Faye.

"Move along," the same omnidirectional voice said.

The white space around me was no longer completely silent. I was somehow being drawn in a single direction and moved without fatigue or a firm sense of time. Eventually, a brown dot appeared in the distance, which gained more definition as I neared. It was a solid mahogany desk, and behind it sat a man wearing a long white robe—the same color as the background.

Standing by the desk was a girl. She was looking down, holding a brown stuffed animal in one hand. She looked up and tilted her head toward me. It was Isabel Remming, the girl on the news. She wore a long sleeve shirt in a floral pattern with a small bow at the neckline. There was no blood on her, no indication that she had been shot in the head.

"Are you Isabel?" I asked her.

She nodded with tears in her eyes.

"Where are we? I want to go home," she said.

The robed man at the desk rose from the chair and smiled at her. "You can't, Isabel. You have left that world. You are with us now." He sat back down.

The man's face was pale enough to blend in with his robe. I wondered if he was an angel.

Isabel was shaking, looking over her shoulder every few seconds.

"You are with us now," the man said to her again. "That bad man can't hurt you anymore."

I reached my hand out to touch her. I couldn't feel her, but my hand stopped where it was supposed to stop, on top of her shoulder.

"Are you okay?" I asked.

She shook her head. "No. Where am I?"

I looked over at the robed man at the desk. "Where are we?"

He waved his hand, inviting me to come closer, his head still looking down at a book.

Unsure why, I grabbed Isabel's hand and took her with me.

"This is the Gate." He looked up as we got to the edge of the desk. "You have left the world of the living."

"You mean we're dead?" I examined myself, then Isabel.

"Yes," he replied. "Everybody asks me that when they get here."

"I'm dead? No, I can't be... I want to go home." She sank her face into her stuffed animal.

"Looks like she needs a minute," the man said.

"Is this Heaven? I just heard my wife back there." I pointed my finger in the direction from which I came, even though I wasn't sure where I was when I heard her voice.

"You seemed to have shuttled back and forth between the two worlds, but you seem to be stably with us now," the man replied calmly. "This isn't Heaven; this is the Gate that leads to it. Here, I check your records, and guide you to Heaven or Hell." He looked down at the large book on his desk and flipped page after page. No matter how many pages he turned from right to left, the stack of paper on the left didn't increase, and the stack on the right didn't decrease.

"Wait. What's going on here?" I placed my hands on the desk and leaned toward him.

He didn't answer and kept on flipping pages.

"What are you looking for?"

"Oh, here. Always the last page," he said even though the stack of paper on the right was still there. "Looks like you had an emergency baptism. You are cleared."

"An emergency baptism?" I said, "I was not baptized. I mean, I was going to be, but…"

"The record shows that after the car crash, you became unconscious and were taken to the hospital."

"How do you know that? Who are you?" I asked the man in the white robe.

"This is my job. I'm what you'd call an angel. When I entered heaven, I decided to serve our gods. Now, I perform various duties, including this one."

"Do you have a name?"

"When you decide to serve the gods, your name becomes irrelevant."

"Not everyone serves the gods in the afterlife?"

"Your questions will be answered when you reach upstairs."

"So you know who I am?" I said to him, in somewhat of a rude tone.

"Of course I do, Mr. Byne. Hershel Byne, age fifty, married to Faye Byne. Should I go on?" He glanced up at me.

"Wait, back up a bit." I shook my head. "When did I get baptized?"

"On the hospital bed. Your wife Faye brought...let's see. Oh yes, Reverend Reed baptized you." He traced the text in the book with his finger as he spoke.

I inched forward to take a peek.

"No,"—he put his hand in my face—"you do not have permission to see the events of the world of the living."

"Wait a minute, aren't we supposed to look after our family from Heaven?"

"You are not in Heaven, yet. This is the Gate. Speaking of which, I need to finish processing you," he said, turning the book to some random page. "Our record shows you had doubts."

"I wasn't raised religious. It's not that I was against it," I said. I was trying to leave my options open. "Do I go to Hell because I didn't believe in Him?"

"If you wish to live with the gods, you'll be allowed to ascend as long as you didn't commit an unforgivable deed." He looked at his book. "And it appears you are clean."

"So God is benevolent." I remembered the argument I read against Pascal's Wager.

"The gods are forgiving and kind. Well, most of them are."

"There's more than one?"

"You are with me because the record shows your last declaration was Catholicism. If you wish to change religious affiliation, you will have to visit a different desk to be processed. But I'd advise you not to pick a malevolent one."

The angel stood up and spread open his right arm, then his left. From the featureless white expanse of space appeared bright lights, evenly spaced on a straight line that stretched well beyond where I could see. Each bright spot multiplied into dots in the perpendicular direction. We were standing in the middle of a perfectly spaced Cartesian grid—an XY-plane. Then just like Star Trek teleportation sequence, desks and robed men appeared at each grid intersection.

"Do you see the man standing over there with a woman in a headdress?" He drew my attention to a row of desks twenty or so to my left. "There starts the other Abrahamic religions: Islam, Samaritanism, Judaism, et cetera."

"Wait, how does it work? Does each religion occupy a different dimension in some sort of parallel universe?"

"If that analogy helps you, yes."

"No," I said firmly. "I don't understand any of this. Is this place…"—I pointed at the white mist under my feet—"somewhere on Earth? Clouds in the sky? Or what?"

The angel wrapped his left hand over his right fist and sighed. "You will have eternity to learn the nature of this world, but I'll give you a different analogy that may tide you over until then. When you were alive and dreamt in your sleep, you were in some sense still a part of the same world, but in another sense not."

"One was real, and the other was not," I replied.

"But when you were dreaming, your mind couldn't tell the difference, could it?"

"You are saying I'm just dreaming right now."

"Like I said, it's just an analogy. Now imagine your dream world was connected to millions of other dream worlds."

What he said reminded me of scientists discussing the possibility that we lived in a computer simulation and nothing was *real*. I remembered trying to imagine an advanced alien civilization with giant computers, each running a simulation of a single individual—*The Sims* game among alien friends.

As I helplessly pondered, he pointed at the grid of desks and continued where he left off, "Beyond the Abrahamic religions are Hinduism, Buddhism, and many others. We are in the middle of a cluster that belongs to Christianity, including Protestants, Anglicans, and whatnots. Throughout history, there have been thousands of separate religious denominations under Christianity alone. Yours is the closest to the Roman Catholic faith. If you follow this row,"—he pointed to a long line of desks behind me—"you will find offshoots of this denomination." He sat back down at his desk. "We try to keep all denominations separate, but group them when they are close enough. It streamlines the processing."

"The processing," I repeated what he said.

"For some religion, it's more about reincarnation, being reborn as a flea or an elephant, which Catholics don't do. Some religions have stricter guidelines for being allowed to go to Heaven. For instance, blasphemy is still considered an unforgivable sin in Islam, and most of Jehovah's Witnesses aren't part of the 144 thousand. We also have to keep up with the changing rules; if we used the old Christian standards, most modern Christians would not make it upstairs, including you. If you insist, you can change your affiliation, but you'll be required to abide by their rules."

I shook my head. "So when...or if I get to Heaven, I can only see and talk to people of the same denomination?"

"Denomination affects the determination of admittance. Once accepted, people of different denominations can interact as long as they mutually agree to do so. Nowadays, Protestants and Catholics tend to get along well, even though they used to be more like the Shia and Sunni of your time."

"What if I choose not to..."

He looked up at me with a serious look. "Not to what?"

"Not to...have an affiliation." My words trailed off.

"Oh, atheism." He raised a corner of his mouth. "It *is* a choice."

"Is there a desk for that?" I looked around the never-ending grid of desks.

"No. Everything just ceases to exist.

"Ceases to exist," I repeated what he said. "Like solitary confinement in total darkness?"

"No. If you think you are in solitary confinement, then it's not *nothing*. If you think, then you still exist. It is not *nothing*."

"*Cogito ergo sum*. I think, therefore I am. René Descartes." I scanned the grid of desks around me, each one a point on a Cartesian coordinate, the mathematical invention typically credited to the same man.

Before the car crash, I had agreed to join the church. I told myself that it was for Faye and the kids. In truth, I was scared. No matter how certain you are in believing that there is no God, when you face the end, you pause.

I looked up, assuming that Heaven was above me. I imagined that a man like Christopher Hitchens wasn't there. At the gate, he probably asked for one more drink and a cigarette, and then told the angel to turn everything off. But maybe, he was curious enough to go up.

"Mr. Byne, you must choose," said the angel. "Eternal white of Heaven, or nothingness. Life everlasting or the end of it all."

I wasn't sure how the world filled with fuzzy white light could get blurrier, but it did. I didn't have to imagine the white—it was all around me. But nothingness? I remembered taking a cave tour when my girls were seven and eight. The guide warned us and then turned off all the lights. The afterimage of the light bulbs that hung on the cave walls lingered for a while, but then we were in complete darkness. But it wasn't nothing. Abby and Nina clung to my legs. I could feel their small hands through my jeans and their heads digging into my waist. Faye hugged me from behind, and I felt her breath on my ear as she said *Wow*.

The angel waited for my answer. He didn't care one or the other; he was just doing his job, logging in another soul to the system. To be honest, I didn't like God. With all the power He is supposed to possess, He cheated me out of years I could've had with my family. At that moment, surrounded by white lights, my heart remained in the dark cave where I felt my family around me.

"I want my Mom and Dad," Isabel tugged on my sleeve.

Faye, Abby, and Nina, all left my thoughts, and the white landscape filled my vision again.

"You will have the chance to see them when you reach Heaven, my child," the angel at the desk smiled at her.

"Isabel Remming, you go by Bella, correct? I'm still waiting for a couple more things on your record, but I'm certain you'll be cleared as well."

Bella clung to me, sandwiching her shabby dog on my leg.

"Everything will be fine when you get upstairs," he said to her.

"Do a lot of people turn down the offer?" I asked the angel.

"Some do. But the decision is yours and yours alone."

Eternity, the word whirled inside me. There were moments in my life that I genuinely wished to last forever, like that day at the beach with my kids or the time I held Faye under the star-studded night on our honeymoon. But when we wish for something to last forever, it is under the premise that it most certainly will not.

What will I do for eternity? Infinite seconds, infinite years?

I thought of that big number that I talked about in my math class: number of possible quantum states in one cubic meter space. Even bigger is a googolplex: $10^{10^{100}}$. One followed by ten billion billion billion billion billion billion billion billion billion billion zeros. What about a Googolplex of googolplexes? All still far smaller than infinity.

"I need more time."

"I understand that, Mr. Byne, but do you know how many come through here every minute?" He flipped the pages of the large book on the desk. "Approximately one hundred and fifty thousand die every day around the globe, so you do the math. You were, in fact, a math teacher, were you not?"

I scratched my head for a second and estimated the number to be about one hundred every minute.

"I want to go, Mr. Byne." Bella yanked on my arm again.

"Your decision will be final." The angel said to her.

She nodded. "My mom told me about Heaven. She told me it's a nice place. She said my Granny is up there watching us...well not *me* anymore. I'm going up."

"I want to see my wife and kids, too." I looked to Bella. She was tightly holding onto her stuffed animal. I smiled at her and patted her head gently. "I will go."

"Good. Now, Mr. Byne, how old would you like to look?"

I cocked my head, wondering what he meant.

He tapped on the desk, and a part of it popped up. He turned the raised wooden piece, revealing a mirror, and I saw my reflection in it.

"You get to pick your age," he said.

"Okay, twenty." The image in the mirror changed into my former scrawny self. I ran my fingers through my full set of hair. "Eleven." I shrunk in height. I had to stand on my tiptoes to catch a glimpse of myself. "Bella, I looked like this when I was your age," I said in a high pitch voice while looking up at her, as I was now shorter than she was. I sounded like the video recordings that Faye took of me on her phone, and I hated it.

Bella lifted the corners of her lips ever so slightly. That was the closest I had seen her come to a smile, but nowhere near those seen in the snapshots of her that were on the news.

I sensed she felt closer to me, so I grabbed her stuffed animal. "What's his name?"

"It's a she. Her name is Tessa."

I turned the dog's face to mine. "I'm Hershel, nice to meet you," I said in my annoying adolescent voice.

"She's just a stuffed animal, Mr. Byne."

"I'm sorry, Bella."

She took Tessa back from me. "It's okay."

She turned to the angel. "I want to be thirty."

"I'm sorry, you can only be as old as when you left the previous world. You have left your physical body now, so you no longer grow or age," he said.

"I'll be fifty," I said. The image in the mirror turned back to what I knew the best: the wrinkled face and the gray peppered-hair, which had receded about an inch. "Clean shaved, though." That was the look I liked best.

"Alright then. If you like, you can change your appearance when you get into Heaven, but this is your default look. You must go now." He tucked the long robe under his buttocks and sat back down on the chair. He twisted the mirror, and it retracted back into the desk.

A golden gate rose from the white mist-covered floor behind the desk. I took Bella's hand in mine, and we walked to it. The stairs behind the gate stretched as far as I could see, disappearing into a point in the sky.

"You can't take her with you," he said. "She needs to do this by herself. She needs to answer a couple of more questions anyway, so you go ahead. She can see you upstairs when she is ready."

She looked frightened. I preferred to stay with her, but it would've been a futile attempt with the guy who seemed to be a stickler for the rules.

"I'll see you upstairs, Bella."

She squished her dog into her chest and nodded.

The gate with its vertical gold bars swung open, and as soon as I stepped inside, it closed behind me. Step by step, I ascended with no fatigue. After a while, I glanced back down, but the golden gate was no longer visible. I looked up again, and a door appeared, almost within my grasp.

Unenlightened

I DIDN'T EVEN have to touch the door; it just opened. The view was no different from before—an endless expanse of white mist. I stepped through the doorway, and it closed slowly behind me and faded into the surrounding.

An eternity of this white shit?

I walked with no sense of an end—what is movement when nothing changes around us? Even in the darkness of space, turning my head would cause the position of the stars to shift. I turned, but nothing changed. I thought, *I'd rather see an endless road than an endless mist.* I remembered a straight road I once drove through the Arizona desert with my hands off the wheel in the moonlit night, and the white mist morphed into a freeway. Fresh yellow dashed centerline was drawn in, and tumbleweed moved across the road toward a cactus on the other side. The stars shined down on me from the clear dark sky with the moonlight on my back. It was beautiful, but somehow had the quality of a planetarium; it was not where I wanted to be. Then the night turned to day, the freeway shrunk in size and curved, and houses grew from the ground and lined the street. It was a summer day in my neighborhood. Everything was there, even the ugly old red Mustang with its collapsed axel sitting on my neighbor's lawn.

"Strange isn't it?" I heard a voice behind me.

I turned and gasped. "James?" It was my old friend James Dublin. "Is it really you? It's been…what a year since you passed?"

"Is that so? For some people, a thousand years feel like a flash in time, and for others, a split second feels like centuries."

"So this is Heaven." I scanned the virtual world of my neighborhood.

"I heard you were coming up," he said. "I think it's nice to have someone greet you when stepping through that door. My father greeted me when I first came here."

"You heard?"

"This is Heaven. Information flows if you let it."

"So you are my guide, so to speak?"

"Yeah, if that's what you want. I have nothing else to do anyway."

"Nothing to do?"

"Heaven is what you make of it. Look around you." He gestured a large circle with his hand.

The houses, street, cars, and trees—everything was gone. "Where did it all go?"

"You weren't thinking about them, so they disappeared. Just think of them again."

I did, and everything came back.

"You'll get used to it," said James.

I thought of Faye—really hard. I imagined her coming out to the devil's strip to wave me goodbye. When Abby and Nina were little, she'd carry one on each arm so the girls could wave to me as I drove away. Those were the days I wished the rear-view mirror had a magnifying capability.

"She isn't here, Hersh. And neither is Abby or Nina."

I didn't know how he knew what I was thinking, but he was right, the neighborhood remained empty except us.

"It doesn't work like that for people who are still alive. Sorry." He put his hand on me.

"So how does it work?"

He smiled. "I'm not 100% sure, but it seems like everyone who comes to Heaven has his or her own world, but the worlds can be connected to share the same space and time—like mine and yours are right now."

"Kind of like multiple simulated worlds?" I said. James and I had talked about the Simulation Hypothesis on the nature of reality after the movie *The Matrix* came out.

"Yeah, kind of like that. Faye doesn't have her world here yet, so no matter how hard you try, you won't find her."

"I thought you were an atheist, James. How did you end up here? "

"I grew up in a Christian family with baptism and all that. At the Gate, I had a decision to make, just like you did. Long story short, I ended up here."

"Sounds like you regret it."

"It doesn't matter whether I do or not. I'm here, Hersh, for eternity. You don't know what that means yet, but you will."

"I think I understand what eternity is, James. Infinite time." I said snidely.

"Knowing numbers and having good number sense are two different things, my friend. Do you remember the kid who broke into my neighbor's house looking for cash to buy drugs? He got life without parole because of a prior assault case."

"Yeah, I remember him."

James nodded. "And we said, 'Can you imagine spending sixty or seventy years behind bars?' I bet he stopped counting the days a long time ago. And that's just one lifetime. Imagine infinite years." He wagged his finger at me. "Being here for even a few months, you'll start to get a sense of how long that is."

"You aren't saying Heaven is like a prison, are you?"

"All I'm saying is just like you don't know what life-in-prison is like until you serve it, you don't understand eternity until you experience it yourself."

"I guess you are right. I don't think even mathematicians and physicists fully understand what infinity is. Feynman famously said, 'If you think you understand quantum mechanics, you don't understand quantum mechanics.' Infinity must be something like that."

He shrugged. "How's Jessica?" he said.

"She misses you. Wait, I thought you'd be watching her from up here."

"Well, I haven't had the nerve to go up a level to do that."

I cocked my head at his reply.

"There are many levels of Heaven. Some call them the Levels of Enlightenment. The first is this." James spread his arms, and the scenery changed into a serene meadow. "The base level. I call it the level for the unenlightened." He strolled down a crooked path, and I followed.

He pointed up with his finger. "Then there is the

second level, where you can view the living. Somewhere above that is the gods' realm. Some say it's infinitely far away. But since we are here for an infinite amount of time, doesn't that mean we all get there eventually?"

"Well, with two infinities… it depends on which one grows faster," I replied as a former math teacher.

"You know what I think?" He turned and shook his finger at me. "It's a ploy to break up eternity, so people don't go nuts. There has to be somewhere to get to, a goal of some sort, I think."

"So what happened to the promise of living with God?" I snipped flowers that grew in the meadow.

"You are much closer to him than before you died. The problem is that when people read the Bible, they assume too many things. Like many people believe the world was created in seven days and the Earth is only ten thousand years old when it's actually over four billion years old. Even theologians conceded that a day in *Genesis* may not be a literal day. Well, surprise! The Bible never said how quickly you would be with God when you reach Heaven. Relative to eternity, even a billion years is short—a mere flash in time. Anyway, I hear some make it to God, so maybe there is a way to circumvent infinity," said James.

"Maybe there is. One of my favorite mathematical results is about adding all positive integers, you know, 1 + 2 + 3, and so on." The Riemann zeta function was what I was thinking.

"I'd say that's infinity, but I bet it's something else."

"It turns out the answer is negative one-twelfth. The sum is infinite, of course, but there is a way to assign minus twelfth to the infinite series."

"Well, that makes no sense, but maybe there is a short-cut to upstairs," he said.

"There must've been millions of disappointed people who expected to meet God immediately upon arrival." I grinned. The scenery was pristine with a hint of mist, like looking through a soft diffusion filter. Every element was perfect: a beautiful meandering creek cutting through the carpet of grass, mountain ridges in the far distance accentuating the divide between the land and the sky, and the fruit trees, which were placed strategically like rocks in a Zen garden, did not have a single wilting flower or decaying leaves on the ground. It reminded me of a painting of the Garden of Eden.

"I've seen a few. But their former priests greeted them and told them that God is grander than anyone on Earth ever imagined. They were then persuaded to begin their pilgrimage to God."

I let go of the flowers I had picked, and they turned into sparkling powder and scattered over the field. I for one wasn't "dying" to see him—even though I did want to know why he cut my life so short.

"Why haven't you gone to see Jessica?"

He fidgeted a bit. "I have my reasons. This is Heaven after all, and we are free to choose. And I chose to wait. It won't be long, twenty or thirty years her time."

It wasn't clear to me what he was thinking. He didn't look happy or sad. On the one hand, he might want to see Jessica as soon as possible, but at the same time, he probably wished her a long happy life in the world of the living.

"James, how do I find the way up to the next level of enlightenment?"

"Hershel, you just got here. I say you should put that on hold and look around. Travel the world."

"Travel?"

"Yeah, the whole world is at your fingertips. You can kill a couple of years doing that."

"A couple of years? That's it?"

"Probably. You said I've only been gone for a year, and I feel like I'm halfway done seeing the world." He stopped on the path that cut through the patch of wildflowers. "Look, another door."

A door, just like the one I had come through, jutted out of the field, making the flowers sway. I thought it'd be Bella, but when the door swung open, it was Duncan. I had to take a second look, as he was quite a bit slimmer than when I saw him last. His hair was shorter and had no grays.

"Hey, look who's here," James strayed from the path, walking through the field to the door.

"James?" Duncan cocked his head. He looked in my direction. "Hershel?"

"Two old friends in one day. If you ask me, I wish God would spread out the joy," said James.

A loss in one world is a score in another.

"Where are we? What the hell is this place?" said Duncan as the door sank beneath the field.

"Good to see you again." James patted Duncan's shoulder.

"Shit, it's you." Duncan examined James' face as if he had just seen a ghost. "The guy down there said I was dead, but I didn't believe him. He let me change how I look. I look like I just got out of college. Is this really Heaven?"

Duncan looked around the flower field. "What are you guys doing here? I never liked nature, hated hiking."

"Oh, come on, Duncan. Not even with all the weight off of you?" said James.

Duncan ignored him and looked at me. "So you didn't take any age off?"

"Nah. You look good, Duncan. So much for making that batch of stout, huh?"

James wrapped his arms around us. "I was just telling Hershel we should travel the world. What do you think?"

Duncan asked about how things worked in Heaven, and we repeated our conversation to bring him up to speed. He was a bit jarred—a little more than I was when I came up. He kept looking around the meadow in disbelief, but eventually, he accepted that he had left the previous world.

"A trip around the world was number one on my bucket list," said Duncan.

"Where should we go, first?" I said.

"Anywhere," said James. "What about Iceland? The Philippines? Thailand? Or maybe the savannah to roam with lions?"

"How about India?" said Duncan. "I always wanted to go there."

I didn't have a problem with that, so I shrugged my shoulders in agreement. A moment later, the wildflowers disappeared, so did the creek that cut through the meadow and the mountain in the far distance. The scenery briefly turned to white and then morphed into an unpaved street in India, with outdoor markets and a roaming cow. Everything was exactly like I imagined it, except it was eerily quiet.

There were no merchants behind the vibrantly colored textiles that decorated the storefronts. The herb shop was empty, so was tailor shop. Fresh vegetables were piled high at a produce market, but no one was there to collect money. The few people who were on the street did not look at us or try to talk. I felt like I was walking through a virtual tour. A guy on a scooter zipped by, and I stepped aside to avoid being hit—not that I could've died again.

"It's like walking through a culture museum," said Duncan.

"I thought it would be busier. Where's everybody?" I added.

"Most in India are Hindu," said James.

"So?" said Duncan.

"Their beliefs are quite different, and many don't feel compelled to interact with us." James picked up a mango from a basket and bit into it. "At least that's what I heard."

"Why not?" asked Duncan.

"Some religious aspects don't mix well. For instance, do you think soldiers who fought each other to death in the Israeli/Palestinian conflict get along up here? Or a Christian killed by an Islamic extremist?"

"I guess not," said Duncan.

"But we see some of them," I said.

"It's sufferance. Kind of like you don't mind seeing tourists in your own town, but you won't go out of your way to talk to them," said James.

"And we are the tourists," said Duncan.

"It's better than complete refusal." James tossed the mango pit on the ground, and it disappeared. He continued down the street and told us a story.

"There was this girl I knew in college. Her name was Jennifer. She was so in love with a guy named Jackson and had been since high school. She used to write *J&J* every-where. But Jackson couldn't stand her. The funny thing was, he was in love with one of her best friends... I don't remember her name now... wait, Allison something."

"Are they in Heaven now?" said Duncan.

"Yeah, they were in a drunk driving accident during their junior year in college. One day, I thought of Jennifer and she thought of me, and we were connected. Her idea of happiness and Heaven was to be with Jackson. No surprise there. After all these years, she was still clinging to that idea. It's a shame. She was a pretty girl. She could've had anybody, just not Jackson."

"And the dude?" asked Duncan.

"She said Jackson didn't want anything to do with her, and they were separated. Even in Heaven, not everyone gets what they want."

"So good for Jackson, bad for Jennifer."

"I guess you could say that. I think Heaven is set up to optimize happiness and minimize misery. She said she was going to start her pilgrimage to join God and shed her past desires. But I think she still believes that she'll be with Jackson when she gets to God."

"The pilgrimage to God? The journey of infinite steps?" I said.

"I'm stuck here for eternity," said James. "Who knows, in a million years or so, maybe I will join the pilgrimage." He laughed.

We walked to the next big intersection, but instead of enjoying the sights of India, I was thinking about a family trip to New York City. Abby had just started walking, but Nina was still in a stroller. At first, Faye and I were so excited to watch Abby walking on her own, planting her face on one show window after another. But a couple of hours later, Abby was in a complete meltdown. We ended up squishing Abby in the stroller and carrying Nina. Faye and I had a big fight over not bringing the second stroller. We had our share of arguments, but they didn't usually last long—the kids were great at loosening the tension, like later that day when we bought hotdogs from a street vendor. As I ate mine with Nina sleeping in my arms, the ketchup and mustard squeezed out of the bun and dribbled onto my shirt. Abby handed me her bib, and we all laughed.

Duncan didn't seem to care about being in India anymore either, so the merchant street disappeared, and we were back in our neighborhood.

"James, you didn't answer my question earlier. How do I get to the next level of enlightenment? To see the world of the living?"

"I'll tell you—it's not for everyone." He paused with a look of concern. "But if you want to go, there is a requirement you must fulfill."

"What kind of requirement?" asked Duncan.

"It's sort of a warning, I think—to make sure that you really want to go through with it."

"What is it? What do I need to do?" I wanted to see my family and I didn't care what the process was.

"It's quite simple really. You need to find and talk to five people who have seen their loved ones through the window of Heaven."

"That's it? Have you talked to five people?" said Duncan.

"I talked with two. That was enough for me to decide not to do it."

He had a gentle smile on his face, but it was clear that he didn't want to talk about it.

"Then what? I mean, if I talk to five and decide to see the world of the living?" I asked him.

"I don't know. I haven't made it that far. But this is Heaven, so you probably just think of a place you want to see."

"Thanks, James." I turned to Duncan. "How about you?"

"I don't know. I just got here. I finally got that damn tube out of my nose, and look at me"—he slapped his gut a couple of times—"the weight loss I always wanted." He grinned. "I'm going to wait a little while. I have eternity, right?"

His tone was sarcastic, maybe even a little disheartened, but I gave him a nod.

"Good luck, Hersh." James patted me on the shoulder and turned his back. "Oh, your friend is coming up."

"My friend?" I had almost forgotten about Bella.

"I'm around. I'll see you later." The houses on the street and James faded into the white mist as he waved his hand goodbye.

"Good luck, Hershel." Duncan shook my hand and bid farewell. He walked in the opposite direction from James and the white mist engulfed him too.

I stood alone on the clouds that stretched into the horizon. The dark blue sky above shifted its hue to red, like the view of a sunrise from the window of an airplane. A hole appeared in the distance, and I was drawn to it. The lump of clouds around the hole morphed into a standard four-pane door with a gold knob. It swung open, and Bella stepped out, turning her head left and right, her Tessa dangling from one hand.

"Bella?" I called with an upper inflection, and as she looked in my direction, the space between us contracted.

"Mr. Byne, I'm happy to see you," she said. "I want to see my mom."

"I'm sure you do. But for that to happen, you have to talk to five people who have seen the world of the living."

"Why, Mr. Byne?"

"It's supposed to help you decide if you really want to see your family or not. At least, that's what I was told."

"Okay, let's do it together then," she said, pulling me forward, whatever forward meant for her.

The color of sunrise brightened to pure white, and then the cotton-like mist around us molded into the shapes of houses and fir trees. But before any of them gained the colors or textures of the suburban neighborhood, a light struck before us, and from it a voice intoned.

"You must go separate ways. Fulfill the requirement on your own terms." Then the light disappeared, and the suburban neighborhood finished materializing. I did not recognize the area at first, but soon realized it was Bella's neighborhood.

"I'm sorry, Bella. Would you like me to stay with you a while?"

"I'm fine, Mr. Byne. I want to see my family."

"Okay then. We'll meet again after talking to five people."

"It's a promise," she said and ran from me, disappearing around the corner house.

i

I STOOD IN Bella's neighborhood, wondering why James stopped with two. I was afraid of what I would discover. I stared at the corner house where she disappeared for a moment longer.

If that little girl can do it, so can I.

As soon as I clenched my fists, my body left the pavement as if there were rockets under my shoes. I flew through the neighborhood, then over the city. The buildings stretched behind me like I was going into hyper speed in a sci-fi movie. Straight ahead of me stood a brick building. I thought I was going to smash into it like a bug hitting the windshield, but somehow I didn't fear it. My body went through a glass window like passing through a hologram and came to an abrupt stop inside the building. The room wobbled back and forth for a few seconds as if the spacetime around me cushioned the rapid deceleration of my travel.

There was a man sitting in a leather chair in front of a fireplace. "Hello, Hershel. I'm Paul." He extended his hand and pointed at the second chair. "Please. Sit down."

"Thank you." Even though sitting was no more comfortable than standing, I sank into the leather seat. It just seemed appropriate. "How did you know my name?"

"I just do. So you want to see the world of the living?" he said, gazing at the flame. The fire lit his face. If I had to guess, he looked like he was in his late thirties.

"Yes. Well, I mean, I don't know. I was told that I had to talk to someone… Have you—"

"Yes, of course. That is why you are here with me. Don't ask me whether I would recommend it or not. All I offer is my story."

"I understand. Thank you for taking the time."

"Ha," he blurted with a laugh. "Time, I have plenty of that." He looked me straight in my eyes with his elbows on his knees.

"So how does this work?"

"You have two options. I can tell you my story, or just show you what I saw, like a simulation of my memory."

"If you don't mind, I'd like to see."

"I thought you would say that." He stood up. "Ready?"

I got back on my feet in a hurry; I had expected a bit more chitchat.

"Yes. Please."

He reached out his hands, and I grabbed them. He looked at me, and my mind got sucked into his eyes. All I saw was an enlarged version of his ocean blue eyes. His pupils widened, and I spiraled into the blackness of them. Like sliding through a dark wormhole, sparks of electricity popped around me. There was a bright light at the end of the tunnel, and it blanched my vision as I went through it. I came to a sudden stop like stepping off from a park slide. The brightness faded, and I found myself standing in a classroom next to Paul.

"What was that? Where are we?"

"Your first trip through somebody else's head? Don't worry. Nothing will hurt you. I promise."

The room was still. We walked down an aisle of the classroom, but no one moved. It was like moving through a still frame of a movie.

"My parents died when I was young, and they didn't leave me much. I put myself through community college. Look at me." He pointed to his younger self, whose pen had stopped at the end of a formula. I recognized it to be the quotient rule for taking the derivative of two functions. "I had so much ambition." He stared at his younger self for a little while. "I had a crappy job during the day and studied here at night. I was sleep deprived, but I ended up saving enough money to transfer to a four-year college."

Like ripping a page out of a picture book and crinkling it, the still frame of the classroom warped and shrunk around us, revealing another scene—this time a tree-lined college campus. We strolled by a water fountain, passing a couple of girls sunbathing on the lawn. I imagined Abby and Nina doing the same when they got to college, and the thought of never being able to visit them at their dormitory choked my thoughts. As Paul walked ahead of me, I kept glancing back at the girls in their bikini tops. If they were my daughters, I would have thrown a towel over them.

"After six and a half years of community college and university, while at one point working two jobs, I graduated."

We walked onto a football field where a large blue tent was set up over rows of white chairs. Fresh-faced graduates in black gowns sat uncomfortably through a speech made by the university president.

"I had a lot of debt, but with a college diploma in my hand, I pushed myself hard and built a business." The scene at graduation was torn before our eyes and replaced with an image of the inside of a large warehouse. Instead of rows of chairs, there were rows of shelves. In place of the podium, where the university president spoke just seconds ago, was a small yellow forklift.

"I took over this office supply chain, and in fifteen years, I was debt free. By my mid-forties, I had accumulated quite a fortune," he said as we walked past a motionless group of people discussing the business. One of them was Paul.

He opened the exit door, but it did not lead outside the warehouse. Instead, like opening a new book, it led to a gazebo in the middle of a pond, where a still figure of Paul in a black tuxedo held a woman in a white wedding gown for a photo shoot.

"I married Beth. Beautiful, isn't she?"

"Wait, this is not what you saw after you died."

"No, these are images of my fond memories. We'll get there, I promise." There was happiness on his face, reminiscing about his youthful life. "It was all good for a while."

"I sense a *but* coming."

He sneered. "After the honeymoon period, things started to get rocky. We tried to work it out, you know, going to marriage counseling. We ended up having a son, and our marriage lasted another couple of years. But then I realized she loved my money more than me. Not surprising in retrospect." He gripped the log fence that surrounded the pond. "We ended up divorcing, and I gave her quite a chunk of my fortune. She was happy, and for me, it was the price of having a trophy wife."

"What happened to your son?"

"I got full custody of Nate."

The brown log fence around the pond turned into a white picket fence, and the gazebo became a house. Paul was in a luxury sedan parked in the driveway and looked a little older than the one I was talking to—the age reversal effect of Heaven was a jarring experience. In the still image, Paul was handing his son, who looked to be about ten, a wad of cash.

"I gave him everything he wanted, something I didn't get from my parents. He had so many toys that every year we had to get rid of some to make room for the new ones. As my business grew, I had less time to spend with him, especially during his teenage years. I think I overcompensated for my absence by throwing money at him."

Snippets of Paul's memory flashed before us as if they were part of a flipbook, like having a pretzel with Nate at a baseball game, lounging on a boat watching Nate swim, and skiing in the Alps together.

"It's such an irony," said Paul. "All the time I spent working, yet these are the things I remember most now that I'm dead."

"When did you die?"

"I had a heart attack when I was sixty-five," he said in his younger look. "Nate was in college then. He did well academically, but he wasn't thrilled about studying. To him, it was something to do for four years. I wanted him to find some inspiration from being in a college. I loved him, and

I wanted the best for his future. You had two children." He looked up at me. "You must know what I mean," he said.

I nodded. I didn't know how he knew that, but I didn't want to interrupt; I just wanted to find out about the window to the world of the living.

"Yes, the window," he said as if he read my mind. "The downside of dying of a heart attack was not having time to plan anything. I didn't get to say *goodbye* to Nate, and I didn't leave any instructions to my employees who depended on me."

"I died in a car crash."

"Sucks, right? My work centered around watching and managing people. So, I just had to see. I talked to five people just like you are talking to me right now. To be honest, I don't remember what I heard—my answer was already *yes*. I went up to the second level of enlightenment and saw them. It's like you are right there, and everything moves in real time. But remember, no one sees you," he said. "You can walk through walls and move across town in an instant." The last still image before us vanished and we stood in the parking lot of a funeral home. "This is what I saw after my death."

He marched right through the cars and headed for the door. I wasn't ready for that, so I walked around them just like I would do if I were still alive. Inside, a little over a hundred people were seated. We approached the silver casket with gold molding and a bouquet of flowers on top.

"I never wore makeup in my entire life. I looked ridiculous."

The white powder they used probably filled in half

the depth of his wrinkles. I didn't want to see myself like that either.

He drew my attention to his ex-wife, who was making small talk with the visitors after they paid their respects to Paul. Nate was at her side, but made no eye contact and said nothing.

Everything looked so real that I almost forgot I was just in Paul's memory. Then someone walked right through me, the back of his head emerging between my eyes.

"Well, at least Beth shed a tear for me."

"Oh come on, I'm sure she misses you."

He snapped his finger, and we were in some law office.

"This was two days later."

Beth was sitting in front of a desk, and the man behind it must have been her lawyer. He said the standard things like, "I'm sorry for your loss" and "If there is anything I can do." Then he told her that he reviewed Paul's will and he was confident that she was still entitled to part of his retirement account, something about a legal loophole in his will.

"There it is." Paul pointed at her face. "Did you see that smirk on her face? Well, that's my ex-wife. I'll be fine if I never see her again."

"And your son?"

"He was crushed."

Paul's conscious transported us back to the funeral service. The scrawny young man next to his ex-wife never looked up.

"I wanted to give him a hug, but I couldn't. It was just an awful feeling. Everyone secretly wishes that people would mourn for you when you die, but there's no joy in actually seeing it. Believe me. If you decide to go see your family, skip your funeral. That's one piece of advice I'll give you."

I imagined Faye in the black dress she wore to James' funeral. The ones that Abby and Nina wore probably won't fit anymore. *Will they be angry with me? What will they say to me?* I have always hated seeing them cry. When Nina was thirteen or so, I accidentally hit her with a hammer when demolishing Lyla's doghouse. She immediately burst into tears, and I felt like throwing up. It was an accident, but it was my fault nonetheless. The car crash was my fault, and I was again making my girls cry. This time, I couldn't even tell them I was sorry.

"So this is it? This is all you saw in the world of the living?"

"Oh, no. I stuck around for a while, a long time afterward, in fact. I wanted to watch over Nate, the way I hadn't when I was alive." Paul turned his back to his casket and walked down the aisle. "Beth had a good lawyer, so she did end up getting some of my inheritance. But most went to Nate, as I wrote in my will." He walked out of the service hall and opened the door to the outside.

Light flashed, and we were back at Paul's house. The garage door opened and I could see a Lotus, fully loaded Jeep, and a big white SUV. Heavy bass boomed as Nate pulled up in a souped-up Honda Civic with neon lights under the car.

"Money and a college kid equal this," Paul said.

We followed him into the house, where music was rattling windows. Young people were everywhere. Empty beer cans littered every available surface. Nate lit up a joint and grabbed a beer from the refrigerator. Paul snapped his finger; the music stopped, and people froze in place. A bowl of chips that someone had knocked off the kitchen island was suspended in midair.

"Watching over someone is a cruel joke, you know." Paul got in the face of his son, drunk and stoned. "I wanted to slap him, but my hand couldn't even move a fly. With money, youth, and partying, managing the business I left for him became a second priority real fast. Eventually, he had to file for bankruptcy. I saw it all happen and there was nothing I could do."

"So you wish you hadn't seen the world of the living?"

He turned to me, and the people at the house party began to disappear one by one. So did the trash, the chinaware from the cabinet, the dining table, the couch in the living room, and even the rug under our feet.

"The last time I saw him was this."

Nate sat on the floor in the middle of the empty room. The only thing left was a TV that was bolted to the wall. The screen was black, reflecting Nate like a mirror.

"I'm sorry," I said to Paul.

"No. This was the best thing I saw." He walked around and stopped in front of Nate. "For the first time, I saw a spark of light in his eyes. I saw a will to make something of himself. A will to dig himself out of this mess. I believed he would be alright, and decided that this would be the last time I'd see him."

"You mean until he dies and joins you here?"

Paul nodded. "I should have just waited in the first place, then listened to his story in its entirety. Peeking at the world of the living is like having surgery without anesthesia and feeling every cut and stitch. It's much more pleasant to hear the doctor say afterward, 'Well, there were some complications, but you pulled through, and everything is fine now.' Don't you think?"

"I suppose you are right, but you could say that you've experienced his life. If he pulls himself up again, it'll be like a sweet victory after a crushing defeat."

"It's up to you to interpret my story. My job is done."

Nate disappeared from the room, and an area rug appeared with a coffee table on it. A lit fireplace replaced the black TV, and a couple of chairs materialized on either side of the table. It was the room where I first met Paul.

"You have four more to go if you so choose. Goodbye, Hershel." He sat in the chair and smiled at me one last time before dissolving into pixels before my eyes. The fireplace, the chairs, and the walls that housed Van Gogh's *Starry Night* and Monet's *Water Lilies,* and the floor under my feet all turned into clouds, and I fell through the vast white mist. I broke through the clouds and coasted over the city below as if I were Superman. It made me think of the first Superman movie, in which he flew around the Earth so fast that he reversed its rotation. For some baffling reason, the reversal of planetary rotation was equivalent to time reversal. It's possible that the film implied that flying faster than light speed caused the time to flow backward, but the Einstein's relativistic equation would actually give imaginary time rather than negative time ($\sqrt{1-(v^2/c^2)}$). Despite being nonsensical, I wished I had such power so that I could pick a different person as my first interview.

My wish wasn't granted.

i^2

A rambler came into focus, and I knew that was my next stop. In the blink of an eye, I found myself sitting across the dining table from a man. He picked up a mug and put it to his lips. After taking a sip, he looked at me.

"You know, Hershel. There was nothing like a fresh cup of coffee in the morning."

Everyone seems to know who I am.

"I have vivid memories of drinking coffee, like how the hot liquid ran down my throat, acidity on the tongue, and the smell…" He ran his nose over the rim of the mug a couple of times and rested it on the country style wooden table. "But now, I'm not sure if I'm really tasting it or imagining it." He pursed his lips. "It feels like a hollow experience. What about you? Do you smell it?"

To be honest, I wasn't paying attention to the aroma in the room, but as soon as he asked, I smelled it. It reminded me of my family sitting at the breakfast table. I could almost taste the bitterness, and I remembered how the sharp coffee breath lingered for hours.

"I'm here to —"

"Yes, I know. I'm Connor, and you came to hear my story." He returned his eyes to the mug.

"My last host knew my name, and why I was there. You do too, but how?"

He looked up and grimaced. "You'll figure it out."

How am I supposed to figure it out? I saw my old friends, teleported to India, flew through the clouds like Superman, but I still haven't got a clue as to what this place is. Is it an alternate dimension, just me gone nuts, or something different entirely?

He put the mug down and crossed his arms. "So what's it gonna be? You want me to just tell you? Or you wanna see?"

It didn't seem like he was going to answer any of my questions, so I just asked to see. He reached his hands across the table and grabbed my hands, and I was down the rabbit hole again.

We were in a gym, where a group of college kids was playing basketball.

"I was an idiot. A life wasted," he said. "I went to college, not because I thought it was a good idea or because I wanted to, but because my parents thought it was something I should do. I hope your daughters don't turn out like me."

"Lots of kids at this age are like that," I said but hoped Abby and Nina would get the most out of their college years.

"I didn't take anything seriously. Do you see the girl by the wall?"

A pretty redhead, wearing super short shorts, was waving at one of the guys on the court. I assumed it was young Connor.

"The only thing I accomplished in college was to get her pregnant. I was nineteen, and Shane was a year younger. Our parents didn't take the news so kindly, to say the least. I didn't know what I was supposed to do besides getting married." He shrugged. "I started working at a restaurant, but I couldn't juggle college and that, so I dropped out. She did, too."

"That's tough."

"She was a good wife, and a good mother to our son, Jacob. I had grown to love her, and we were happy."

We exited out of the gym into an apartment. I was getting used to sudden changes of scenery. A coffee table sat between a TV and a couch where young Connor slept with his legs hanging over one end. Jacob watched TV while sitting on the edge of the coffee table with a rattle in his mouth.

"We moved into this crappy apartment. The rent was cheap, but freaking cold in the winter and unbearable in the summer. When I turned twenty-one, I took a job at a bar because it paid better. Working nights and sleeping during the day, I didn't see Shane much or spend much time with Jacob."

The room reminded me of the first apartment I ever rented, where the blinds spared me the view of the dumpster. At the time, I was proud of having a place that I paid for on my own, but I was glad I didn't start a family there.

The scene changed to a large private room with lots of dining tables. Most had drinks in their hands. They seemed to be having a good time, many with tilt-head-backward laughs, but Connor looked serious. Jacob was crying, and Shane looked like she wanted to get out of there.

"Where are we?" I said

"My five-year high school reunion. I was the only one with a kid. That's my high school buddy David sitting with us. He had a startup business in Phoenix, and he asked me if I wanted to come work for him. I acted tough as shit, you know. I told him we were doing fine and said *no* to his offer. Of course, soon after that, I lost my bartending job, and I ended up having to get two part-time jobs. Both minimum wage jobs, just to make ends meet. As soon as Jacob started kindergarten, Shane got a job too. It was real hard sometimes, even to eat. But what did I expect, right? No degree, no skills."

"So what happened to you? I mean, how did you get here?"

"I told you. I was an idiot. I had one too many drinks one night, got in the car, then BAM"—he slapped his hands together—"and that was it. I crashed my car into a tree on my way home."

"That's how I got here," I said to him. "I mean not drunk, but a car accident."

He lifted a corner of his mouth. "I was all confused when I got to this place. I wanted to see my family. One guy I talked to… Jeff, I think that was his name, he advised not to see my own funeral, so I skipped that. I saw Shane and Jacob a little later."

We were now standing in the kitchen of a small house with Shane and Jacob sitting at the table. She held a coffee cup that had lost all of its steam, and Jacob was drawing circles in a bowl with his spoon instead of eating his soggy cereal.

"My son was thirteen when I died. Shane couldn't

afford the apartment anymore, so they moved into her mom's house."

Jacob got up and threw his spoon into the bowl, splashing milk all over the table.

"You need to clean this up," Shane said. But the boy ignored her and left the kitchen.

We followed Jacob upstairs and into his bedroom. He picked up the picture of him and Connor on the dresser. He stared at it, squeezing the edge of the frame.

"I hate you." He threw the picture at the wall.

No father should ever see that. I felt great guilt in making Connor relive that moment.

Jacob sobbed and went to the other side of the room to clean up the mess he had made. He picked the picture out of the shattered glass. Tears rolled down his cheek and wet the photograph until Connor's face became warped from the tears. He kneeled down on his knees, and the broken glass went through his jeans.

"Jacob, get up." His mom came up to his room after hearing the shattering sound. "Oh my god, you are bleeding."

"See? I'm not there anymore, but somehow I still managed to screw everything up," said Connor.

"You can't blame yourself for that?"

"Why not? I provided that environment. His failing is my fault. My son is in high school now and pretty messed up."

We were outside the front gate of Jacob's high school. He was the last to walk out the door. He lifted the shoulder straps of his backpack to his cheek and scurried along the concrete wall of the building as if to avoid being seen by the crowd of students who hung out by the bus pickup zone. Three blocks from the school, he walked along the chain-linked fence surrounding an abandoned playground. He stopped mid-stride when he saw a couple of boys ahead. He turned into the park where the grass was overgrown.

The boys followed and intercepted Jacob.

"Hey Jacob," one of them said. "Are those the only jeans you have?"

"They must be. It has the same fucking ketchup stain from yesterday," the second boy said.

"Leave me alone, alright," said Jacob. His greasy hair, which hadn't been cut in a long time, covered half of his face.

"We don't need to see this," I said to Connor, but he gritted his teeth and said nothing.

One of the boys pushed Jacob. "I'm just trying to be your friend, man."

The other spit on Jacob's pants. "Now, that should help you remember to wash your jeans. You're welcome."

Jacob pushed back at the spitter.

"Oh, you wanna fight?"

I remembered when Abby came home with a bruised cheek in first grade. Faye and I were in the midst of switching jobs, and we had to cut down on spending. All of the hand-me-downs from her cousins ran out, so one day she had to wear a stained dress, a bit like Jacob. She said some girl teased her about it at a recess, and they got into a fight. *What would I have done if I were there at that playground watching Abby get hit?*

"Stop," I screamed at the boys.

"There is nothing we can do, Hershel. Remember that."

The boy drove his fist into Jacob's abdomen. Jacob collapsed into the fetal position. The other boy kicked dirt in Jacob's face. The two punks laughed and left the scene.

"That's enough," I said to Connor and closed my eyes.

When I opened my eyes, we were back at the rambler. Connor was sitting at the table just like when I first met him. He rolled the bottom of his mug against the table in a circular motion.

Faye, how are you going to pay for everything? My life insurance…is it enough? The girls' college tuition? How are you going to pay for it now that I'm gone? Can the girls manage school and working to cover their tuitions? Will they drop out of college like Conner did?

"So much for watching over someone from Heaven, right?" said Conner.

"Do you still go back to see your family?"

He shook his head *no*. "When I did, all I thought about were *what ifs*. What if I stayed in college? What if I took the chance and moved to Phoenix to work for David's company? What if I…" The words trailed, and he shook his head in disgust. "All I get from watching them is a feeling of regret, just a constant reminder of my failures. I wished I could have punched those kids"—he made a fist and held it in front of his face—"but then what's the point, right? It wouldn't change the fact that I can't provide for my son." He swung his fist down at the table, but stopped right before hitting it; instead, with tears in his eyes, he just tapped his fist on the tabletop.

Watching the world of the living with no power to influence it. It's like watching a horror movie and screaming at the dumb girl for going back inside the slaughterhouse. There's nothing we can do, but we shout at them anyways.

"I wish there was a way to change their world," I said.

"I heard it's possible to change the world of the living if you go beyond the second level of enlightenment." He took another sip from his mug and began rolling its bottom on the table again.

"How?" I stopped his hand from playing with the mug.

He looked up at me. "Like I said, I heard about it. I don't know anything more. Besides, if it were easy, everyone would be doing it, right? What's the chance that a guy like me would succeed?"

"I hope everything works out for your family, Connor."

"The last time I went to see them, my son was in community college. Shane got a new job, and they eat less canned food these days. All I can do is to hope for the best and wait it out. I just close my eyes and clear my mind, and days pass without pain or grief. In fifty, sixty, or seventy years, maybe I'll see them again." He closed his eyes and took a long deep breath.

I crossed my arms and tilted my head back. The ceiling of the house cleared, and white clouds drifted overhead.

"This isn't what I imagined Heaven to be."

"No one really thinks about what Heaven will be like for more than a minute when they are alive. They never take it to its logical conclusion," he said with his eyes still closed. "Well, that's my story. You need to move along now."

The whiteness swept in, engulfing Connor in its blinding light.

Why did God let Connor watch his son like that? What will I see? Is this the warning that James was talking about?

Negative Positivity

"NO ONE SEEMS happy about it," I whispered to the clouds.

"For every one of us, there is a story, and there are so many souls here," a woman spoke from behind me. "I, for one, don't regret seeing the world of the living."

"You must be my third." I turned toward her voice.

"I'm Kristen. Nice to meet you, Hershel."

I stared at the stunning woman, whose long white dress with a hint of pink was accentuated by the soft diffused light of Heaven. She was the type of woman who would grace the cover of a beauty magazine: a model with a perpetual smile and flawless skin that everyone's eyes would be drawn to as they walk through a cashier line.

"So you are glad you saw it?"

"Not at first." She grabbed a chain out of thin air, and the chain grew downward to a porch swing that appeared behind her. She sat and gently rocked back and forth as the rest of a house materialized around us.

I perched on the short wall that wrapped around the porch of the craftsman-style house to listen to her story.

"I was traveling with my husband on a train when my time came. He was a math professor, and I was a psychologist, so we used to fly all over the world for conferences. To change things a bit, we thought we'd take a slow train trip across the country to celebrate our anniversary. We should have taken another flight."

"What happened?"

"Just a depressed teenager. He parked his car on the track, and our train hit it and derailed. My leg got crushed, and a pipe went through me—a broken handrail, I think it was. I lost so much blood so quickly; I didn't have the strength to move." She kept rocking the porch swing. "Ben pulled himself over to me and freed my leg. I remember looking at him…he was sweating and grunting. He touched my cheek with his bloody hand, and said, 'Stay with me.' I tried to keep my eyes open. I wanted to tell him that I loved him, but I drifted."

"I'm sorry."

She shook her head sideways, smiling. "It's all over now. The past is the past. But you can imagine why I had to see him." She paused momentarily and saw me nod.

"Come." She got off the porch swing and reached for my hand.

I felt a jolt as I looked into her eyes, and I knew I was in her memory already. She helped me get off the ledge, and we walked into the house.

"This was our house. It wasn't very big, but it served us well for forty years."

I looked at her youthful face again as she moved her hair out of her eyes.

"Right, you picked your younger self."

"Men age well. 'Distinguished,' some would say. But us women spend an awful amount of time putting on makeup to look older when we are young and devote even more time trying to look younger when we are old. The PC police would say, 'love yourself at any age,' but…"

"I knew someone who counted her age as an anniversary of her twenty-ninth birthday."

"Exactly." She cracked a flawless smile and spread her arms as if to say *look-at-me*.

"You didn't have children?"

"No. We worked, that was our life. By the time we thought about it…it just didn't seem right." She led me through the living room, the kitchen, and into the family room at the back of the house. A man was sitting in a wheelchair.

"That's Ben, five days after I died and the night before my funeral. The train crash had put him in a wheelchair. Our friend dropped him off at our house, and it took him ten minutes to wheel himself down the hallway into this room."

His eyes were red and swollen from crying. He moved slowly along a wall of pictures.

"This is a picture from our thirtieth-anniversary celebration." She pointed at the one in a white frame as Ben passed by in his wheelchair. "He took me on a fishing trip in the Caribbean."

Maybe I was supposed to be looking at the fish in their hands, but instead, I compared the image of Kristen in the photograph with the one standing in front of me—I thought she had aged well.

She moved behind Ben as he strained to turn the wheel.

"When I came to see him after I died, I just followed him around the house as he cried."

Ben stopped at a bookshelf and picked up a photo album.

"I sat next to him like this." She settled on the love seat next to his wheelchair and gazed at him as he flipped through the old album. "He didn't know I was watching him, of course. If he did, I would have told him to flip the pages a little slower. It's funny how vivid my memories were as I looked at those photos. That's from our trip to Italy." She pointed at one of the pictures on the page before he flipped it two seconds later.

After a while, Ben fetched another album from the bookshelf and rolled himself back near the love seat. The pictures in that album looked a lot older than those he had looked at earlier.

"We were sweethearts from high school, you know."

He clawed his fingers at the pictures as a teardrop fell on the page. He wiped it with his sleeve before turning the page.

"Oh, Ben." She tried to put her hand on him, but it went right through him.

"Did you go to your funeral?"

"I did."

The room spun around us. We now stood at the entrance to the funeral parlor, which had been decorated by rows of flowers sent by people he knew all around the world.

"For your sake, I'll relive this once more." She said as she led me to her funeral service.

"If it pains you, we don't need to do this."

"It'll help you make your decision." She led me down

the main aisle. She stopped by a couple. "This is Kathy and her husband, Michael. She was a colleague of mine."

Kathy was holding her husband's hand. "It's still hard to believe she is gone. I just had lunch with her a couple of weeks ago," she said.

"Oh, you mean the lunch when she told you that your grant proposal was subpar? You seemed pretty upset about that."

"Well, she hadn't gotten a grant herself for a couple of years," whispered Kathy. "I didn't take her comments too seriously."

"She got the job because of her husband, right?" said Michael.

"Come on, Michael. She was nice."

"Hey, your words, not mine."

"It's not great to hear people talk about you, is it?" said Kristen as she turned to me.

"Are you mad at Kathy?"

"No. I've said things about her in the past—not to her face, of course. It's not her fault that I was listening."

She walked to the front row where Ben was doing his best to smile as some friends told an old story about Kristen, something about her falling into a pool.

"Not that story again. Sorry, Ben." She smiled at him.

She had a longing look as she watched Ben. She was reliving the moment for me, but she looked like she was witnessing the whole thing for the first time. She reached her hand to Ben's face, trying to hold it without going through his cheek.

"You said you were happy to see the world of the living," I said to her, "I thought this would be a happier story."

"It's all relative, Hershel. Death comes to everyone, and a funeral is not a happy occasion. The trick is to accept it for what it is."

"So, what happened next?"

She turned to me, and the service hall changed back to the family room of her house. She led the way up the stairs, where a custom-made wheelchair lift had been installed. She gestured me into a bedroom where Ben slept with a nightlight on. On the nightstand next to his side of the bed were an alarm clock and a four-picture collage of him and her together, with her necklace hanging from one corner. On the table on the other side was a picture of Kristen and a fluted vase with a single red rose.

"Every day since I died, he bought flowers to put in this vase. When he found a picture of us having a picnic, he bought two daisies. When he remembered the summer we cleaned up our backyard, he plucked morning glory. Today he chose a rose because it was the anniversary of our first date. Every night before going to bed, he took that picture of me in his hands and told me he loved me. I never knew he had such a sentimental side. Hearing his voice was worth it for me. I promised him that I'd watch over him."

"But you are with me. You don't watch over him anymore?"

"He found out he had colon cancer. It was pretty advanced. I was angry about my death, but in a way, I was lucky that I died before he did."

The neatly kept room changed into a cluttered one, and sunlight poured in from the window. Ben lay in bed, smacking his lips like he had dry mouth. A home nurse came in and lifted a corner of his comforter to check his diaper.

I cringed at the sight.

"The doctor gave him a thirty percent chance of making it a year. He chose hospice care over chemotherapy. I wished he had fought, but…"

"You watched him die?"

"Yes. I made a promise to watch over him. If I had stopped, then it would have been a lie." She paused and scowled. "People came to say *hello*, putting on a smile, then left with sadness, more like pity really. It took a long time for him to die—well, a lot longer than he had hoped. It's ironic. When you find out you might die, you do everything to stay alive, pray to God even. But when all hope's gone and you wish for a quick death, God doesn't grant you that either. I told him I loved him the whole time I stayed by his side, but he didn't hear me. All he heard was the ticking of his wristwatch, which only served to tell him the time of his meals, spoonful of mashed up food. He cried every time the nurse had to change him. In the end, he basically starved himself. I knew what he was thinking: nothing in, nothing out. It was hard to watch, but a promise is a promise. Not that it changed anything. I was relieved and happy when he finally took his last breath."

That's how I was supposed to go—dignity taken away with each bite of puree and every change of soiled pads. Maybe I got lucky with the crash.

"Where is he now?" I asked.

"He is here, in Heaven. Before I came to talk to you, he said he was going fishing."

"So you would recommend seeing the world of the living, then?"

"It's not my job to say. All I can tell you is my story."

I looked up at her, trying to sense a genuine expression, but behind her beauty lay an empty stare. "Right, just your story." I sighed.

We fell through the floor of the bedroom and found ourselves back on the porch. She sat down on the swing and began to rock. I felt a great sadness as I recalled the look on her husband's face as he lay on the bed.

"Death is sad, but that's not why you are here with me, Hershel."

I concluded that seeing the world of the living was an overall positive experience for Kristen. I thought of James only talking to two people. Maybe if he had talked to another, he would have changed his mind. Besides, Kristen was my third and I was already more than halfway to my five. Concorde Fallacy? Probably.

"My time with you is up," said Kristen. "Good luck, Hershel." She gave one more kick to get the porch swing moving and then rocked with her head down. With each oscillation, Kristen and her house faded into the white clouds.

Two more to go.

Paradise

THE WHITE CLOUDS turned into white walls and trapped me inside a small room. There was an examination table in the middle of a small room, a round stool next to it, and a sphygmomanometer hanging from the wall.

Hospital?

"Yeah." A boy emerged from the white wall. "Hello, Mr. Byne. I'm Joshua. I'm seven—well, I was."

"Hello, Joshua. Nice to meet you." I squatted a bit and shook his hand. He was a skinny boy, quite a bit shorter than typical seven-year-olds. "Seven, you said?"

He touched his hair and dragged his hand down his face all the way to his chest. "This is what I looked like when I was five and a half."

"Where are we?"

"This is the last place I remember. I was sleepy all the time. I remember everyone crying, but it made me happy that they were all here."

"You got sick, didn't you?"

He nodded. "They told me there was something wrong with my blood. They told me I had leukemia. My body hurt all the time." He spun once in place; he grew a bit taller, and his face puffed up. His hair fell from his scalp and rained onto the floor, disappearing as soon as it hit the tiles. "I hated how I looked. I didn't want to go to school even when I could. They said it was from the medicine that was supposed to make me feel better."

"Oh, I'm sorry." I didn't know what else to say.

I remembered how Reverend Reed explained why God allows evil in the world using the immunization analogy. *But why? Do we need the suffering of little ones like Joshua instead of monsters like Jon Nadson?*

"At first, everyone said, 'You are a tough boy, you can beat this,' and 'What do you want to do when you are done with treatment?' Then, there was none of that. They started to talk about Heaven and God taking me to make me feel better. I told them I didn't want God to take me; I wanted him to make me feel better so I can play catch with my dad and my brother, Jack. They told me that I was too young to know how great God is, and how lucky I was to be able to meet him first. They said I was going to a happy place." He looked up at me. "Do you know how to get there?"

"Isn't this the happy place they talked about?"

He looked down at the floor and shook his head *no.*

"Joshua, you must have seen your family after you died."

"Yeah." He turned around and pressed his hand against the white wall, and it swung open like a door. He shrunk to his five-and-a-half stature with a full set of hair, and I followed him into the next room. It was a typical boy's bedroom, painted blue and green, robots on top of the dresser, and baseball bed sheets.

"This was my room. I loved it. My parents let me pick the

colors, and I helped them paint it, too." He ran to the corner of the room and pointed at a glob of dried paint near the baseboard. "I messed up a little here, but my dad said not to worry about it." He grinned a little with just one corner of his mouth.

He skirted around his bed and sat on it. "Jack and I would jump on my bed and have a wrestling match or shoot a basketball." A small ball appeared in his hand, and he shot it into the hoop hung at the top of the door. As soon as it passed through the net, it disappeared.

"Every night, my mom sat on my bed to read me stories, and my dad and I talked about baseball as he tucked me in. He always let me stay up a few extra minutes.

"What happened when you saw them again?"

"You wanna see what I saw?"

I almost said *yes*, but then I remembered the faces of Paul, Conner, and Kristen. I didn't want Joshua to relive anything he didn't want to see again. "You don't need to show me. Just tell me what happened."

"Okay. They were all in here." He ran his hand on the comforter, straightening the crinkles. "They all sat on my bed crying, crying lots. I just wanted to hug and kiss them. But they couldn't see me and I couldn't touch them. Jack sat between my mom and dad. They gave Jack lots of hugs. Then, they all fell asleep on my bed. I just wanted to kick Jack out so I could lie there, too."

"It must've been hard for you to see that."

"They talked about me all the time," said Joshua, "but it always made them cry." He didn't look up as he spoke. "But then, they started to talk about me less and less. They took Jack to a baseball game; they had sodas and hot dogs, even ice cream. They looked happy without me."

"Oh, Joshua. I know it's hard for you to understand. Your parents love you very much and miss you more than you can imagine. I had two girls, and I miss them, too."

I felt a massive blow in my gut when the word *had* rolled out of my mouth like I had accepted it. In time, their memory of my life will fade, they will get used to having Thanksgiving dinner without me. *If I can't deal with this sickening thought, how could Joshua?*

"You are always in their thoughts even when they don't say it."

He looked up at me angry with pursed lips. "Then why did they give my room to Jack? That was my room, my happy place. They hardly talk about me anymore, except crying each year on my birthday. I wish I never looked." He pounded on his bed.

Trying to explain death to a kid is hard, especially when we don't understand it that well as adults. As I sat next to Joshua, I recalled Nina's pastel orange bedroom with an empty hamster cage in the corner. Little Hammy died when Abby and Nina were about Joshua's age, maybe a bit younger. It didn't matter what I said to them, only time healed their sadness. As my girls got older, they eventually grasped the concept of life and death on their own terms. But Joshua was trapped as a child and would never grow older.

Would Joshua ever learn to cope? Would he ever mature here?

He tugged at my sleeve. "So where is the happy place we go when we die? How do I get there?"

"Well, …" I searched for an answer, but none came to me. I had just gotten to Heaven, and in fact, Joshua had gone farther than I had. But I was the adult in the room, so I did what adults do to kids sometimes—draw their attention to something else and pretend we know what we are doing.

"When's the last time you slept?" I said.

"I don't know. I never feel tired here."

"I know just what you need to do. Lie down on the bed, Joshua."

He put his feet up on the bed, and I helped slide his body to the middle.

"Have you ever been a tiny bit sad, maybe for not getting a toy you wanted or losing a game to your friend? Well, you felt better the next day after a good night's sleep, right?"

"Yes." He closed his eyes.

"Not seeing your family is hard." I patted his head. "It's going to take lots of sleep, I think. So if you wake up and still feel sad, close your eyes again."

"Okay." He clasped his hands over his chest."

"Sleep tight, Joshua. You'll be in a better place." I stroked his cheek, and he took a deep breath. As his conscious faded, so did Joshua.

Did I cheat him? Deep down, I knew he would still feel sad when he woke up. I wondered how many nights I must sleep to feel at ease for not being able to talk to my family again.

I held onto Joshua's memory for a bit longer, and the empty bedroom stayed with me. The robot on the dresser had lost its arm from repeated use, the basketball hoop had a cracked backboard, and an old baseball was tucked inside a seasoned glove—this place was his paradise. I couldn't recall what my room looked like at his age, but I remembered my college room: loudspeakers, a swimsuit calendar, and a bottle of vodka that I bought with my fake I.D. The dorm room was smaller than Joshua's and had a dingy dresser and a sagging mattress, but it was a launch pad for a brighter future: a house to own, a car to drive, a dog, wife, and kids. Suddenly, I realized that Joshua hadn't outgrown his precious innocence—he wasn't old enough to have dreams for his future. What divine lessons did Joshua learn in his seven mortal years to prepare him for Heaven? Bella was just a little older than Joshua, so there was no reason her situation should be much different. I remembered seeing her bedroom on the website that her parents set up, and with that thought, Joshua's bed morphed into hers, with Tessa laying on top. The Robots on the dresser were replaced by stuffed animals and baseball themes with hearts.

Maybe she will decide not to see the world of the living.

But *I* still wanted to see my family; I had to plow on. *One more.*

Oblivion

THE BED SHEETS turned into sand that trickled to the floor like the sand in an hourglass. The mattress, the box spring, and even the wooden bed frame followed. The carpeted floor became a beach, and the walls of the house vanished into the sea and sky. It wasn't like the cold shore of Puget Sound that I frequented, with its seaweed covered rocks and the Olympic Mountains across the water. It was just a uniform sandy beach with crashing waves and a swaying grass field nearby. A woman appeared by the water's edge, looking out to sea.

"Hello there," I called to her.

"Hello, Hershel. I'm Mary." She parted her graying hair that was beating in the wind.

"Finally, someone who looks closer to my age," I said. Then I smacked my head for saying it out loud.

"It's quite alright." She laughed. I initially picked my younger self, but it didn't feel right to me."

While Kristen had the aura of my wife when she was young, Mary reminded me of Faye in her late forties. Abby had once suggested Faye dye her hair, but I liked her gray.

A running joke was that I didn't want it to look like I was dating someone half my age, but in truth, I never wished for her to look younger.

"Is this where you lived?" I said to Mary.

"Not far from here. It's not like we could afford a house right on the beach, especially with all my medical bills. You came to hear my story, correct?"

It was obvious that she wasn't there for the small talk, so I said *yes*.

"I had a dream job and a wonderful husband; everything was perfect except for a single missing letter."

I probably looked dumbfounded because she chuckled.

"I had a mutation in one of my genes—just one missing letter in my DNA. I was destined to die young. I just didn't know it." She moved the hair that blew in her face by the ocean wind.

"By the time I found a lump in my breast, it was too late. I told Kirk—oh how handsome he was—that he should move on with his life after I was gone."

I didn't get to say that to Faye. I thought about it, but I also thought I had a little more time.

She made eye contact with me like she knew that I was thinking about Faye. "I think it's the sort of thing that people say to their loved ones when they are dying. He had his whole life ahead of him. I didn't want him to dwell in the past."

"But you went to see him?"

"Yes, I did. I left that world too soon, and I wasn't ready to part with it." She grimaced. "It was hard for him. He mourned my death for three years. I wanted him to pick himself up and move on. I screamed at him, but of course, he couldn't hear me. Then it happened." She looked away from me.

"What happened?"

She sighed and turned back to face me. "Here, take my hand."

I gazed into her eyes and dove into her memories. Clusters of what appeared to be neurons, like the ones that I had seen in science documentary films, were flashing all around me. They coalesced to form pictures, like images of her and Kirk on their wedding day at a lakeside dock, Thanksgiving dinner at her parent's house, a night out with their close friends, and the gentle kiss that Kirk gave her on a withered log at the beach...all rushed by me. I came to a sudden stop at a restaurant. Kirk sat at a table for two, across from a woman. A waiter walked through me and poured them wine. Kirk and his date gave each other awkward smiles and clanged their glasses.

"She was one of his old friends, recently divorced. It turned out she always had a crush on him, and she finally asked him out on a date. It was something I wished would happen, you know, for him to move on. The night before this, he spent all evening going through every photo album we had. He didn't say anything, but I knew... He always had that look when he was doing something he wasn't so proud of. I sat next to him and told him it was okay to go on a date."

"So you were happy for him?"

"I was...but it was strange. There he was, the love of my life, sharing a bottle of wine with someone else. It was the same one he always ordered for me. He wasn't cheating, I knew that. But it wasn't something I should've wanted to see."

"So that was it? That's when you stopped watching over him."

"No. She wasn't the one for him. He dated her out of courtesy. But it was a start. He began to date more; he seemed happier, and I was happy about that."

The scene changed, and we were in a dark movie theater where Kirk shared a bucket of popcorn with a woman. Then a few moments later, we were walking through a park alongside Kirk, who was holding the hand of yet another woman. My mind drifted as I wondered about Faye and her single male friends. In place of the oak and maple trees in Mary's memory, I thought of ferns and firs. But no matter how hard I tried, Faye didn't appear in front of me, just the ill feeling of imagining her with some other man.

Mary waved her hand in front of me, and I was out of my thoughts. She took my hand and led me to a southern colonial house. We strolled into the garden and peeked through a bay window where Kirk and the woman from the park were having a cup of tea.

"That's Jackie," said Mary.

They were sitting across from an older couple on a couch. Laughter escaped through the open windows.

"He fell in love again. And that's him meeting her parents for the first time." Mary moved to the other side of the bay window, where she could see Kirk's face. "I had this belief that I would never really be replaced. I thought he would date others, but I'd always be the love of his life. I was wrong. He married Jackie six months later…it took us three years to get married."

"I'm sorry," I said, remembering saying the same to Paul, Connor, Kristen, and Joshua.

She shook her head sideways. "It's how it is. I was being disingenuous when I told him to move on." She took my hand, and we walked under an arbor that supported creeping grapevines.

"This is the night before he married her," she said, and the picturesque lawn browned and became a hardwood floor, the cedar fence turned into the walls of a bedroom.

Kirk sat at a desk, looking at pictures. Among a dozen or so picture frames were three of Mary. He tucked the stand of the first frame and placed it in a box. He took another and laid it on top of the first. He picked up the last picture; Mary and Kirk were laughing underneath an arbor with clusters of white flowers. "Mary, I hope you'll give me your blessing," he said to the picture in his hand.

"I said yes, of course. Not that he could hear me."

He stared at it for a while then set it in the corner of the desk, behind a picture of him and Jackie.

"That's my place now," said Mary.

I thought about the wall of family pictures in my house. Since I was usually the one taking the pictures, they were mostly of Faye, Abby, and Nina. But there was one that was special to me. It was a spontaneous family photo taken by a passerby—the horizon was tilted, and the background azalea bush had lost most of its flowers, but our smiles made up for them. I swallowed the lump in my throat and asked Mary, "So that was it?"

"No, but I'd rather not relive it."

"Of course."

We left the bedroom and returned to the white sand beach. The wind stirred her hair, and she tucked both sides behind her ears. She walked to the water's edge, and I followed.

"Every night when he made love to her, I felt like a piece of me faded from his memory. I know that's how things should be. I thought"—she dabbed corners of her eyes with her finger—"a day would come when he would pack away the last picture of me on his desk, and I didn't want to see that."

"So you'll wait until he joins you here?"

"Then what? I was with him for sixteen years. If they have a long life together, it'd be forty years, maybe more. I watched and read so many love stories when I was alive." She paused and looked at me. "You know the cliché, 'I'll wait for you in Heaven.'" She huffed. "It doesn't work out that way."

I stared at her for a long time without having anything clever or comforting to say. *How long will that picture of me stay on the wall? Will Faye remarry? Will her new love last longer than ours?*

"Kirk is a borderline atheist, so I'm not even counting on him entering Heaven when his time comes. Maybe he'd be better off if he didn't."

"Why do you say that?"

"You are new here, but it's just a matter of time before you realize that there is nothing here."

"Nothing? How about your old friends? Family members who died before you? Things, places, everything you ever wanted?"

"Yes, of course, but how many times can you listen to the same joke or relive the greatest moments of your life? I think even a thousand years is too long in this place. This place has everything, but eternity dilutes them all."

"So what do you do when you aren't talking to someone like me?"

"I meditate with nothing around me. That's what many do. Days, weeks, months, even years go by. When I come out of meditation, it's all the same. Sometimes, a fragment of a memory pulls me decades backward and forces me to relive the moment all over again. My preacher used to say what we hold dear as mortals doesn't compare to being with God and we should leave everything of the old world behind. Someday, I will shed everything and be left with nothing but white all around me."

"I just got here. I'm not ready to let go."

"You are like me, Hershel. You left that world too soon." She began wading into the water. Waves splashed her legs, erasing her from below. She trod deeper and deeper without looking back.

"Thank you for your time," I said to her, but the ocean breeze swept my words across the coastline.

A towering wave swallowed her into the ocean. The wave crashed, but before the water reached my feet, it turned into a gust of wind and the sandy beach into a puff of clouds.

Perfection

I HAD FULFILLED my requirement for seeing the world of the living, but my sentiment was like the amorphous white haze that surrounded me. Suddenly, I remembered my promise to Bella to meet after we both finished our requirement.

The clouds receded, and I found myself standing by the trunk of a large oak tree. The white under my feet turned to freshly cut grass, every blade perfect, and not a single clover in sight. Beyond a stretch of the green field was a carousel. A familiar carnival tune rang, and the wooden horses bobbed up and down as they circled with no one on them. Just outside the umbrella of the oak tree was Bella, resting on a cast iron park bench that was big enough to seat four adults. She squished herself against an armrest with her head on her arm, staring at a lone tulip that grew a few steps in front of the bench.

"Hi Bella, how did it go? Did you hear five stories?"

She didn't raise her head but squeezed a *yes* through her lips that were squished against her arm.

I sat next to her, leaving enough space for her to sit up comfortably if she chose to do so. "What did you decide?"

She shrugged, neither *yes* nor *no*. She sat up. "You said you have kids, right, Mr. Byne?"

I told her I had two daughters, their names, and ages.

"Is that why you helped me at the Gate?"

"I'm not sure. I was watching you on the news while driving. I got into a car crash right when you were shot."

"Do you think that's why we are together? Because we died at the same time?"

I didn't know the answer.

"Do you think my parents saw me die on TV?"

"I—." I almost answered her question but stopped. "I saw them on TV about a week ago. They love you so much, and they just wanted you to come back home."

"When my cousin died, my mom said he would be okay because he gets to spend more time in Heaven." She pursed her lips. "It's not fair. What's so great about this place?"

I looked down at Bella who was scowling with her arms crossed. "Death is hard, and adults try to make it easier for children."

"By lying to us?"

I had two thoughts: "It's not a lie if you believe it"—a quote from *Seinfeld* or "It's hard to admit that we don't know." I told her the latter.

"One of my five was a girl my age. She was also kidnapped and killed. She said her parents were sad, but they were glad it was over…that she was in a better place. This place!" Bella framed the view of the tree and carousel with open hands. "You're gonna say I'm being a baby, but I don't want to be here. I want to be home."

"I want to be home, too." I ran my hand over her hair.

A hint of calm returned to her face—maybe that was her best attempt at acknowledging my effort.

"Do you think this is the Heaven that people talked about? I don't want this. I want my family. My friends. Are you going to see the world of the living, Mr. Byne?"

It was time to tally up the stories from Paul, Connor, Kristen, Joshua, and Mary. I gave the stories of Connor and Joshua a *negative one* each, and that of Kristen a *positive one*. I scored Paul as neutral, so I gave it a zero. That brought the sum to *negative one*. Mary was difficult because her story made me think of Faye the most. Mary was not merry, but she did wish for her husband to move on and she saw exactly that. So even though it didn't feel right, I scored her story as positive, which brought the total tally to zero. Maybe it wasn't about the score. Like James said, maybe it was all about warnings—God saying, "Are you sure?" But with the even score and trepidation that I couldn't shake off, I searched for anything to break the tie. Then I remembered Ben, Kristen's husband.

"Bella, I want to see one more person."

"I'll go with you."

"Okay." I put my hand on her shoulder.

The grass around the carousel turned into water, and it swallowed the horses all at once. The field turned into a lake, and the ripples reached the shore just a few yards from where we sat. An older man materialized by the water's edge, sitting on a camping stool with a fishing rod in his hand.

"That has to be Ben."

"Yes, it's me." The man turned his head toward me.

"I heard about you from—"

"My wife, yes I know. You know the best part of fishing here, Hershel?" He returned his attention to the lake. "The line is always tied correctly, the lures are always the right kind, and the sinker is always optimal. Perfect, perfect, perfect."

"It is Heaven, I hear." I walked toward him and sat on a stool that grew out of the ground beside him.

Ben laughed aloud. "You know what's the worst part of fishing here?" He glanced at me sideways. "It's too perfect."

"Huh?"

"I used to love coming to this lake, dipping a line or two, for hours on end. Most of the time, I came up empty. Frustrating as hell, but it was okay because it's part of the sport. I always thought that the lack of a reward was necessary to make the times when I actually hooked a fish that much sweeter."

"It's not like that anymore?"

"Like you said, this is Heaven." He stood up and tossed out a line; the lure pierced the surface with a minimal splash. "A trout, a rainbow trout," he said. The line became taut and the rod flexed. "Bigger," he said, and the rod flexed more. He turned the handle on the reel, taking his time, shifting his fishing rod from left to right, and back again. The fish flapped in the water as its dorsal fin broke the surface. He took one step into the lake, grabbed the end of the line, and pulled up a trout the size of his arm.

"That's an awesome fish you got there," I said.

"Shit. It takes the fun out of it if you ask me." He jiggled the hook once, and the fish splashed back into the water. He tossed the lure back in, and said, "Tuna."

"Tuna? It's a lake."

"I know, but what's the difference." The fishing rod arched and he began reeling in again. "It doesn't even matter if I turn the reel." He stuck the rod into the holder on the ground, and a tuna the size of a motorcycle jumped out of the water and skidded sideways to our feet.

"Holy sh—"

"I told you. I call this the downside of perfection. We judge perfection through imperfection, don't you agree?"

"How so?"

"Well, let's say you just had the most delicious mango, perfectly sweet with the right amount of tanginess and a smooth velvet-like texture, not too firm or too soft. It brings you such happiness that for a moment you only think about the mango, like nothing else in the world matters. Now imagine that all the mangos in the world taste exactly like it. It is no longer a perfect mango, just ordinary. We weren't made to live in a perfect world, and catching any fish I want, at any time is just like that."

Can't you wish for randomness to get some of the surprise back?

"I've fished all my life, and I can tell you there is nothing random about catching a fish. It's about knowing their behavior and the water. It's a game of trickery and a test of your reflexes against theirs. I was a mathematician, just like you, and I tried modeling the art of fishing with math. I worked out formulas with variables to model luck and such, to try to give it some sense of a 'surprise'"—he made quotation marks with his hands—"but it had nothing to with my skill or my knowledge of fish."

"Funny, I thought fishing was just something to do while having a beer in the sun."

"Ha, ha, ha. That was a great bonus. But even that sucks here. You haven't had a beer since you got here, have you?"

"No, not yet."

He reached into the cooler and grabbed a brown bottle. "What do you like?"

"There was this local IPA I liked, really hoppy, but mild in bitterness. It was called—"

"Palate Cleanser IPA." He turned the bottle to show me the familiar label.

"Yeah, that's it. How did you know?"

"You'll figure it out," he said and handed me the beer. The bottle cap evaporated into the mist.

I tipped my head back and had a gulp—at least I thought I did. I remembered the taste and the fizz, but couldn't feel anything. *This must've been what Connor meant about his coffee.*

"See, it sucks, doesn't it. All your life, you wished to have a body that would last forever, not the flesh and bones or nerves and muscles that eventually give out. Now our memories and souls are eternal without any of that organic stuff. But all the blissful experiences we used to cherish were due to tingles in our nerves, and without them, things aren't the same." He removed a knife from his fishing vest. "Do you like Tuna?"

"I used to," I replied.

He held the knife's blade, gesturing me to take it. "Cut it open."

I shook my head *no*. "I never gutted a fish before, let alone a tuna. I've seen it on TV though, and it was a bloodbath."

"Nah." Ben gripped the knife handle, tilted his stool

toward the fish, and made a single incision along the side of the tuna.

The slit widened on its own, and he shoved his hand into the belly of the fish and yanked out a platter of sashimi, glistering with freshness, served with a delicate mound of green wasabi and a small dish of soy sauce.

"No mess at all." The knife morphed into a pair of chopsticks, and he put a slice into his mouth. "It just melts in your mouth." He kicked the tuna. Its wound sealed shut, and it jumped back into the water. "Hot sake goes better with sashimi." The bottle of beer in his hand turned into a small cup of sake.

"Why do you do it then? I mean… come here to fish and have a drink?"

"To reminisce, I suppose. That's the thing about being human, we always want what we don't have; and once we have it, we miss the time when we didn't."

"My mom said you get to have everything you want in Heaven." Bella joined us; she must have gotten tired of waiting. "So it's true."

"Hello there. Bella, is it? It's true. If you want a doll-house or designer clothes, you can have it."

"I never cared much about dolls or clothes."

"Ha, that was quite a sexist thing for me to say. I apologize." Ben laughed. "Lots of people who come to Heaven gather the stuff they always wanted, you know, fancy cars, private jet, diamond necklace, and whatnots. But when they realize everyone can have the same things, they see no joy in having them. Yet for some, not having everything still makes them feel inferior to others. Feeling envious is bad, but being envied is great. That's human nature, even in Heaven."

"So much for leaving life on Earth to live with God in Heaven," I said.

"Maybe we all need to learn to let these things go." He laughed. "But what's the rush, right? I could relive this shit for a million years to come and still have plenty of time left to be enlightened."

"What does enlightened mean, mister?"

"To know what's truly important, and get rid of everything else. At least that's one version I hear," Ben said to her.

"I just want to be with my parents and my brother."

"Well, …I'm sorry darling," said Ben. "You'll have to wait a while for that. But as important as that seems, some say that is something you *want* and not what is necessary."

"I don't understand."

"Neither do I, Bella," I said. "I always thought family came first. Maybe we still have a lot to learn." I played the *I'm-as-clueless-as-you-are* card with Bella, a little trick adults use when trying to make kids feel okay for not understanding something. But this time, I didn't understand it either.

"So, are you going to go see your family, Mr. Byne?"

"I…"

"Still undecided, Hershel?" Ben said mockingly. "I'll let you in on a secret." He chugged the rest of sake and licked his lips. "Everyone ends up going."

"Excuse me?"

"You are on the fence. Fifty-fifty like a coin toss—a head you go and a tail you don't. You'll flip a coin tomorrow and do the same. How many times will you get tails before getting a head? It doesn't have to be fifty-fifty. All nonzero probabilities multiplied by eternity equals certainty. You should remember that."

"Then what was the point of meeting five people?"

"It's like the warning label on the back of your beer. It says it can kill you, but you drink it anyway. Besides, you didn't come to see me for my opinion. You came here to stall until your heart is ready."

I smirked and turned to Bella. "I'm going to see my family."

"Then I'm going, too."

"I don't want to influence your decision, Bella."

"I want to see my mom." She looked at me and said, "But I'm a little scared."

"Me, too."

"Good luck, Hershel." Ben grabbed a fishing pole and waved goodbye with the other hand. With each ripple that reached the water's edge, the lake faded further into the white mist and the blue sky filled with white clouds.

I looked to Bella; she was holding Tessa tightly against her chest.

"To the world of the living."

As soon as I said that, we blasted upwards and broke through the thick layer of clouds.

"Welcome to the next level of enlightenment." A woman said as she finished materializing before our eyes. She sat at a desk.

"Is this the Gate to Heaven?" asked Bella.

I understood why she asked—the desk looked identical to the one we saw at the Gate.

"No, this is a different gate. One level up. You already are in Heaven, dear."

"Are you an angel?" Bella asked the woman.

"You can call me that, my dear. Are you here to visit the world of the living or start the pilgrimage?"

"I want to see my parents."

"And you, Hershel?"

"The same. I mean…I want to see my family, too. But I thought I would accompany Bella first."

The angel turned to Bella, "Are you sure you want Mr. Byne to go with you?"

Bella nodded, holding onto my hand.

Two doors appeared behind the angel. "Through the door to the right."

"Where does the door on the left go?" asked Bella.

"The passage to the gods. The start of the pilgrimage."

Bella pulled me to the right door.

"Once you pass through the door, just think of a place you want to go," said the angel. "Take your time. I'll see you back here soon."

Purgatory

THE DOOR OPENED, and we were in front of Bella's brown house on a cul-de-sac. The street leading to the house was packed with cars and TV station vans.

"Go away," Bella yelled at the people hanging around.

Most were either talking on their phones while staring at the large bay window with curtains drawn, or feverishly typing on their mobile devices with their backs against their cars.

Bella stepped up to the front porch and reached for the doorknob, but instead of turning it, her hand went right through the red door with chipped paint. She looked at me with half of her right arm invisible beyond the door's surface. I gestured her to walk through it. She did, and I followed.

We climbed the half flight of stairs of the split-level house to the living room, where a television was playing the news. In the corner of the screen was an image of her house.

"Nicky," Bella called to the boy by the bay window, who was peeking outside through the gap in the curtains. He did not move. She called again, but he did not answer.

"They can't hear or see us, Bella."

She shifted her body like she wanted to dash towards him, but I held her back.

"Is that your little brother?"

She didn't answer, but I assumed he was.

He pulled the curtains together, making the two sides overlap in the middle. "Assholes," he said. I was a little shocked to hear such a word from a little boy, but not as much as when he walked straight through us.

We turned around and followed him. He walked into a bedroom where his mom sat on the bed, resting her back on the headboard with a tissue box beside her. He hopped up next to her.

"...It has been twenty-four hours since the tragic end to the life of Isabel Remming, and Jon Nadson is still in critical condition." A small television in the bedroom was playing the same news as the one in the living room, but the sounds from the two TVs were slightly out of sync.

"Burn in Hell!" her mother screamed at the face of Jon Nadson on the screen. The cross on the wall above the headboard rattled.

"Mom?" Bella called to her as she tried to move the tissue box to sit on the bed. But no matter how hard she tried, it did not move, not even the slightest flutter of the thin tissue. She cried, waving her arms to get her mother's attention.

"Can we turn the channel, Mom?" Nicky said as he scooted closer to her.

"Yeah, sorry." She picked up the remote and pressed the up button until a cartoon program came on. She blew her nose and added the dirty tissue to the heap of used ones on the nightstand beside her.

Bella climbed up on the bed but made no dent on the comforter. She tried to pry her brother off their mother. "Move!" she screamed. She wailed and flopped on the other side of her mom, sharing the same space with the tissue box. Her mom plucked two more tissues from the box, not knowing her hand sliced through Bella's heart in the process.

"She can't see you," I said to Bella as she clenched her mother's shirt at the chest.

Determined, Bella got on all fours in front of her mother's face and peered into her eyes. "I'm right here," she said, but her mom's eyes only reflected the images on the TV screen.

"My Bella…" Her mom sobbed and blew her nose again.

"Why can't you see me, Mommy?" Bella's head drooped like a withered flower.

From outside came the sound of a car pulling into the driveway, and a moment later, the front door opened. Someone came up the stairs, and the TV in the living room turned off.

"Honey? Nicky?" a man said.

"Dad!" Bella said.

"We're in here," said Nicky.

Bella got off the bed. Her dad came to the bedroom door, and she ran to him. She spread her arms wide to catch his waist, but she wound up behind him in the hallway.

Her mom waved him over, and he joined her and Nicky on the bed.

"I'm here!" Bella screamed and sobbed.

When Nina was six, she wanted to help me clean up the garage. Faye had taken Abby to a birthday party, and I needed to tidy it up and watch Nina at the same time. At that age, "help" was a fun activity and not yet a chore. She dropped a mallet from the workbench onto her pinky toe, ending up with a small fracture. I tried to calm her, saying *it'll be okay* and *it'll go away in a minute*, but it did no good. She needed Faye, not me. I held Bella like I held Nina that day, fully aware that I was quite useless.

Her father switched the television back to the news. "Sorry, Nicky," he said.

A reporter in a pink business suit was talking about Joseph Nadson, the father of Jon Nadson, who was being held by the police for knowingly aiding his son in human trafficking. "The police said, he kept repeating that his son was a good boy."

Bella's dad threw the tissue box at the TV. "A fucking good boy? He fucking took her, you fucking asshole."

"Ned." Her mom held Nicky close.

"I'm sorry," he said to Nicky.

"Where's Bella?" Nicky looked up at his mom.

"She is in Heaven, sweetie. She is in a happy place now."

"I don't want to be in Heaven. I want to be with you," Bella shouted.

Her dad got a phone call and stepped out of the room, so her mom changed the TV channel back to the cartoon. I left Bella and followed her dad.

"…Where do they live?" I heard him whisper into the phone, as he headed down to the basement.

"A fucking trailer park? Fucking figures." He paced around the basement as he talked.

He stopped in the corner where an old oak cabinet stood with a padlock. He reached into his pocket and removed his keys.

"Can you fucking believe this guy? He has the fucking nerve to say that his son is a fucking good boy." He toggled the linked keys and found the one needed to open the cabinet.

Inside were two black handguns, a hunting rifle, and a few boxes of bullets. Bella joined me in the basement.

"Bella, you should go upstairs," I told her.

"Daddy? What are you doing?"

He didn't flinch at her words, but instead activated speaker mode on his phone and set it on a shelf inside the gun cabinet. "I'm gonna fucking kill them both." He grabbed the rifle.

The man on the phone yelled, "Ned, calm down. Don't do anything stupid."

Ned put the rifle back on the rack and grabbed a handgun.

"I hear he's in real bad shape," said the man on the phone. "They don't think he'll make it through the night. God will take care of the rest, you hear?"

Ned picked up the phone and ended the call without replying. With his phone in his left hand and the gun in his right, he pressed both against his head and wailed without sound, mucus bridging his upper and lower teeth of this opened mouth. He leaned against the wall of the basement, but his body slid to the laminate floor and curled into fetal position. Tears puddled by the side of his face and thick saliva drooled from his mouth as he widened his jaws as if he were screaming. He banged the gun on his temple and cried quietly.

"Daddy, stop. Please stop. I'm okay." She sat in front of him and cried, but their tears were in different dimensions.

"Bella." I reached out to her.

"I want to be alone now, Mr. Byne."

Before entering the world of the living, I honestly thought I would be able to comfort Bella—I was wrong. I stared at her for a moment longer. I remembered Paul's story. He said everyone wants their loved ones to mourn their death, but no one should watch it. I became frightened to see my family, but as soon as I thought of them, I was transported to my own neighborhood.

It was a sunny day, but no one was outside. With great hesitation, I walked up my driveway. I got to the front door with a gold knob that had lost its luster. I remembered the day when I installed it seven or eight years ago: Abby and Nina were laughing, taking turns trying out the new set of keys. I had used the door every day without much thought, but now every little thing seemed to bring back memories. The vertical scratches on the door were made by Lyla as she begged to be let in after a long walk. The mailbox that hung on the siding was one of the first things Faye bought when we moved into the house. The house number, the doorknocker, the flower pots…all had a story. But then the image of Bella crying swept into my thoughts.

The door seemed to be staring back at me now, just like the water taunted me on my first high dive at the city pool, but I had made the choice to be there. I summoned the courage to go through the door. I imagined Faye's face as I touched the knob.

Bright white lights flashed before my eyes, bleaching everything in my sight. Then I was in complete darkness, the blackest of the blacks.

Interference

A PAIN, WORSE than a burst appendix, spread through my abdomen. I wanted to scream, but I was unable to move. An ensemble of sounds filled the darkness, but at first, I couldn't distinguish one from another. I picked one and focused on it, like trying to listen for the bass player in a heavy metal band. It was a rhythmic beep that coincided with the throb inside me—it had to be a heart monitor.

Am I at a hospital?

I began to assign individual elements of the noise fog to familiar things: a pump, a toilet flush, casters rolling on the floor, high heels, the clatter of plastic blinds, and the crows outside the window. There were several voices too. Warmth swept up my left arm; the pain subsided, and the voices became clearer.

One of them was a news anchor on the TV. "Breaking news, Jon Nadson has died at the hospital."

"Where's Abby?"

Faye!

"Check her location on your phone."

Nina!

I wanted to call out their names, but my throat was stuffed. I tried to raise my hand, but it wouldn't move.

"48th and 275th. Where is she? I thought she went to the cabin with her friends."

"That's where…"

"Where what?" Faye said.

"That's near Robert's house."

The phone rang.

"Abby?" Faye answered.

"Mom? I'm…by Robert's——I'm sorry," I heard Abby's voice coming from the phone. She was breathing heavy as she spoke.

"Calm down. What's going on?"

"He hit me. He—— Oh no, he's —— his car."

Then there was a cracking sound, like a phone hitting the pavement.

I tried to scream, but the tube down my throat got in the way.

"Abby? Abby!" said Faye.

My chest tightened up, and I heard the heart monitor sped up.

"Faye," I tried to squeeze out her name, but I could only babble with my lips around the tube. The heart monitor blipped in erratic rhythms.

"Hershel!" I heard Faye's voice and felt her shaking me. "Dad!"

I heard footsteps.

"Get the doctor," someone said.

The tightness in my chest spread to my shoulders and up my neck. The sound of the flatlined heart monitor became fainter and fainter.

A pinpoint of light in the darkness expanded until the white mist engulfed me like a tsunami. I found myself able to move freely and without any tube in my throat. A golden gate materialized in front of me and opened, revealing the stairs behind it.

The Angel at the Gate to Heaven spoke to me from behind, "Hershel Byne, we already cleared you, so you may climb the stairs again if you so choose."

I looked back and forth between him and the gate. "What? What's going on?"

"This happens all the time."

"What happens all the time?"

"Coming in and out of the afterlife. Modern medicine is making more work for us. Back in the day, when someone died, he remained dead. Nowadays, a jolt to the heart or an injection in the arm can shuttle people back and forth between the two worlds. But do not worry. You just have to renew your choice at this gate, and off you go."

"Off I go? Send me back!"

"I can't do that, Mr. Byne. But you can return to Heaven if you wish…unless you changed your mind, of course."

I pounded on my chest as if I could revive myself and return to the world of the living.

"It's pointless, Mr. Byne."

No matter how hard I hit my chest, there was no physical pain, but in its place was the overwhelming sense of despair.

"For your minor inconvenience, you have a chance to choose again, Mr. Byne. Eternal white of Heaven, or nothingness? Life everlasting or the end of it all?"

"I'm going up. I need to see Abby. She's in trouble."

"I'm sorry, Mr. Byne. You can go see her, but you won't be able to alter the world of the living."

"I still need to see her." I didn't believe him—I didn't want to believe him. I dashed through the gate and ran up the stairs.

I burst through the door at the top of the stairway.

"Back again?" said James.

"I've got to see Abby."

"It's not worth it, Hershel. It'll only bring you pain."

"I don't have time for this, sorry."

"You have endless time," he said as I ran from him.

Running turned into rocketing upwards, and I broke through to the second level of enlightenment. The angel at the second gate simply pointed at the door on the right. I barged through it.

I entered a dark intersection. The streetlight was just bright enough to read the two perpendicular green signs on a post. They read 48th Ave. and 275th St. I ran up and down 48th Avenue at non-human speed, fast enough for houses to blur, but I couldn't find Abby. I went back to the 275th intersection. I spotted something shining under the streetlight, and I went near it. It was Abby's phone. I looked down 275th Street, and there she was.

Abby was running—crying. She held her side like she was fighting a cramp in her stomach. Glancing back at where she came from, she hid behind a tree.

"Abby, what's going on? Are you alright?" I shouted at her, but she didn't acknowledge my presence.

"Oh no," she said.

A car drove past the tree, and then came to a screeching halt. The driver's door swung open, and Robert got out of the car.

"Abby, come back here." He pointed at his feet.

"Leave me alone," she screamed and ran back towards 48th Ave.

"You bitch," he said and got back into his car.

I followed her, but the sound of clattering aluminum cans made me look back. Robert made a quick three-point turn, pushing the recycle bin up on the curb in the process. I stopped chasing after her and got in front of his damn car with my arms spread wide.

"Stop," I screamed.

The headlights beamed in my face. The engine revved, but I stood my ground. Less than ten yards away, his eyes were directed at me, but through me—I was the only one playing a game of chicken. I jumped to the side and flew through another recycle bin. Lying on the curb, I saw Abby make a left turn. Robert's car failed to corner, and it skidded to a stop on a narrow part of the street with cars parked on both sides.

Robert yelled from the car, "I'm sorry. I just want to talk."

"Leave me alone," Abby shouted back.

His car was jammed diagonally on the street with less than a foot of space at both bumpers. He jockeyed the car back and forth to get out of the jam. The head of the car cleared and he was about to make the turn to go after Abby.

I jumped into the passenger seat, right through the door. "Leave her alone."

Robert's eyes were fixed on Abby running in the distance.

He floored the gas pedal, and his head slammed against the headrest. The residential area abruptly ended as we came right up behind her. She made a quick turn into an abandoned lot littered with old rusted lawnmowers. He slammed on the brakes, but the car's momentum dragged us past the entrance. He put his hand on the headrest of the passenger seat, slicing his hand through my face in the process. He backed the car up, shifted it into first gear, and drove into the junkyard—pure adrenaline fueling the anger in his eyes.

"Stop, you little shit." I tried to jam the gears, but I couldn't move the stick shift.

Robert sped up, and the car joggled like skis on moguls.

Abby glanced back. She slipped between two lawnmowers and then jumped over a small heap of yard tools. The shaft of a weedwacker caught the tip of her toe, and she flew forward, landing behind a tractor.

The car slammed against the lawnmowers, and he lost control of the steering wheel. The front wheels rode up on the junk pile, and we were briefly off the ground.

"Fuck!" He locked his elbows, and the car bounced once before it slammed into a tree.

The hood of the car popped up, and the windshield cracked. I went through the glass, the sheet metal, and the tree, tumbling to a stop by a broken riding lawn mower. I rushed to Abby. She lay in the dirt with her hair covering part of her face. I screamed at her to get up. A blade of grass moved by her mouth—she was still alive.

I walked to the side of the car. Robert wasn't moving. Blood from his forehead was smudged on the airbag, but it appeared to be just a minor cut. The warm breath from his mouth condensed into dew on the airbag. I returned to Abby and screamed for help against the star-studded sky.

"Mr. Byne," Bella tugged at my elbow.

I looked down at her and suddenly remembered that I was just an observer from Heaven.

"When did you get here?" I said to Bella.

"Just now. I don't know what to do." She looked around. "What happened here?"

I ignored her and ran out to the street. "Where are the goddamn police?" I ran back to the car and made sure Robert wasn't moving, then returned to Abby.

"Abby, wake up." I tried to look at her eyes through her hair.

"It doesn't work, Mr. Byne. I yelled and yelled at my dad, but he didn't answer. I screamed at my mother, my brother…nobody heard me."

"I've got to reach the next level of enlightenment."

"And do what, Mr. Byne?"

"I'm going to find God, and ask him for the power to change things in this world."

"I want to go with you."

"I don't know if it will work. I can't promise you anything."

"My dad is going to do something bad. I don't want him to get into trouble."

Neither Robert nor Abby moved. I rested my hand on Abby's cheek. *Hang in there. I'll be back.*

"Okay. Let's go." I took Bella's hand and looked up at the starlit sky.

We rocketed upwards until the junkyard became the

size of a pinhead. The night sky brightened to pure white, and we were back in Heaven.

The angel at the desk swiveled her chair and looked at us. "That was quick," she said. "Did you see everything you wanted to see?"

I stormed toward her, stopping inches from her face. "I heard there's a way to reach beyond the second level of enlightenment. How do I get there?"

"Do you think you are the only one in the history of humanity who has wanted to change the world of the living? If it were easy, everyone would do it, and the world would be thrown into chaos."

"But there is a way?"

"You must reach a level of enlightenment equal to that of the gods."

"How do we get there?" said Bella.

"I cannot tell you how to get there. I can only show you where to begin your pilgrimage."

"Where?" I demanded.

"Through the Path of the Unclaimed."

"What the hell is that?"

"No need to be rude," she said. "You think you are in a hurry, but trust me, it's not that urgent." She swiveled her chair back to face the desk.

I walked around the desk and placed my hands on it.

"This is urgent."

She looked up at me. "You still think that time flows the same here, but I can assure you that it does not."

"But—"

"There's no point in trying to convince you. I've seen your type too many times." She pointed at the door on the left behind her. "Through the Path of the Unclaimed is the road to the realm of gods. But once you get there, you may no longer have the desire to change anything."

"Are you sure you want to come with me?" I said to Bella.

Bella kissed Tessa on the nose and rested the stuffed animal on the angel's desk. She looked up at me and nodded.

Pilgrimage

I TURNED THE golden doorknob and pushed the door open. Beyond the sharp edges of the doorframe that cut through the bright and pure white of Heaven lay a dimly lit gray haze. Bella stuck her hand into the doorway, and it disappeared as if no light could return. She glanced up at me then jumped into the haze. I reached my hand out to grab her but missed. With my own hand now deep inside, I called to Bella, but she didn't reply. I held my breath as I crossed over to the other side, and exhaled into the hazy gray air. Through the black doorframe behind me was not the bright white of Heaven, but a muted glow. Bella nudged me to the side and closed the door.

The space was gray, but not dark. We could see things clearly, but the air felt stiff, and the silence felt more prominent. A wide path up ahead was lined on both sides with endless rows of shelves, and everything vanished into a bright speck of white light in the far distance like a perspective drawing. To our right, a spotlight illuminated a counter where a woman stood with her hands crossed in front of her waist.

She approached us. "This is the Path of the Unclaimed.

This is where your pilgrimage to the Realm of Gods will begin."

"Who are you?" Bella cocked her head.

"I serve the gods."

"Another angel?" I examined her from head to toe.

She wore a long black gown with just the tips of her shoes poking out at the bottom. Her long straight black hair blended into the gown.

"If you want to call me that, it's fine. I'm your guide. Follow me."

She led the way down the middle of the path, which was blacker than asphalt, toward the shelves.

"How do we start this pilgrimage?" I said.

"The moment you stepped through that door, you began."

"Where does this path go? Does this lead to God?"

"Everyone asks the same question."

"And the answer?" It was rude, but I was in a hurry to get back to Abby.

"You take one step forward, then another, and another. Move forward, toward infinity. Beyond infinity lies what you seek."

"Infinity? Beyond? What am I? Buzz Lightyear?"

Bella chuckled.

"Seriously?" I said. "That will take an infinite amount of time."

"Infinite number of steps. Time is irrelevant. If each step takes no time at all, how long does it take to reach the end?" said the guide.

Infinity times zero…undefined.

We reached the first row of shelves and continued. Each row consisted of repeating shelving units, which were a bit taller than an average person and twenty meters or so in length. They seem to go on forever to the right and left of the central path.

"How many steps have you taken?" she asked.

"I don't know. I wasn't counting."

"See it's not hard, is it? It'll get easier, I promise."

Bella ventured down an aisle and picked up a jar from the shelf. "What's this?"

The guide caught up to Bella and took the jar from her hand. "Nameless and unclaimed."

I picked up another jar just like it. "An embryo?"

"Looks like from the end of the first trimester," the guide said.

"You mean it's an aborted fetus?"

"Let's see…" She flipped the jar I had been holding in my hand upside down and read the label on the bottom. "Spontaneous miscarriage. We have so many of these nowadays." She ventured further down the aisle and picked up another jar. "See this?"

It looked empty. I flipped it over and read the label: Frozen, pre-implantation.

There was a small section in the middle of the jar that acted like a magnifying lens. A tiny dot floated in the middle of the jar.

"What does that mean?" said Bella.

"It's a fairly new phenomenon. Ever since man figured out how to store embryos, and people began to claim that life starts at conception, the ones that die in the freezer or a petri dish end up here as well. They were given serial numbers but no names. Without thoughts or souls, they don't belong in Heaven proper, so we store them here."

"Doesn't an emb—ryo grow into a person?" said Bella.

"Once it dies on Earth, it can't grow here in Heaven. Just like you won't age, my child."

Bella picked up another jar and put it up to her eye.

"This one looks like a tiny fish."

"We all look like little fish when we are this small, my child."

"Are these alive?" asked Bella.

"You ask an irrelevant question. Are you?" Our guide walked to a path between shelving units and crossed to the next row and the next. "Those are the lucky ones. Come," she said as she picked up speed.

Bella and I did our best to keep up with her, almost at sprinting speed.

Our guide slowed down, and we walked into a large area filled with cribs instead of shelves.

"Hello, Sister," she said to a woman in a white nurse's uniform.

In the crib closest to us was a baby with a disproportionally small head and his intestines spilling outside of his abdomen. Bella hid behind me. The sign on the crib read, "Name: John. Age: one day. Trisomy 18"

The sister put a blanket over the baby and rocked the crib back and forth as he wailed.

"Is he in pain?" I asked.

"In Heaven, you talk because that's what you were capable of doing when you died," said our guide. "Little John cries because that's what he was capable of doing when he died."

The sister placed her hand on baby John. "He is stuck being one day old, waiting for his parents to come to claim him."

"Probably not, Sister." said our guide. She tucked her hand back inside the long black gown. "They hardly ever do."

"No?"

"People wish for babies like John to rest in Heaven, but the memory fades by the time they die. Many don't even attempt the pilgrimage right away but remain at the base level of Heaven. And those who do, they just walk past here." The guide bowed to the nurse and walked away.

Baby John with a red face kept crying. Looking at his physique, I found it hard to imagine that he wasn't crying out in pain. We wandered through what seemed to be an endless field of cribs. Some babies slept in peace, and some wiggled their hands and feet as mobiles above them turned to lullabies.

Bella tugged at me. "Mr. Byne." Her eyes said she wanted to move on. So we hurried and caught up with the guide.

"I can't believe they are not claimed," I said to the guide.

She stopped and pulled a book from the inside of her gown. She opened it in the middle and flipped several pages forward. Just like the book of the angel at the Gate of Heaven, the size of the left and right portions of the book didn't change with each page turned. She scanned a page with her finger, stopping about three quarters down. She snapped the book shut and swiped her hand left at the field of cribs. We remained still, but the cribs zipped by us as if they were on a high-speed rail. Soon the crib sector was gone, and rows of shelves hurtled past us once again. I squeezed my elbows against my side in fear of them being scraped. She then pushed her hand forward, and the motion shifted to the perpendicular direction. I straightened my spine, tucked my chin in, and watched shelves flying by at the tip of my nose. Our guide stood unaffected as shelves passed through her as if she was in a separate dimension. She put her hand down, and all movements ceased. Beside me, Bella let out a sigh as if she just survived a roller coaster ride from hell.

Our guide walked down the adjacent aisle and stopped in front of a small fish bowl. "Do you remember these?" She picked it up and showed us a pair of fish circling each other.

"Goldfish? They come here, too?"

"These are the ones you got at a carnival when your daughters were four and five."

"Oh, I remember. They didn't live very long. They were pretty weak from being in the plastic bag all day. Faye told the kids that they were going to Heaven."

"This is a section of the Unclaimed that some call the toilet cemetery. Would you like to claim them?"

I didn't know how to respond.

"I didn't think so. Do you think that someone would want to carry their miscarried fetus the size of a lemon wherever they go? Or wear a necklace with a locket of a fish-like embryo, helplessly wiggling its emerging limbs? We're just glad that people don't claim life begins with a sperm or an egg."

"That'll be a lot of jars," I said.

She smirked. "A lot more."

"I had a bunny," Bella said. "Her name was Pepper. Is she here?"

She opened the book again and found the page.

"Follow me." She walked back down the aisle, and we followed.

Rows of shelves began moving past us again, and we crossed the asphalt-black central path to the other side with yet more shelves. Abruptly, we burst out onto a wide-open landscape organized into square grids of fenced grass patches and lush vegetable gardens. We came to a stop at one of many garden patches. A white rabbit with black spots was digging up a carrot. When it saw us, it cocked its head with the carrot in its mouth.

"Pepper?"

"Would you like to claim her?" the guide said.

"Yes."

"Pepper will join you at the base level if you decide to return there."

"I can't just take her with me now?"

"You came here for the pilgrimage. If you wish to continue, you must leave everything behind."

Pilgrimage. I remembered why we were there. *Abby.*

"Bella, I have to go."

"I'm going with you, Mr. Byne."

"So no Pepper then?" The guide did not seem one bit surprised. "You see how this place keeps growing."

"We need to return to the main path." I began walking down the dirt trail between white fences.

The scenery changed around us like rewinding the videotape that captured the footage of us getting to the Pepper's lot. We were back on the main path with the beginning of the pilgrimage behind and the bright singularity ahead of us. Several people walked past us toward the light. They did not say a word, and they became smaller and smaller as they walked away from us.

"What you seek is beyond that light," said the guide.

Bella touched the end of a shelf. "But these shelves look like they go on forever. How will we ever reach the end?"

"They do go on for a long time, my child."

"But there is a finite number of lives ever lost, correct? These rows of shelves… they must end at some point," I said.

"Imagine trying to read all the books in the world. Could you ever really read them all when new books are being written faster than you can read?"

The question reminded me of the time we visited New York Public Library. Nina had just started to read on her own, and she was ambitious to read them all. Abby, being a year older, told Nina that she was dumb for thinking that was possible.

"That's impossible," said Bella.

I told Bella about an interesting math problem related to this, where an ant walks on a stretchy one-meter rope. As the ant moves one centimeter forward, the rope stretches to two meters. When the ant moves another centimeter, the rope becomes three meters long, and so on. Our intuition tells us that the ant will never reach the end of the rope, but it eventually does! It does so in about 10^{43} iterations. If each centimeter takes one second, it would take the ant 10^{35} years, a lot longer than the age of the universe (13.7×10^9 years). But if each step took the shortest amount of time allowed by quantum mechanics (the Planck time), which is coincidentally about 10^{-43} second, it would only take the ant about one second to reach the end.

"So it's a race then," said Bella. "If we walk fast, we'll reach the end."

The guide laughed at Bella, just like how Abby laughed at Nina at the library.

"You can think of this place as a symbol for lingering

memories of your past lives. As you shed your memories and all the emotions that you once possessed as human, this black path will begin to turn white, and you will notice these shelves less and less."

"And God is at the end, right?" I said to the guide.

"The greatness of God is infinite. All you can do is to march one step at a time."

"This is a trick, isn't it? No one ever makes it. Am I right?"

"Many give up and return, but some do reach ultimate enlightenment. Count the steps, like counting sheep to fall asleep. You may get there."

"One step forward, then another… One plus one plus one," I mumbled as I imagined an endless sequence like I used to write on the whiteboard in class.

"How many was that?" said the guide.

"Three," replied Bella.

"Keep counting, my child. I have more souls to guide. Good-bye, Mr. Byne. Good-bye, Bella." She walked back toward the entrance, and her body faded into the gray air.

"Mr. Byne, we need to try."

"Okay." I took her hand and began our march.

I usually got bored with counting past a hundred or so, and this was no exception. I visualized the sequence again, but this time after the summation symbol, Σ. *One plus one plus one plus one…a divergent series.* I stopped.

"Why are you stopping, Mr. Byne?"

"Can it be that simple?" I muttered.

"What's simple?"

"You can't walk one step at a time to infinity."

"But we are doing it. Those people ahead of us are doing it."

"1+1+1+1 forever. Do you know what that sum is Bella?"

"I'm only eleven, but I know that's infinity. Whatever that means."

"The sum diverges and tends to infinity." I began walking back towards the entrance.

"Where are you going? We have to go this way."

"Bella, I studied math in college. Sometimes, when an infinite sum diverges, there is a way to assign a meaningful value to the sequence."

"I don't get it, Mr. Byne."

"There is something called the regularized sum of a divergent series. It's related to the Riemann zeta function." I was sure she wasn't nodding, but I just kept talking as if she understood. "Riemann zeta function,"—I swiped my hand in front of me, and the formula appeared against the gray air—"What the…"

"How did you do that?"

"I just thought of writing the equation out."

Bella moved her finger in a semi-circle, and she drew a seven-colored rainbow. "Cool."

I stared at the equation that I drew mentally and continued with my thought.

"The zeta function, which is a sum of…"

$$\zeta(s) = 1 + \frac{1}{2^s} + \frac{1}{3^s} + \frac{1}{4^s} + \cdots = \sum_{n=1}^{\infty} \frac{1}{n^s}$$

"If s is minus two, for example, this becomes 1+4+9+16+25+ and so on. This, of course, diverges to infinity, but if you regularize the sum, it becomes zero."

"Zero?"

"Correct. Another example is when s is minus one. Then it becomes…"

The sum appeared in front of us. "1+2+3+4+5+…"

"Like all numbers?" said Bella.

"Well, it's the sum of all *positive integers*, and the regularized sum is negative one-twelfth." The equation in the gray air became: $1+2+3+4+5+… = -\frac{1}{12}$. "This result is even used in physics, like the Casimir effect."

I glanced back at Bella, and she just shrugged her shoulders.

"I don't understand anything you said, Mr. Byne."

"I don't fully understand it either. But if this crazy math can explain the physical world, like the Casimir effect, then there must be some truth to it. I mean the world is full of things that defy our intuitions, like quantum theory, general relativity, evaporating black holes, and the possibility of extra dimensions in space. If a counterintuitive idea can be proven, it doesn't matter even if *I*"—I pointed at myself—"don't understand it."

"What does that have to do with us?" she said.

"In the zeta function, if s is zero, then it becomes 1+1+1+1+1+…" The formula in the air updated as I spoke.

"One step after another?"

"Exactly. Okay, the details aren't important, but it also has a regularized sum."

Math can save your life…even in Heaven!

We ran back the way we came. When we neared the door, the guide was standing at the counter.

"Gave up already?" she said.

"No. I think I found a shortcut."

"Have you? Not a lot of people do. And those who know don't typically come to Heaven in the first place."

"So you know the answer."

"Of course. I serve the Creator."

"Why didn't you tell me?"

"It's not my place to tell." Her answer was short and dry.

"Is it really that simple?"

"Simple? That's quite relative, don't you think? Enlightened, maybe?" She said with a sarcastic smile.

"But I'm sure some people might do it by accident from time to time," I said.

"It must be done deliberately and consciously, which requires one to have an understanding."

I looked at the door. "That's where we need to go," I said to Bella.

"Good luck, Hershel. Remember, it's not a real sum, so it doesn't work all the time."

"What are we going to do, Mr. Byne?"

I pressed my back against the door and told Bella to do the same.

"The regularized sum of $1+1+1$ forever is minus one half. We'll take a half step backward. Are you ready?" I said to Bella.

She nodded.

"Okay, here we go." I squeezed her hand.

Our heels went right through the door, and we took a half step backward. The intersection of our calves and the door glowed like rings of fire. I no longer felt the door on my back, so I shifted my weight backward until my body aligned with the core of the door. The door's surface burst into lights, and a swirl of colors filled the gray air. Then the door ripped through our bodies and hauled white mist with it. The door stopped in the vast expanse of pure white and grew to the size of a two-story building. Bella and I looked at each other and silently agreed to move closer.

Lightning struck the door and split it down the middle. My heart jumped, and I squeezed Bella in my arms. We waited for the door to open, but instead wrought iron began to creep inwards from its edges like ivy. White mist thickened above the door, from which two steel swords materialized. The creeping wrought iron formed a pair of sheaths that crossed in the center of the split door. The swords began to spin, roaring like giant turbines, and Bella covered her ears. The doorknob liquefied and molten gold poured out like a fountain. It flowed to the four corners of the door, where it took the shape of dragons. They unfurled their wings as their tails elongated around the doorframe in a clockwise direction. The swords stopped spinning, and Bella uncovered her ears. The golden dragons tilted their heads and glared at us.

Bang! The swords drove themselves into the iron sheaths in the middle of the door, and Bella jumped with a shriek. The dragons dug their claws into the door, faced the center, and scorched the surface with their fiery breaths, magically turning the wrought iron into shimmering gold.

Fallen Angel

THE DRAGONS MADE of liquefied gold stopped breathing fire at the crossed swords and solidified into statues. Bella left my side and approached the door, checking the dragons for any movement with each step. Before she reached the door, I pulled her back, deciding that I should be the one to touch the door first. I kicked the tail of the dragon on the bottom left, then tapped its head with the tip of my finger. It didn't move, and I sighed in relief. Bella pushed the door, first with her hand, then her shoulder. I stood on my tiptoes to touch the sheath of a sword, thinking that the crossed swords were keeping the door shut, but only the first joint of my fingers could reach the bottom of it. I looked around for ways to get to the hilt of the sword, but it appeared hopeless.

"Great." She puffed. "We make it here, but we can't open it."

I banged on the door, but it was like pounding on a concrete wall, it didn't even make a sound.

"Hello?" Bella yelled at the seam of the two halves of the door.

I stepped away from the door that was freestanding in the white mist. I walked around it and saw that the other side was pitch black. Bella reached out her hand to the black backside, but her hand didn't stop at the surface, it disappeared into the darkness. She looked at me, took one sharp breath, and ran into the black.

"Bella, wait," I yelled. "Bella?"

After she disappeared, I kept calling her name. I didn't dare to go into the darkness myself. Then, Bella tapped me on my shoulder from behind.

"It doesn't go anywhere," she said. "I came out the front."

I stood at the edge of the door so that I could see both its front and back by tilting my head. I stuck my hand into the dark side and watched it poke out the decorative side. It didn't work the other way around.

"It's no use, Mr. Byne."

"Did you think you could just walk through that door?" A voice came from all directions.

"Who's there?" said Bella.

"I am the Angel of Light." The voice focused.

We moved to the front of the door to follow the voice.

Blinding light from above hit the misty white ground. From out of the halo of exploding light walked a man, handsome with shoulder length blonde hair and a neatly trimmed beard. He wore a white gown with gold stitching; a tall clergy collar accentuated his height.

"My name is Hershel. We are here to —"

He raised a finger at me and turned his gaze to Bella. "Hello, Bella. I've been expecting you."

"You were expecting me?"

"Yes, of course. You have suffered an awful death," he said to her. Then he turned to me. "You were clever enough to come this far, but the door will not open for you, no matter how long you wait."

"It is a door." I banged on it. "It has to open somehow."

"Just like minus one half and infinity are not equivalent, this door isn't the same as the one you would have reached the long way. What do you hope to find on the other side anyway?" He stroked his beard.

"God, answers, and the power to change the world of the living."

"Um, maybe you will."

"Have you been inside?" said Bella.

"Of course, I have. I am his loyal servant."

"Can you let us in?" I said with some urgency. "My daughter is in—"

"Abigail… Yes, I know."

"Then can you?"

"No, only the gods and stewards like myself can cross through this door. Well, there is a way in, but—"

"How? How do we get in?" I stepped closer to him.

"I thought you would ask. But I cannot guarantee that you will like the path."

"I will do anything."

"Me, too," said Bella.

"Alright then. The path is through Hell."

"Hell?"

"Yes, there is a hidden passage there that will grant you access to this door." He paused and looked at Bella and me sequentially.

"Ok, how do we get to Hell?" I said.

"I am the Angel of Light, the light to guide you through the darkness. But, walking through Hell isn't enough. You must also complete a task."

Bella and I looked at each other, then at the Angel of Light.

"To emerge back from Hell, you must gain a new level of enlightenment, equal to the one you would have gotten on your pilgrimage."

"What do I need to do?"

"You must save a soul," he said.

"You mean, save someone from Hell?"

"Yes. That will be an act worthy of entering the Gods' Realm. But, you must understand the risk."

"Like what?" asked Bella.

"There is a chance that you will fail."

"Are you saying we could end up in Hell after being admitted into Heaven?" I said.

"Yes. You've heard of the fallen angels, no? On the other hand, there is also a chance that someone in Hell can be saved. Don't you think that God is indeed merciful?"

"I don't care about the risk," said Bella. "I need to stop my dad from getting into trouble."

"And you, Mr. Byne?"

"I will go. I need to help Abby." I gave Bella a nod.

"Alright then." He removed a folded piece of paper from the inside pocket of his white gown. It unfurled into the size of a newspaper on its own. Old cursive script filled the page—too decorative to decipher at a normal reading pace. The first word, written in large font, was *Contract*. I had no desire to read the rest, so instead moved my eyes diagonally to the bottom of the page.

"Sign your name here." He pointed at the line with a black feather pen.

As I hesitated, Bella took the pen and wrote her name in block letters. She handed me the pen, and I signed my name under hers.

"Good," he said.

The large contract folded itself back up. He tucked the contract in his gown. He raised his hands and waved them downward. Like dry ice vapor blown by hot breath, the white mist under our feet moved away from us, revealing a pitch black hole that appeared to have no bottom. We were levitating over it.

He looked up and raised his hands. "I am the Angel of Light. The contract has been signed. Hershel Byne and Isabel Remming, two souls from Heaven, will plunge into the depths of Hell, and I shall be their guide."

A spiral staircase made of black onyx rose from the hole. It came to a stop when the first step contacted Bella's feet and the second step touched mine. Only two turns around the central pillar were all I could see in the pit of darkness.

The Angel of Light crossed his hands behind his back and descended into the dark space until he landed on the staircase ahead of us. "Follow me."

Bella and I placed our hands on the central pillar of the spiral staircase and began our descent. The Angel of Light held up his palm, and a small fire appeared to light our way. After making several turns, the white portal above us had shrunk to the size of a needle hole.

"There is no going back now," he said as he sped up.

The pitch of the spiral stairs increased, and Bella had to jump down to the next step. Then the treads began to angle downward.

"Mr. Byne?" I heard her trembling voice behind me.

"Keep up." The Angel laughed.

It became too steep even for me to find the next tread without hopping down. Bella screamed and fell right past me. I tried to catch her, but I missed and slipped too. My butt hit a step and bounced off onto the next. Then all the treads fused together, and the staircase became a slide. The central pillar disappeared, and I was flung outward. We were like coins on a pitch-black gravity well, sliding down in spiral orbits toward the center. Bella was screaming ahead of me; she was revolving faster and faster. The flame of the Angel was near the bottom of the vortex, and as the flame vanished into the abyss, so did Bella. In total darkness, my rotation down the spiral intensified. I pressed my hands on my head and cried out as I plunged vertically down the vortex.

All of a sudden, like a coin dropping out of a funnel, all sense of motion ceased. There was nothing to see, no sense of up or down, only silence.

Is this Hell?

"Almost." The omnidirectional voice of the Angel pierced through me.

Is this nothingness?

"*Cogito ergo sum.* Close your eyes."

I found it pointless, but I complied.

"Now open them."

Still dark, but not pitch black. Instead of floating in the void, I was standing on a surface, shiny like a black piano. There was a faint orange glow ahead, and I moved toward it.

It was the guiding flame of the Angel, floating over his

hand, and Bella was standing next to him. Behind them was an enormous stone double door, lodged in an endless black wall.

"Here we are." He turned to the door and pressed his fiery hand on its seam. Flames flooded the gap between the double door and spread all around its edges. The door rumbled and began to open, revealing the raging inferno inside.

The Angel of Light walked in and split the flames down the middle like Moses parted the Red Sea. Walls of fire grew tall like tidal waves on both side of the parted path and converged to form a tunnel of flames.

Bella clung to me and swatted the flames that came close.

"Do not worry, my child. You are quite safe from the flames. Come."

As the corridor descended, the flaming ceiling rose higher and higher. The blazing walls diverged, widening the path.

"Who comes to this place?" I asked.

"All sorts."

"Would I have come here if I hadn't joined the church before I died?"

"No, not even those who commit blasphemy come here nowadays."

"I thought that was the unforgivable sin."

"Even when the atheists who denounced the existence of God come to this place, they realize that they were wrong. They accept the existence of an afterlife and God himself. With acceptance, they are saved."

"Pascal's Wager: the benevolent God."

"Precisely. Some are malevolent though."

"How about the seven deadly sins?"

"Some are outdated. Gluttony and Sloth?" He hooted as he kept walking. "Half your countrymen would be down here, and how would we punish them? Immobilize them and stuff their mouths with salted turkey?

"Lust and Envy, that depends," he said in a more serious tone. "Some are just human nature. We used to have people here for adultery, fornication, homosexuality, and such. Those days are long gone. A sign of the times."

"How about Wrath?"

"Those committing acts of violence, like murderers and rapists…" He stopped mid-stride. "He doesn't like them, so they are popular residents of this underworld. Funny though, if you think about it—He killed millions himself."

"He? You mean God?"

"Have you read the Bible?"

"Oh, you mean the Old Testament."

"He killed millions, the Flood of Noah, Sodom and Gomorrah… God is God, old or new. What sins are left?" He tapped his chin a couple of times.

"Greed and Pride?" said Bella.

I looked at her with surprise.

"Sunday school," she replied.

"Oh, yes. Those are punished, especially when one places personal gain over the lives of others. These types of people may never have pulled the trigger of a gun, physically stolen food from the poor, or taken medicine from the sick. But they are fully aware that their actions cost the lives of many. Are they sorry?" he said rhetorically. "Oh no. They hide behind words like *authority, naiveté,* and *business,* and smile over their escalating wealth and power. Humans are so quick to punish those who commit an act of wrath but too kind to those with greed, too forgiving to those who claim to be above others. But if it were the other way around, there would be fewer souls down here for sure."

"Huh?" Bella cocked her head.

"People with greed are the type who fear imprisonment and death. Those who commit the sin of wrath, not as much. But in any case, the murderers and rapists are the most common inhabitants here."

"I hope they suffer for a long time," said Bella.

"They do, my child. Forever. Well, until they eventually make it out of here."

"If they are here forever, how would they ever get out?" said Bella.

"There are different sizes of *forever*." The Angel smiled at her.

"Like different types of infinity?" I said.

"Yes, I forgot you were a mathematician."

"Infinity is infinity, isn't that true?" said Bella.

"Well, Bella, some infinities are bigger than others." I tried my best to explain, "For instance, there is an infinite number of integers—you can count those, like one, two, three. But the set of real numbers, like ones with decimals, is not countable, and it is bigger than that of integers."

"How much bigger?"

"Infinitely bigger." I turned to the Angel of Light. "So they can suffer in Hell forever, but that *forever* is infinitely shorter than the eternity of Heaven?"

"If you want to rationalize it like that, sure."

"Do they go to Heaven when they get out of Hell? Like the one who killed me?" She had both hands clenched into fists.

"No, they go straight to the path of the pilgrimage."

"Which lasts forever," I said. *Argh*.

"It does make your head hurt, doesn't it. I speak figuratively, of course." He appeared to be entertained.

The cardinality of time in Heaven and Hell? Who would've thought?

The shiny black floor reflected the violent burst of flames above us, but it was quiet, tranquil almost. There was no lake of fire or screams of agony.

"This is not what I imagined."

He crossed his hands in front. "You expected fire everywhere?"

"Yes, sort of."

"There's no need to make the likes of you, or those who come to punish the sinners, suffer in flames."

"I thought demons punished the people sent to Hell," said Bella.

The Angel rubbed Bella's cheek with the back of his finger, and she cringed at his touch. "There are so many sinners here, my child. And we need at least one soul in charge of tormenting each sinner."

"Where do the punishers come from?" I asked.

"They are easy to come by. The more horrid the sin committed, the more souls line up to take their turn in revenge. Which reminds me of the reason why you are here. You are here to save a soul."

"But there is no one here," said Bella.

"Hell is not like a prison with a common gathering space. It's more like solitary confinement. It is much more punishing that way."

"How do we find a sinner?" I asked.

"You will need a guide." He snapped his fingers.

A loud thundering sound came from above. A swirl of fire, like the eye of Jupiter, raged over our heads and then careened downward. It hit the black onyx floor next to us, and the flames dissipated.

A small creature kneeled before him. "Master, I'm at your service," it said in a cackling voice.

"Rise, my loyal servant."

The creature's skin was gray. It had a long tail with a spade-shaped tip that seemed to have a mind of its own, and a pair of wings on its permanently hunched back. It raised its long ears and twisted its neck to glare at us over its shoulder.

A demon?

"He is a servant of this world." The Angel stroked the head of the spade-tailed creature. Then he raised his hand to the ceiling, and swirls of flames came down. He grabbed the flames and threw them over his shoulder like a cape. He levitated and said to the demon, "Show them around, then bring them back to me."

The fiery cloak whirled around him like a tornado and snatched him up into the blaze above.

Theodicy

A CAST-IRON DOOR rose from the floor ahead of us, just the door with nothing behind it.

"This way." The demon unfurled his bat-like wings and flew toward the door. It stuck its two-inch long nail on the end of its finger into the keyhole and twisted it. It thrashed its wings, and the gust of wind blew the door open.

Like passing through a portal into another world, we moved from the uniform black floor with nothing around us to the inside of a room where a violent flame engulfed a wooden scaffold. A young woman stood by the fire with a torch in her hand.

"You have a visitor, Eleanor," said the demon.

"I'm Hershel, and this is Bella."

"Welcome," she said, throwing the torch into the towering flame.

"Are you a sinner?" said Bella.

"No, I'm his tormentor." She raised her hands to the fire, and as she lowered them, the flames extinguished.

A skeleton was shackled to the stake with its skull resting on its collarbone. The last bit of charcoaled flesh fell off its bones and crumbled into ashes as it hit the ground.

Bella clung to me, burying her face into my side.

"Who is that?" I asked.

"Adam was his name. He made my life a living hell."

"So you burned him?"

"He'll be back."

Powdered with black soot, the skeleton whitened and red fibers sprouted from it. The growing mass thickened into muscles, and eyeballs grew in the empty sockets of the skull. The skin that had begun to cover the body hadn't spread to his face yet, leaving the eyes bulged out with growing muscles surrounding them. He dropped his blood-red jaw and gasped for air.

"For what he did, no amount of torment will bring me peace."

I held Bella tightly. It wasn't a sight to be seen by an eleven-year-old—I wasn't ready for it either. "What did he do to you?"

Eleanor patted Bella's hair and looked at me. "She shouldn't see this." She reached her hand out to me.

I took her hand and succumbed to the familiar sensation of being drawn into someone's mind. We were now in the kitchen of a house from medieval times.

"This was my house."

A woman entered the house with a handsome young man. It was not Adam.

"Is that you?"

She nodded. "It was our first anniversary. We splurged and bought wine to celebrate. But then, they came." She pointed at the door as the couple exchanged a kiss.

The door blasted open, and three men barged in. "Is that her?" one of them said.

"Yeah, that's her," said another.

Two men grabbed Eleanor by the arms and dragged her to the door. The third man pointed a knife at her husband.

"Why are you taking her!" her husband yelled.

"She is a witch," said the man with the knife as he slowly backed toward the door.

Eleanor banged her feet and screamed as the men pulled her from the house.

"She is my wife. She is not a witch."

"She will confess, you will see." The man with the knife closed the door.

"A witch hunt," I said to Eleanor beside me.

"Yes. There were countless more like me, all in the name of God," she said, devoid of emotion.

"Who is Adam?"

"The priest." She diverted her eyes away from me.

We were no longer in her house but in a dungeon. Eleanor's wrists were bound with a rope and hooked to a pole above her head.

"You don't have to relive this."

"No. You need to see this." She turned to me with tightened lips. "You must understand. Deprived of food and sleep, I lived in my own filth. I prayed to be rescued. I prayed for my husband to come and set me free. One day, the priest brought my husband to see me. Seeing my soiled dress and matted hair, he cried. He told me to confess, then left the room."

The door to the dungeon opened, and two men

entered. One man hoisted her up, and the other unhooked her wrists from the pole.

"Please, no," begged Eleanor as the men dragged her out of the cell.

Her heels left tracks on the floor, and we followed them into another room. A man was adding a log to a fire. He gestured the two men to spread her arms apart. He grabbed a bucket of water and splashed her. She shook her head to rid the water from her face. Muddy water dribbled from her hair to her already soiled dress.

"That's Adam, the priest," said Eleanor.

He squeezed her two cheeks together. "You have been accused of being a witch. Do you confess?" He pressed so hard that his thumb slipped inside of her mouth. With a look of disgust, he wiped his thumb on the collar of her dress.

"This is a mistake. I am not a witch." She shivered in her wet clothes.

"Of course, a witch would deny it. I can assure you,"— he grabbed her by the neck—" this will not be pleasant."

"Please…" She struggled for a breath. "I am not a witch."

He slipped a knife under the strings that held her dress closed. She tried to pull her arms to her chest to keep the dress from falling off her body, but the two men ripped the top of her dress off. She covered her breasts with one hand and held onto her skirt with the other, but the men tore that off, too.

"No. Please, Father." She crossed her legs as the men pulled her undergarments down.

The two men grabbed her wrists and spread her arms apart again.

"Such a beauty." The priest squeezed her breast and sneered as she moaned. "Witches have gotten so sophisticated in infiltrating our society."

"I am not a witch!"

"Confess!" He slapped her face hard with the back of his hand.

Standing beside me, Eleanor watched herself being beaten. Without shifting her gaze, she said, "There was no way out. But I didn't know that then."

The priest told his assistants to move her to a metal chair in the corner of the room, where they tied her hands to the armrests and her ankles to the legs of the chair. Her bare bottom was against the cold iron seat that had a stove-like compartment below it.

"Performing sexual acts with the devil?"

"I did no such things," she said with a hoarse voice.

He fetched a burning piece of wood from the fire with a pair of tongs.

"Please, no."

"Do you confess?"

She shook in fear, slapping her bound hands against the armrest. She pushed herself against the backrest as if she could escape if she pushed hard enough.

He inserted the burning wood in the seat pocket. She tried to raise herself off the seat, but the men pressed her down. The seat under her began to glow red, and she screamed, rattling the chair off the floor.

I had to look away.

"I confess. I confess," she shouted.

It took longer than a minute for them to untie her. The men pried her from the hot iron seat like ripping meat off an ungreased pan. I felt ill from her screams. She fell unconscious as her body hit the floor with a thud.

"I can't even imagine —"

"This wasn't the end." She kept her eyes on her naked self, lying on the dirt, but she tightened her grip on my hand. "He gloated that he was right. He tortured me for two more days, right up until my execution. I was barely alive when they finally burned me over green wood. He said a slow burn would cleanse the blood of a witch. The flame devoured my legs. Luckily, the smoke killed me before the fire reached the rest of my body."

She let go of my hand, and we were out of her memory and back in Hell. Adam, bound to the stake, had full skin now, and hair was growing out of his head. The burned logs under his feet had regenerated and became stacked up into a scaffold. He arched his head backward and gasped for air.

"Eleanor. I'm sorry." He yanked on his shackles.

She didn't acknowledge him but instead turned to me. "I waited and waited for him to die. It was contaminated water that killed him. He died lying in his own feces, but not before he tortured and killed five more women like me." She picked up a stick, and a piece of tarred cloth wrapped itself around the tip. "For someone like him, Hell is too kind."

The torch spontaneously ignited, and she shoved it into the bottom of the stacked logs. The fire crackled, and smoke rose.

"How many more times?" he yelled.

"Until your blood runs clear and the flame cleanses my soul," she replied.

Bella buried her face against my side again and covered her ears as his scream intensified. His skin blistered and the blood seeping through his cracked skin bubbled. The shackles stopped rattling, and the flame engulfed his agony.

The orange flame illuminated Eleanor's face, staring at Adam with the same empty look. "You know, the ironic thing is—"

The demon shrilled. It grabbed Bella's and my hands and yanked us toward the door.

"The ironic thing is what?" I turned to her as we were dragged out of the room.

She didn't answer.

The door closed in my face, and another appeared behind us. The demon swung its spade-shaped tail and pointed it at the next door. "Stay focused on the tour."

The demon unlocked the second door with his fingernail and blew the door open with his wings.

A woman holding a long ball-tipped whip stood in front of a man tied to X-shaped beams with his arms and legs spread wide. His back was slashed and smeared with blood that had darkened. His legs were shaking, and his shackled wrists held up the weight of his sagging body. She cracked the whip at him, and he grunted, arching his back and rattling the chains that bound his limbs. She turned to us. Her eyes were sunken, with dark bags underneath. She sobbed and took another swing at the man.

"Are you okay?" Bella asked the woman.

"I'm fine." She hung her head low and raised the whip for another strike.

"What's your name?" said Bella.

"Zoe."

"What did he do to you?" Bella approached her.

"This pig stole my life from me. 'My little Zoe,' he used to call me." She whipped him again. The man let out a short grunt through the gag that covered his mouth.

"He was my uncle. I trusted him." She whipped him three more times in quick succession.

A segment of flesh hung from his back exposing a white rib underneath. With his legs no longer supporting his weight, his arms stretched downward, and the grunting ceased.

"He molested you, didn't he?" I said.

Zoe nodded. "He had his eyes on me from the time I was little, younger than you." She looked to Bella.

"Did he kill you, too?" said Bella.

"Not physically, but it's all the same to me. No matter how far away I ran or what I did, I was haunted by what he did to me. I trusted no one, and I was always alone. I started taking anti-depressants. One day, I took too many, mixed with alcohol. Such a wasted life. I was broken, and nothing could've fixed me, all because of him."

"Why aren't you in Heaven?" I asked.

"I was in Heaven," she said, "I even started the pilgrimage. Peace at last, if you can call it that."

"So how did you end up here?"

"I was notified that this pig had finally died." She pointed at her dead uncle with her chin.

The spilled blood returned to his body, and every slash on his back began to heal. His trembling legs straightened to carry the weight of his body. He took a breath through the gag.

"At first, I ignored the news and kept moving toward the light. I walked and walked, but nothing changed. I knew I was supposed to leave everything behind to reach the end—the place of ultimate enlightenment, I was told—but I couldn't. My anger pulled me back from where I wanted to go, and the light at the end never got closer. That's when I saw him… You saw him too, didn't you? That's why you are here."

"Who?" said Bella.

"The Angel of Light," she said in a sarcastic tone.

The demon's tail swayed to get her attention, and she pursed her lips.

"He offered to help me. He said I needed to deal with my past to move on. I said *no* at first, but then I realized he was right, so I took his offer."

"P-lee-th-sh-op," her uncle said through the gag.

"You found him like this?" I asked.

"No. When I came here, my uncle was punishing another man."

"Your uncle was a punisher?" said Bella.

"Yes. As a boy, he was abused by his pastor. When I first came to Hell, I saw him punching his pastor with metal knuckles. Covered in splattered blood, he turned to me. One look and he knew it was his turn."

"What happened to the pastor?"

"Do you think my uncle was the only one he molested?" She turned up a corner of her mouth. "There was a line of souls waiting for revenge. Some had knives and others guns, all fighting to take the place of my uncle.

"As the pastor was dragged to a different room, the beams rose from the floor, and the shackles bound my uncle's hands and feet like they are now. He said it was his pastor's fault. I didn't want to hear his excuses. I spat in his face and kicked him in the groin. He begged for forgiveness, but it was too late for that. I snapped my fingers, and he was gagged. All at once, those terrible memories flooded my mind as vivid as ever, every cut inside of me, the taste of his…thing, the shame. My hatred for him turned into this whip. The rage kept growing inside of me until I couldn't contain it anymore. I cracked the whip at him, tearing his flesh like he tore the inside of me. I felt a small release of anger. That's when the door closed. I've been here ever since."

"Zoe, plee-th n-o mor," her uncle said through the gag.

Zoe cracked the whip at him, and blood oozed from a fresh vertical slash on his back. He heaved and banged his fists against the beams, rattling the shackles.

I placed my hand on her whip, and she faced me. In her eyes, I saw a scared girl in her striped underwear, staring at a wall with her chin resting on top of her knees. Zoe slapped my hand away, and a blaze of fire in her eyes engulfed the image of the little girl.

"I'm not his little Zoe anymore." Her hand quivered.

"Can you ever forgive him?" I didn't believe that she could, but I asked her anyway.

She didn't answer; the quiver in her hand spread to the rest of her body. "I don't see a way out of here."

"Maybe when you find closure, you can go back to—"

"You don't understand. *He* is the reason I'm here!" She cracked the whip at her uncle again and again in a fast figure eight, each one harder than the one before. I told her to stop, but instead, she began shouting.

"Time to go." The demon flew up, covered our faces with his wings, and ushered us out the door.

The door closed behind us and disappeared. The demon was getting ready to open another.

"Why can't we talk to them? Why do you push us out?"

"This tour is like a preview." It cackled. "You can see her again if you wish. But for now, we need to move along."

Inside the third door was a man tied to a chair.

"Matt, this has gone on long enough. Let me go," he said.

Matt twirled a police baton by its short handle as he circled the man in the chair.

"Long enough? Have you no guilt, Phil? Why do you think you are here?" Matt thrust the end of the baton into the man's abdomen.

"What's your story, Mister?" said Bella. "Why do you hurt him?"

"This scumbag took everything I had. Everything."

"Look, it was just business. You were the one who signed the paper without understanding the consequences."

"You knew the loan was shit, but you sold it anyway." Matt delivered another blow.

"Look,"—Phil heaved and coughed—"the system isn't set up to protect against stupidity. Dimwits like you kept me in business. I didn't do anything illegal. Was it unethical? Maybe,"—he shrugged his shoulder mockingly—"but you know what? I wanted a nice car and a nice beach house with a pool. Sorry you didn't get to have what I had," Phil said defiantly.

"What happened to you?" I grabbed Matt's hand as he was about to deliver another blow.

"He jacked up the interest. I lost my job. I lost my house. I got sick from the stress. I couldn't afford the treatment. By the time I was rolled into the emergency room, it was too late."

"Blame your doctors, blame the government, or better yet, blame yourself. Guys like you focus on having things you can't afford and ignore the fine print. You shouldered the risk, and I got big returns. That's all."

"Do you know how many lives you ruined? There will be a line behind me who would love to punish you." Matt slammed the blunt end of the baton against Phil's face.

Phil moved his jaws back and forth and raised his bloody face. "Go ahead. Hit me again. I don't fucking care. I'm getting used to it anyway."

"My family still lives in a homeless shelter because of you." He punched Phil with his bare knuckles.

"You saw your family?" said Bella.

Matt nodded. "There's no way they can dig themselves out of that life… And it's all because of this guy's greed, his complete lack of empathy."

"How about this?" The demon handed Matt a knife. "Punishment is more effective if you rotate the tools."

Matt took the knife and placed the blade against Phil's face.

"Oh, come on, Matt," said Phil.

Matt stared at himself in the knife's surface. "He deserves eternity in this place. But not this." He dropped the knife.

"You signed the contract," said the demon. "He might not have slit your throat,"—the demon got in Matt's face— "but you know, if it weren't for this unremorseful man, you would still be alive. You'd still be with your wife, your son. Imagine all the family dinners you are missing, your son opening presents under a Christmas tree." The demon picked up the knife with its spade-shaped tail and placed it back in Matt's hand. "It is all his fault. He deserves this. You said it yourself; there will be a line of souls waiting to take a crack at this miserable thing. He isn't even worth being called a man."

Matt gripped the knife tight.

"Do it," said the demon as it stepped aside.

"Come on, Matt. Not the knife. Just hit me again."

Matt grabbed Phil's hair and tipped his head backward, holding the tip of the blade over Phil's right eye.

"This is for my family." He slowly stabbed his eyeball as Phil screamed.

The back of the chair hit the floor, and Matt got down on his knees gripping the knife with both hands. "Give me back my life. My wife. My son." He stabbed the man's chest with every word.

"Time to go," said the demon and we were pushed out of the room again.

"Is physical torture appropriate for a man like that?" I asked the demon as I faced yet another door.

"This is Hell, and I'm a demon. Are you really asking *me* that?" It laughed aloud in its cackling voice. "We used to have people here for having an affair, or just looking at another man the wrong way. This is Hell, and we have a reputation to keep." It unlocked the fourth door. "See what you think of this next one."

As soon as we walked into the room, there was a gunshot. Half of the victim's head was blown off, and smoke drifted out of the shotgun barrel.

"Hershel. That's your name, right?"

"Yes. And you are?"

"Colin. And you must be Bella. This isn't a sight for a little girl like you,"— he unlatched the double barrel shotgun and loaded it with more shells—"but you better get used to it."

The mutilated head of the man began to regenerate.

"The asshole in the chair here is Dwight Paige, a former head of the American Firearms Association."

The last drop of blood returned to Dwight's skull, and his skin regenerated. He inhaled and opened his eyes. "Colin, that's enough."

"Enough?" said Colin. "Enough what? Enough people killed because of you?"

"Look, I didn't kill your grandson. Some lunatic did. I didn't even sell the weapon that killed him."

Colin turned to us. "Can you believe this guy? Not a single drop of remorse in him." He fired a shot at Dwight's left knee. The bullet shattered his kneecap and splintered the wooden leg of the chair behind it.

"Goddammit," Dwight shouted, tightening the muscles of his bound arms to fight the pain.

"If he didn't kill your grandson, then who did?" I asked.

"There was a shooting at a mall. Some guy shot eleven people while shouting 'End of days.'"

"So why aren't you tormenting that guy?"

"The mall shooter was a mental patient. I don't think he knew what he was doing. Besides, my grandson was killed by a bullet from another man with an open carry permit.

That man, a fully bearded redneck, unloaded his entire clip at the shooter. One of the bullets hit my grandson's neck, and he died two days later."

"So why him?" Bella asked Colin.

Colin shoved the smoking barrel into Dwight's other knee. "This guy's mission was to tell millions that they should carry a gun at all times—'the good guys' he used to call them. He just wanted to sell more guns at the expense of innocent people. Your good guy killed my grandson!" He blasted Dwight's other knee.

Dwight rocked in the chair, screaming. "I didn't care about the gun sales, you half brain fuck. It was all about maintaining influence over the stupid rednecks who love to hold onto their guns. It was like herding sheep—easy, and with power, money just flowed in."

"How did you end up here?" I asked Colin.

"I died from a stroke and got recruited to this place. I was given a choice between the mentally ill shooter and this piece of crap, who had just died from a private jet crash. The mental patient was remorseful. He said he fell through the cracks in the system, not getting the medication that he needed. In fact, he said he deserved to be punished for what he had done. He asked for forgiveness but didn't beg for mercy. I couldn't imagine torturing him for all eternity. But this piece of shit"—Colin reloaded his weapon and swung it fast to close the barrel—"went on the news and called the death of my grandson 'a casualty of freedom.' What an asshole this one is. Given the choice between the two, I didn't flinch. I took a gun and shot him in the face right then. I've been stuck here ever since."

He placed the nozzle of the gun at Dwight's chest and

emptied both barrels. The blasts knocked the chair over, and a puddle of blood oozed on the black onyx floor.

"What about the guy who shot your grandson?"

"The redneck? He's still alive. I will get him when he dies. It turns out the 'good' guy with the gun dreamt of being a hero, like in the action movies. No fucking surprise there. He didn't care about the victims; he just seized the chance of emptying his clip in public."

"What happened to the one who shot eleven people? The mental patient?" said Bella.

"Those who were slain didn't care if he was remorseful. They lined up to take on the burden of Hell's duty."

"A burden?" I said.

The demon spread its wings and pointed its tail at Colin, and he froze.

"The tour is over now." The demon shot its spade-tipped tail at the door. The tail elongated like a rope tied to an arrow and pierced the door. It shortened its tail, and the door hurtled toward us.

Reflexively, I protected Bella from the oncoming door. I closed my eyes right before the impact, but nothing happened. When I opened my eyes, the demon was gone. Bella and I were back in the empty black space with the fire roaring above us.

Penrose Triangle

"HELLO. HELLO," I called out as I spun in place.

The flame and its perfect reflection against the glassy black floor converged at the horizon. Being sandwiched by the fire, the boundless space paradoxically felt constricting. Bella clung to me, and I wrapped my arm around her.

Flame swirled like an eye of a storm above us, and the vortex grew downward like a tornado looking for a landing. The fiery tip met the floor, and the flame roared.

"How was the tour?" the voice of the Angel of Light came from within. He walked out in his white gown, his hair swaying in the blazing convection, unaffected by the fire. He spread his arms open, and the flame swept upward to the ceiling.

"Did you find a soul to save?"

"How can I choose? I cannot sympathize with anyone I met."

"Um. Now, isn't that a problem?" He stroked his chin.

"I want to go back. I don't want to be here," said Bella.

"My child, do you not remember what I told you before coming here? You do remember,"—he looked to me—"don't you, Hershel?"

"You tricked us," said Bella.

"Tricked? I do not recall that. Did you not read the contract?" He bent at the waist to look Bella straight in the eyes. "You knew the risk."

She averted his stare.

"You said, if we save a soul, then we can see the gods," I said.

"Indeed. I did say that. But I never promised that I would tell you how. Now did I?"

Suddenly, the kindness I had seen in him when we first met disappeared. The outline of his face looked sharper than I remembered. "Who are you?"

He ignored me and placed his finger under Bella's chin, lifting her face up.

"Do you remember how you died, my child?"

"Of course, I do. He shot me."

"Rise, Jon Nadson." He raised his hand to summon the dead.

From the pitch-black floor, a circular pit of flames rose. Walls rose silently around us until they reached the ceiling. We were now in an isolated room just like the others we had seen on the tour. Nadson emerged from the fire, screaming, clawing at his face, and arching his back as the fire devoured him. The piercing scream ceased as his flesh turned into smoldering embers. As the last bit of orange glow waned, the gray mass crumbled off his bones.

"He is now a prisoner of Hell. Unless, of course, you save him."

Muscles reformed over his skeleton and a fresh layer of skin wrapped his body. As hair grew in, his eyes opened. He scanned the area and found Bella. "You little bitch." He tried to lunge at her, but barbed wires shot up from below, gripped his wrists, and yanked him back to the floor.

"You can no longer hurt her. No matter how hard you try, Jon Nadson," said the Angel of Light.

Naked and on his knees, he gritted his teeth as blood trickled from where the barbed wire dug into his forearms. He looked up at Bella. "Isabel Remming. If you had kept your mouth shut, I could've sold you on the first day. Instead, I got stuck with you for weeks. It's all your fault."

"You have seen this type, haven't you, my child? Unrepentant, self-righteous, and cruel. If anyone deserves to be here, it's someone like him," the Angel said.

"Why don't you come a little closer, Isabel? Let's have some fun, huh?"

"You shut your mouth." I stormed closer to Nadson.

"Are you the one who will strike him first, Hershel? Are you going to take her job?" The Angel gave me a piercing look.

I had my fist raised, but lowered it as I took a step backward.

"I didn't think so," he said and turned to Bella. He reached into his gown and removed a gun. "Here, my child. Take it. Shoot him wherever you want."

She took it and slid her finger inside the trigger guard.

"No, Bella."

She glared at me, and the menacing look on her face held me back. She raised the gun. Her hands were shaking.

"Ok, ok, Isabel. I was just kidding. I'm sorry."

"He is not sorry, my child. I can assure you of that. Now do it."

"Bella, no!" I reached for her, but the Angel shoved me to the side.

She stepped forward and aimed the nozzle at his head, her finger pressed against the trigger.

"Such a quick and painless death? Why don't you aim a little lower where it really hurts? Remember what he did to you?"

She kept her trembling aim at his head, but her eyes unfocused.

"Of course you do," said the Angel with a smirk.

The weight of the gun dragged her aim downward to his neck and then to his tattooed chest. She kept her blank stare as the nozzle continued to move lower to the middle of his six-pack abdomen. It stopped at his groin.

"Pull the trigger, my child." His voice made her jump.

Her eyes focused and her finger twitched on the trigger.

I pried in between her and the Angel and put my hand on the gun. "Bella, don't do it."

Her face wrinkled, and her head sank. The gun swung down to her side like a pendulum.

"She'll come around," the Angel said.

"Who are you? I thought you were the Angel of Light, here to guide us through this place."

"Yes, indeed. I am the Angel of Light, although I have other names. But you must have assumed that *guide* meant *help*." He sneered.

"Wait a minute. What other names?"

"Some call me Lucifer, the most beautiful angel of all."

"Lucifer, you mean Satan?"

"Some call me that too."

"You are the Devil?" said Bella.

"I am the most loyal servant of God. No insults please, my child."

"But you are the Devil," Bella repeated.

"He values my service. I provide the contrast to make his work look better. Heaven cannot exist without Hell. People aspire for eternal happiness because they imagine the alternative—Hell," he said, slowly pressing his tongue against his upper teeth.

"You are not a loyal servant of God." I wanted to get in his face, but my feet wouldn't move.

"I endure the hatred of mankind. I receive no rewards, yet I do my job. If I'm not loyal, I don't know who is."

"You are a murderer." Bella backed away from him.

He laughed. "It has been said, 'The greatest trick of Satan was to convince people that he didn't exist.' You've heard that before, haven't you?" He paused. "Wrong!" he shouted. "The greatest trick was for God to blame me for all his wrongdoings."

"But you killed people. I read it in the Bible," said Bella.

"What all ten or so?" He huffed. "In my defense, I had God's blessing, even for those few. On the other hand, He flooded the Earth and unleashed plagues. Killing ten versus millions? Human ignorance blesses the Almighty."

"What do you want from us?" I stood closer to Bella.

"Men, women…and nowadays children, so many sinners. There aren't enough demons to torment them. But for every sinner, there are enough afflicted souls willing to carry out their revenge. They are so easy to find. One trip to the path of the pilgrimage, I can round them up like a flock of birds."

He began circling us. "You, on the other hand, were clever enough to skip the pilgrimage and reach the door to Gods' Realm. I had to pry you away.

"So you lied to us?"

"No lies, just a little misdirection. The contract holds true. If you save a soul, you can proceed. But chances are, you will abide by my decree."

"I won't." She dropped the gun on the floor.

"Oh no?" He resumed pacing. "After hearing the news of your tragic death, millions felt the rage inside of them. As Jon Nadson spent the day on the hospital bed, people said, 'Give him death,'"—he pumped his fist in the air— "to a murderer whom they knew nothing about. And when they learned of his death, they all wished he'd burn in Hell for eternity." He looked right at me. "Revenge is at the core of all humans; your bones are made of it, and your blood feeds it with pride and anger, all the while your mind tries to suppress the burning hatred with ideas like fairness and justice. And your pretty skin"—he ran his long finger down Bella's neck to her shoulder—"hides all the turmoil within, so when you look in the mirror, you only see self-righteousness."

"Not everyone is like that." I looked straight at Lucifer—he wasn't an angel in my eyes anymore.

"Reasoning is your saving grace, but believe me, emotions trump all. Do you believe a serial killer deserves a death sentence?"

"Yes," I answered.

"How about men who are convicted of murders, but didn't commit?"

"Of course not."

"But how do you know who committed a crime and who didn't?"

"Level of certainty."

"Certainty? That's funny, especially coming from a mathematician like you. Where do you draw the line? 90 percent confidence? 95 or 99.9 percent? Juries, witnesses, and expert forensic scientists have all declared innocent men guilty beyond a reasonable doubt, but you can never be 100 percent sure." He raised his voice. "Execution is driven by your inner being, your uncontrollable desire for vengeance. You still don't believe me, do you?"

He raised his palm in front of Nadson's face and pushed him away. The bound and naked body receded until the black wall swallowed him. He raised his hand again, and flames descended from the ceiling above. A column of fire raged in front of us with a man inside. As the flames dissipated, the bald man with blistered skin raised his head.

"Do you know this young man?"

His hair and eyebrows regrew, and I gasped—it was Robert Wilkin.

"For a mere minute of gratification,"—Lucifer grabbed Robert by the gag in his mouth—"he attacked your daughter Abigail."

"Where's Abby? Is she alright?"

"He chased her down in his car."

"Where's Abby?" I screamed at Satan.

"Pretty girl, wasn't she, Robert? A precious thing."

A knife appeared in Lucifer's hand, and he turned to me. "Here, take it. Gouge his eyes for seeing your daughter with ill intent. Cut off the hands that struck your daughter."

I grabbed Robert by the hair and pulled his head backward. As I peered into his eyes, a fog of darkness began to engulf my vision. I closed my eyes and shook my head.

"Open your eyes and look into his. He'll show you what happened to your precious girl."

I gritted my teeth and looked into his eyes. It was like looking through a thick cloud. I dipped my head lower and saw a living room through the ceiling. Robert and Abby were on the couch. He leaned into her and slid his hand over her jeans. She told Robert to stop and pushed him away. He slapped her on the face and pinned her down. She started to scream and kicked the coffee table, spilling their drinks.

"Oh, Daddy," said Lucifer. "Look at the fear on her face. He didn't care about her. Now take it." He placed the knife in my hand.

The vision of Abby disappeared. I placed the tip of the blade right below Robert's left eye.

"Remember Zoe?" Lucifer whispered into my ear. "Abigail will be scarred for life, all because of this man, and you couldn't do anything about it."

I pressed the blade down until there was a triangular depression of skin; he grunted through the gag.

"Mr. Byne?" I heard Bella's pleading voice from behind. "Why is it okay for you to hurt him?"

I released the pressure on the knife and looked back at her.

"Is it because you are an adult and I'm not?"

"That's right," I shouted, immediately regretting it.

Bella backed away from me and shivered. A tear streaked down her cheek like the time when she saw her dad in the basement of her house.

"I didn't mean to— "

"I don't want you to do it." She shook her head.

I saw Abby in Bella's eyes and became numb. The knife's

handle rolled off my fingers, and the blade clanged on the black floor. As I pulled on Robert's hair, it slipped off his skull like a wig. He didn't flinch. I looked at his face—it was no longer him, but a hairless plastic mannequin.

"What happened to him? Where did he go?"

"Sometimes even my tricks fail," said Lucifer.

"A trick? He isn't here, is he? He's still alive."

"Does it matter? You saw what you wanted to see and it almost justified hurting him. Maybe what happened to your daughter was worse than what you imagined. What would you have done then?"

"Abby…where's she? Is she still alive?"

Lucifer held his palms up in the shape of a cup, and an image of Abby floated over them. She was still lying next to the tree.

"How long has she been out?"

"You just left her. A few seconds ago, her time."

"That can't be. It's been hours, days maybe."

"That's just your perception of time. It has no relevance to time in the world of the living. Time is an illusion after all."

I stared at the image of Abby. "Do something. Please." I pleaded with Satan—the Devil!

"I don't do that sort of thing. I won't mind having Robert here if he dies, however. Maybe your daughter will become his punisher…when she dies, of course."

"No, she won't. I need to get out of here." I searched for an exit, but every direction looked the same—solid black walls.

"You are not going anywhere. You still haven't fulfilled the requirement."

"God, please save her." I looked up and saw nothing but roaring flames.

"Why plead to God for help? He is no more powerful than I." He shook his head.

"Then you save her."

"I have no will to do so."

"You are no god, not even an angel," I shouted at Lucifer, then immediately realized that I just insulted Satan, like taunting a hungry lion.

"When is the last time a work of God saved a life? Not just dumb luck but a true miracle? Then again, you can't tell the difference between the two, can you?"

"We hear about miracles all the time," said Bella. "This one time, a school bus full of children lost control on a bridge. They could have fallen to their death, but the suspension cables stopped the bus. I saw it teetering on the edge on the TV. Everyone said it was a pure miracle."

He laughed. "That's the beauty of that damn thing you call God. He doesn't have to do anything. He gets credit for all the good, and I get credit for the bad. Why didn't he prevent the bus from losing control in the first place, huh? To test their faith, right? To measure their worth by the number of prayers?"

"He saved those children because He can and wanted to. That's what my preacher told us."

"Oh, the omnipotent god." Lucifer waved his hands in the air as if to ridicule. "He is all knowing, too, isn't he? He knew every minute detail that contributed to that accident. What if the brake lamp came on that morning before the children got on the bus? What if the driver had ten more minutes of sleep the night before? What if the clouds dissipated a little sooner to dry the road? Why do bad things happen at all? He would have known about every tragedy that would occur from the very first moment of creation. He could have changed the master plan so that nobody would have to know words like *pain* and *suffering*, but no"—he wagged his finger at us—"He chose this miserable world, a world in which school children were made terrified of plunging to the bottom of the river, screaming for their moms and dads as their bus teetered on the edge. And for what?"

"To teach us a lesson?" I said.

"Like immunizing children, Hershel? Reverend Reed told you that, right?" He laughed. "How about shocking dogs to teach them not to cross an invisible line? I've heard them all."

"It is to teach us that we must pray to God for the good of the world," said Bella.

"Pray? If God already knows what is going to happen, what is the point of praying, my child? If your little voice"—he pinched Bella's cheeks—"can change his mind, his master plan for the world, then he didn't really know what was going to happen. By praying, you are attempting to singlehandedly prove that God isn't all-knowing. Do you think your little hands"—he picked up her hands and forced them to clasp at her chest—"have the power to make God do what *you* want him to do? Accept this, my child." His voice escalated with each word. "It's either He is powerless and clueless, or He wanted a world of suffering, where people beg senselessly for his mercy." He pushed her hands to the floor. "And you think I'm the Devil."

Bella rubbed her wrist and stepped back into me.

Lucifer took a deep breath and his anger faded. "Putting philosophy aside, we have work to do. Don't we, my child?" He waved his hand at the mannequin, and it hurtled into the black wall. He then flicked his finger in a quick beckoning gesture, and the wall spat out Nadson. The barbwires around his wrists dragged him across the piano-black floor as if there was an invisible Titan pulling on them. Nadson's body came to a stop right in front of us, and the barbwires became anchored to the floor.

"I'm in need of an assistant," said Lucifer. "To give him what he deserves, and who is more appropriate than you, my child." A tail appeared from underneath his white gown and picked up the knife that I had dropped. "Do you think your murderer should go unpunished? After all he did to you? He deserves to suffer." He handed the knife to her. "Make him understand your suffering. You may even be able to draw out sorrow and regret from this wicked man."

She gripped the knife but shook her head sideways.

"No? You won't do it? I know someone who will."

"Who?" She raised her head.

"Your father."

"He is not dead. We saw him," I said.

"True, but he will die eventually—it's inevitable. Mark my words, my child. A father will never forget losing his daughter, especially a death like yours. With all the gory details of your death played mercilessly on the news, the sound and the image of your last moment are seared in his memory. They eat away at your father from the inside. Only the vision of Jon Nadson in Hell grants him a small measure of consolation, and his hatred fuels the imaginary flames. He prays to God to punish him. No, he demands it." Lucifer's voice intensified like a dramatic sermon. "Even when you are forgotten by the rest of the world, every little girl he sees will bring it all back. A man like your father will beg me to take this job. He will want to break his bones one by one, slice him bit by bit. Oh yes, he will."

"No… Daddy."

"So you see, my child? If you don't take this job, I will just wait for your father to join us here. Do you want him to punish your murderer for you, or do you think you should take it upon yourself?"

Bella raised the knife.

"Now slice him and seal his fate, my child. It is what everyone wants."

"Bella. No. You don't know what your father will do. He is trying to trick you."

"Mr. Byne, he is right. My dad will do this. You saw him with the gun."

I grabbed Bella by the arms and squatted to look straight into her eyes. She was trembling. She tried to look away, so I shook her to get her attention. "We just saw Zoe, Eleanor, Matt, and Colin. You didn't want me to become like them, and that's why you stopped me, right?"

She glanced at Nadson over my shoulder.

"Look,"—I shook her again—"I'm a father too, but I didn't hurt Robert."

"It's different," she shouted. "Abby is still alive. I'm dead!" She pushed me away. "You don't know what he did to me. They will examine my dead body. My dad will know."

"Yes, he will, my child."

"Police don't release that kind of information to the family, Bella."

"Perhaps what your father imagines is worse than what actually happened." Lucifer walked around Bella and bent at his waist to whisper in her ear. "I think it is. Much, much worse."

"Stop." I sprang and tried to tackle Lucifer, but my body went straight through him.

"It is not wise to attack someone like me, Hershel."

"Bella, don't do this. You will be stuck here forever."

"I don't want my dad to be stuck here, either."

"I'm a father, so I know. If he knew you sacrificed yourself to spare him, he would suffer even more. He would not want to see you become the servant of this…Devil." I pointed my finger at Lucifer.

"Nonsense. If you don't do this, my child, you will regret it forever. You will live with the guilt of sealing your father's fate forever."

"We don't know that. No matter how smart we are, we can't predict the future. When your father comes to Heaven, you can warn him."

Bella threw the knife on the floor.

"Oh, the voice of reason." He threw his hands up in the air. "It does not belong here."

"You prey on the innocent?" I said.

"Innocent…perhaps. But she is a cog in the cycle of hate and revenge. Her death is fuel to perpetuate a beautiful system of suffering that is as old as humanity itself."

"It doesn't have to be this way." I kicked the knife beyond his reach.

"No, but it is. Jealous and vindictive, you are a reflection of your Almighty. He wanted humans to suffer. Yearning for revenge is part of who you are, pure and simple."

"He preached for love," Bella shouted.

"There is no vengeance without love! The stronger the love, the more painful the loss. The punishment must match the sin; only death suits the one who brought death."

"An eye for an eye—" I muttered.

"Man is blind."

"It shouldn't be the way," I said.

"But it is what you want." He brought his hands together and turned his palms upwards. A hologram of a man in a prison cell came into view. "This one was convicted and sentenced to death for the torture and killing of five men, six women, and twelve children. He watched them scream until they passed out, in a dungeon much like the one where Eleanor was tortured. Imagine the pure agony that he inflicted on the innocents."

I could hear Eleanor's scream again, the rattling of the metal chair.

"Don't you think he deserves to be put to death?"

"Yes," I said without hesitation.

"That's right. People will spend millions of dollars to keep him alive, even hire a watchman to make sure he won't kill himself so that *they* can kill him in the end. All the theatrics won't bring back the victims. His death will bring no change to the world. Deterrence? That's a delusion. The families of the victims count the days to his final breath, wishing the execution will go wrong and he'll suffer more than he's supposed to." He paused for a moment and smiled with arrogance. "But if you want to break the cycle, I say let him live. Make him serve society in some way. Allow him to have a meaningful, happy life."

"No way."

Lucifer grinned. "As a mathematician, you must have come across a Penrose Triangle."

"Of course. So what?" I replied, not knowing where he was going with it.

"Have you seen one, my child?" he said to Bella.

He pointed to our left, and a sculpture of a Penrose triangle rose from the floor: three square beams connected end to end in the shape of an equilateral triangle.

"It's just a triangle," said Bella.

"Look carefully, my child. Follow the surface of a beam around the triangle."

She traced around the triangle several times with her eyes and cocked her head. "That's impossible. The top of one goes under another…something's not right."

"It's just an optical illusion," I said to Bella. "The same idea was used in the famous artwork called *Waterfall* by M.C. Escher—maybe you've seen that one. If you step to the side,"—I took five wide steps to my left and beckoned her to come to me—"see, it's not a triangle anymore."

"Oh, I see." Bella saw the triangle split at the top corner, looking like an unfolded paperclip, and then returned to where she had been standing to see the trick again.

I followed her back and admired the illusion too.

"That is my point." Lucifer gloated.

"What's your point?" I said.

"There are many locations from which to view this sculpture, but there is only one place where it makes sense, where the sculpture conveys its purpose. After you broke the illusion by stepping aside, you returned to see it again. You will always return. There are many ways to deal with evils in the world, but you always return to retribution. To end the cycle of evil is to step away,"—he swept his hand and made the triangle lose its illusion—"but you can't. It is in your nature."

He raised his palm, and the hologram of the serial killer floated over his hand again—the killer sneered at me with a look that said *I'll-kill-you-too*, and the images of mutilated bodies ran through my head.

"What are the odds that this man can be rehabilitated?" said Lucifer. "Certainly not zero…a chance for bettering the world even."

The image of the scruffy killer in a prison cell disappeared and was replaced with a scene at a café, where he sat in a business suit—he looked like an ordinary man.

"But can you imagine him enjoying his golden years, while the families of the victims continue to suffer?" said Lucifer.

I cringed at the thought. Words like *justice*, *closure*, and *punishment* came to mind.

"See, you simply cannot allow this man to have his redemption. Where is your compassion for this man?"

I remembered watching a documentary about the Norwegian prison system where a murderer is treated like any other citizen, and his standard of living is higher than a low income family in the U.S. They said the purpose of the prison system is to keep the public safe, and the country's recidivism rate is the lowest in the world—logically it made a lot of sense. But what if that murderer had killed my family? The clash between logic and emotion inside of me had no immediate resolution.

"God help us," I said.

Lucifer laughed, tilting his head backward. "God made

all animals on Earth, but man is the only species ever to roam the Earth who kills for reasons other than to eat."

"Male lions kill the cubs of other males," I said, trying to lay a counterpoint to anything he said.

"They do so out of instinct, for the survival of their bloodline. But you,"—he pointed his finger at my chest— "men kill out of spite, for retribution, for power unrelated to your procreation. In his image, you were made. What does that say about your God?" He lifted my chin with the tip of his finger.

I averted my eyes and saw Bella—her eyes fixated on Nadson.

Lucifer turned to her. "So, you see, my child. You know that nothing can take you back to your parents. But you can't help but feel the rage boiling inside of you every time you stare at his face." He pumped his fist. "You think about roasting him, skinning him from head to toe, removing his nails one by one, and gouging his eyes. Why is that, my child?"

"Because I'm angry and it will make me feel good." Bella curled her fingers into fists.

"That's right. Then do it." The knife I had kicked away flew through the air and Lucifer snatched it. "Just look at him, and give in to your desire." He hoisted Nadson's face with his tail that slipped out from underneath his white gown. "He is not sorry for what he did to you. He is just sorry that he was caught, that he died." He handed her the knife.

"That's not true, Isabel," pleaded Nadson. "I'm sorry."

"He will say anything. But remember: when he screwed up, it was your fault. He almost cut your pretty face with a broken bottle, didn't he?"

Bella inched closer to Nadson.

"He scored your ankle with a knife." Lucifer touched Bella's foot with his tail. "He said, 'This won't devalue you.' Remember?"

Bella parted Nadson's hair with the knife.

"Come on, Isabel. I said I'm sorry."

"You made me eat dog food, then laughed when I gagged." She ran the tip of the blade along his face.

"Bella, don't do it." I stepped forward, but Lucifer put his arm in front of me.

"Why stop her? He deserves it. She wants to do it. It's a win-win."

"Why don't you laugh at me again? I'll even make your smile wider." She slid the knife inside his mouth.

"Now, we are onto something," said Lucifer.

"Bella. Listen to me. This is what the Devil wants you to do. It is not what *you* want."

"How do you know what I want?" She pointed the knife at me.

"I know that you don't want to spend eternity in a dungeon with him. He can't hurt you anymore. But with every cut you make, you will lose yourself. You aren't a devil or a demon. You are better. You are better than he is." I pointed at Nadson. "Don't let your hatred and anger define who you are."

"You don't know what he did to me," she yelled at me. "He deserves this."

"Bella," I said as calmly as I could. "You'll become him. It'll just be you and him stuck in this empty room for all eternity…trapped with the one you hate the most in the whole world. Imagine a hundred years, a million even, just the two of you."

She dropped the knife. She swiped her hand at Nadson's face, and he vanished into the darkness.

I struck down Lucifer's arm and reached Bella. "Your dad will be proud of you. I am proud of you."

"You've found a way," said Lucifer. "You must see the irony though. She didn't defeat the vindictiveness in her heart; she simply succumbed to fear."

A bright light flashed above us and bored a hole through the flames. A scroll descended along the beam of light and landed in Lucifer's hand. He unrolled and read it.

"What does it say?"

"It seems that I have failed to recruit you, Isabel Remming…this time at least." He rolled the scroll back up and handed it to me. "And you, Hershel Byne. It seems that you have saved a soul."

"I can return? And Bella?"

"That scroll is the key to the Gods' Realm. It is for you and you only. Bella will return to the base level of Heaven. She can wait for her family there or return to the pilgrimage."

"God sent this?"

"God? Maybe it's from the Creator himself."

"The Creator?"

"There are so many gods in this world. Have you never wondered who created them all?"

"If there is a creator of the gods, who created him? And if he exists…" *Infinite regress.*

"There is always a sensible answer to the *what-came-before-it* problem. But you must reach the next level of enlightenment to find the answer." He pointed to the scroll in my hand. "Now go. I cannot keep you any longer."

He turned to Bella. "You did well, my child. I confess that I do not find joy in imprisoning the likes of you."

"Then why do it?" said Bella.

"Out of necessity, my child. I cannot rely only on sinners to perpetuate the cycle of hatred and punishment. As it turns out, it's quite easy to make good people do bad things."

"I don't believe that." I shook my head, but a doubt clawed at my heart.

"There is darkness in the heart of every man, and I am a mere reflection of that fact. Accept it, for you cannot defeat what you fail to recognize. But I assure you, I will be here for a long time."

The column of light that brought down the scroll widened.

"Step in, Isabel Remming. You are going back to Heaven."

"It isn't a nice place."

"Call my name, my child. I will come to get you anytime." He ran his six-inch long finger through her hair.

She brushed his finger aside. "I will not work for you."

"Good luck, Bella," I said.

"Mr. Byne. If you see God, ask him to stop my dad from doing terrible things. And if you ever see my dad, tell him to be happy and that I'm okay."

"I will, Bella."

"You be careful. I'll see you again, Mr. Byne." She stepped backward into the light.

The column of light intensified, bleaching her dress white and blending her pale skin into the light.

Good-bye, Bella. Thank you.

The white mist swirled around her and receded upward into the abyss of the flames above. When I returned my attention to the black space around me, Lucifer was gone.

"Find the path of the Drained Souls." The voice of Lucifer echoed.

As the last echo of his voice tapered off, there was total silence. All that remained were the red light from the flames above and my reflection on the polished black floor. Lost, like the first time I found myself with white mist all around me, I walked aimlessly.

Up ahead, there was a cluster of freestanding doors, all ajar.

666

I GRABBED THE doorframe closest to me and pushed the door open a bit more to peek inside. Through it was Eleanor's room, a column of fire casting a long wavering shadow behind her.

"We meet again, Hershel," she said without moving her gaze away from the fire that began to lose its strength.

I let go of the doorframe and reluctantly stepped inside. "When the demon dragged us out, you said something about irony. I didn't get a chance to hear what you meant."

"The demon didn't want me to persuade you not to follow my path." She turned to me as I got closer. "Since you're here again, you must've refused to become someone like me. There aren't many like you."

"Do you regret it?" I was more than half sure what her answer would be, but I had to hear it from her.

"It's hard to say." She squatted down and hugged her legs. "After all these years... what year is it?"

"Twenty-eighteen."

"Almost four hundred years..." She buried her chin to her knees. The flame died, and the ashes began to return to

Adam's bones. "I still hate him. And the irony is I'm stuck here with the man I despise."

I was right.

Immediately, I felt ashamed of even thinking that in front of Eleanor.

"You don't know what it's like to be tortured like that for no reason at all. He enjoyed it, this monster."

The gray mass that thickened around Adam's skeleton blushed and quivered.

"After something like that, when Satan asks if you want revenge, you take it. You don't hesitate for even a split second."

"You've suffered enough."

"I'm tired of this, Hershel." The words leaked out of her mouth like the last bit of air from a deflated balloon.

"Then stop. Save yourself." I reached out my hand, and she took it.

"I have tried, but—" She looked up at Adam who had fully regenerated.

He smirked. "You were my favorite, Eleanor."

"He does that, and it all comes back." She stepped forward, and the stake that bound him morphed into a chair, which tied his hands at the back and his bare feet to its legs. "The night before he burned me at stake, he scalded my feet."

A tub of boiling water rose from the black floor.

"A bath again, Eleanor? Bring it on. It's fading anyway."

"What's fading?" I said to Adam.

"My memory of pain," he replied. "My real body has been eaten away by the worms long ago."

"Shut up!" She slapped him across his face.

He wiggled his jaws back and forth. "The pain I feel here

is based on my experiences while living: a broken arm when I fell from a tree, being burned by spilled tea or accidentally touching a hot coal, slicing my finger with with a carving knife, or smashing my finger while hammering a nail. But the pain I feel become less and less as my memories fade. How many times has it been, Eleanor? A thousand? Ten thousand?"

"Shut up," she yelled.

"Why do this?" I asked her.

"Because he still remembers how he tortured me."

He smirked, almost gloating. "I remember your witchy skin blistering over the coals, oh it was so red and ugly after that. It just popped when my knife touched it; I could see the muscles tightening underneath. It was a shame…you had such young beautiful skin."

"His memories of my torment amplify his own pain." Her knuckles turned white. "And as long as I remember it, I can make all the pain and fear come back to him. Fading pain?" She gripped his jaw and twisted it. "I can assure you it'll be as fresh as the first time!"

She squeezed his face so hard that his chin slipped out of her fingers.

He wiggled his jaw. "Come on, Eleanor, stop."

"*I* still remember it all like it was yesterday. A pain so intense that you lose yourself." She tilted the chair from behind and scooted it forward so that his feet hovered over the boiling water.

"This isn't real. This doesn't hurt. This isn't real. This doesn't hurt," he chanted.

She leaned towards his ear. "Remember? You said you didn't want to cook my feet. You just wanted my skin to peel.'" She lowered his feet into the tub.

His heels touched the bubbling water. "No," he yelled. She let go of the chair and dunked him ankle deep. He screamed with his mouth agape at the flaming ceiling. He screamed until he passed out.

I felt ill, not only from seeing the suffering of a man but also for the fact I was growing accustomed to witnessing it. "How long must this go on, Eleanor?"

"There's no chance of forgiveness. My only hope is that someday I can forget. The real irony is I have to relive my memories to torment him." She got his feet out of the boiling water and tipped the chair on its side.

"Why don't you remember your husband, your family? Love and happiness instead?"

"They were drained of me long ago. Pain and anger are all I have left. Once they are gone, I will rest."

I couldn't have saved her, even if I had tried.

"Goodbye, Hershel." She looked away—she was done with me.

The sudden emotional distance from her translated into the physical space between us. I found myself on the other side of the doorframe and watched the door close. The door rattled a few times and then was swallowed by the black floor.

I walked toward the next closest door and found Zoe inside.

"You're back," she said to me.

"I'm getting out of here if I can find the path of Drained Souls. Why don't you come with me?"

"My place is here. I'm bound by the contract."

"What is in the contract?"

She snorted. "Nobody reads it until it's too late. It says I will remain his tormenter until the end of times or my conscience fades away." She cracked her whip at her uncle. "Where's that little girl you were with?"

"She returned to Heaven."

"She made a better choice than I did. Stupid me."

"No chance of forgiveness?"

"Every once in a while, I remove the gag from his mouth and watch him drool. He says the same thing…that he is sorry. Then he adds that he was a victim too. Kind of makes the apology seem less sincere, no?"

"Lucifer said his job is to keep the cycle of sin and hatred going. Maybe it's up to us to end it."

"This pig stole my life, and my hatred locked me here, robbing me of a better place. I hate him even more."

"But if you stop—"

"Then what? The pilgrimage? How long were you there before he snatched you? I walked until there was nothing but endless white mist, second after second, hour after hour, year after year. When I closed my eyes, I heard the Bible being recited cover to cover and back again. When I opened my eyes, it was all the same, like I hadn't taken a single step. Unlike the pilgrimage, I can release my anger here. I can feel my soul being emptied drop by drop with every crack of the whip. Someday, I'll be empty… I'm hopeful for that."

"You wish for *nothingness*?"

"Ironic, isn't it. I could've just said *no* at the gate. But now I must work to drain all thoughts and emotions to become an empty shell. The path you seek is where I'll go eventually."

"I couldn't have saved you, even if I tried."

"You weren't meant to get out of here…if it wasn't for that little girl."

I looked up at the flames and imagined Bella surrounded by white lights.

"You go along now. I have a job to do."

"I'm sorry, Zoe."

"Don't be." She began whipping him again. "Goodbye."

With every exchange of the cracking whip and the
grunt of her molester, the space between us stretched and
the one behind me contracted until I was out the door.

As the floor swallowed Zoe's door, I faced two more. I
walked past them, pulling each one closed without looking
in. *Find some closure, guys.*

The ubiquitous and nebulous flames reflecting off the pitch
black floor began to flow like a jet stream over the Pacific
Ocean. I took a step in the direction of the flow, and the
reflected flames sank on both sides, forming mountains
made of fire with the ridgeline under my feet. I picked up
one of my feet and tried to tap on the space away from
the ridge—the floor was still there. It was just an optical
illusion, but I didn't stray. I kept my eyes on the ridgeline
and marched forward with the scroll in my hand. Eventually, the Alps of fire led me to the mouth of a tunnel with
an orange glow. As I stepped into it, the reflected flames
behind me returned to its amorphous form. The tunnel
was what I had always imagined of Hell—jagged ground
made of scorched rocks, steam venting from fissures, and
the echoes of moaning souls.

This better not be another trick of yours, Lucifer!

But the glowing rocks that paved the path weren't hot,
neither was the venting steam. As I progressed through
the tunnel, the moaning became progressively louder and

started to sound more like hums or unintelligible chants. The tunnel opened up into a cavern with a long winding path to a suspension bridge. There was something odd about the bridge that stretched over a river of lava: not only did it sway from left to right, but also every part of it seemed to flinch and jiggle.

The rocks around the perimeter of the tunnel behind me encroached inward. Instinctively, the thought of going back crossed my mind, but the hole quickly became too small—one of few instances when my indecisiveness helped me, I think. It also made the restless bridge my only way out.

As I got close, I gasped.

The bridge was made of human bodies, all naked with lifeless expressions. Four or five bodies, lying side by side, spanned the width of the bridge; they were staggered by a half body length in a head to feet orientation. Children lay perpendicular, crosslinking the strands of naked bodies. Their muscles twitched involuntarily as the hot lava beneath them moved the surrounding air by convection. I couldn't tell how many layers of bodies made the bridge, but the lava below wasn't visible through the mass.

"Are you all alright?" I shouted at them.

No one replied, not even tilting his or her head in my direction. I tapped an arm near the base of the bridge with my foot—it was stiff as a log. I raised it with the tip of my foot as far as my knee would bend and let go. It snapped back like a rubber band and the vibration propagated down the bridge, their bodies bobbing up and down ever so slightly.

I figured that they were the Drained Souls.

Along the sides of the bridge were human guardrails,

standing with their heads hung low and holding hands. The first soul that formed the right guardrail was a young woman; her pale skin glowed from the lava below. I lifted her head with the joint of my middle finger and then parted her long, red curly hair that covered her body all the way to her belly button. Her eyes were open, but they did not focus on me. On my left was an old man; the wrinkled skin of his chest sagged over his belly and his thin peppered hair barely covered his head. He had the same look. I stretched my arms wide to hold onto both of them and summon the courage to cross. I took my first step onto the bridge; it swayed but was stable. I said *sorry* to the woman under my foot, took a deep breath, and planted my other foot on the bridge. Hunching my back, I plodded forward with one careful step after another. A blob of lava erupted on my left, and I tightened my grip on the handrails. When I glanced back, a row of new bodies stood at the end of the bridge. They didn't follow me; instead, they burrowed themselves into the bridge, and I felt the bridge shift forward.

"Help me," said the slender woman under me, like she was talking in her sleep.

I took my foot off of her and stepped on the thigh of another. "Take me," that one said.

I felt the handrails move.

"Help me," the man to my right said.

"How?" I said, but he just repeated the same thing.

Not everyone I touched moved or spoke. To those who did, I asked for their names and how they got there, but no one answered—they all had the same empty stare. I tried not to step on anyone's face although it probably wouldn't have made any difference. I started to feel more relaxed about walking on the moaning souls, and when lava erupted to my right, I noticed that there was a bridge just like the one I was on. An eruption behind it revealed yet another bridge in the far distance. On my left, the view was the same.

"How far to the end?" said an old lady who was my right handrail.

"About halfway," I said.

"How far to the end?" she repeated.

When I was less than five steps away from reaching the end of the bridge, a boy reached out his hand. "Take me with you."

"Cheater!" The bridge shook in anger.

I stepped over him and secured my footing.

The boy cried again, "Take me with you."

I couldn't resist. I turned around, grabbed him by the arm, and yanked him out of the bridge.

"Cheater!" The bodies surrounding the boy clawed at him, but their fingers slid off his smooth skin.

"Are you okay?" I said to the boy, but he didn't reply.

The woman directly under his feet wrapped her hand around one of his ankles, and another man yanked his other foot down. The boy lost balance and fell backward, slipping out of my hand. As soon as his back hit the bridge, the drained souls crowd-surfed him toward the start of the bridge.

"No, please!" he screamed.

"I'm sorry," I yelled as the tide of arms swept him away. It was all my fault that he had to start over.

I stepped away from the turbulent souls and found solid ground. At the seam of the bridge and rock, a head of an old soul rose, and his arm emerged like a zombie crawling out from his grave. I didn't take his hands, but stepped back and watched. He dug his nails into the rock and climbed out of the mass of bodies. He stood and mumbled something.

"What did you say?"

He turned to me and said, "At last." What I heard was English, but his mouth moved differently, like watching a dubbed movie.

"How long did it take you to cross the bridge?" I said to the man.

He looked back at the bridge. "I don't know."

"When did you die?"

"I served the great Pharaoh Khufu." He began walking along the path away from the bridge.

I asked him some more questions as I followed, but he showed no interest in answering them. His stride hastened with excitement as the path led us into yet another tunnel. The glow of heated rock was dimming behind us, and just before the darkness swallowed us, the tunnel dead-ended at the bottom of a dry well with white light pouring in from above.

"No." He collapsed to his knees as he looked up at the column of light.

The vertical hole was about a body length in diameter, and every square inch of the cylindrical wall was covered with naked souls. They moaned and shifted, never finding a comfortable position under the weight of the others above them.

The Egyptian man crawled on the ground to the wall of the well. A woman ascended a body length, leaving a space for him to join the multi-layered mass. He stood up and wedged his body inside it. As he did, bodies wiggled, shifted, and shoved him into the back. He waited thousands of years to cross the bridge only to find the wait was not over. It reminded me of the disappointed look on Abby's face when we took her to the Disneyland for the first time. After waiting for an hour in the hot sun for a ride, we entered the building only to find the line inside was even longer.

Abby! I gripped the scroll tight, and the sound of crinkled paper reverberated up the hole.

"You have a scroll," a woman on the outermost surface of the human wall said to me. Her eyes were wide open, yet her stare was empty and her dark gray pupils fixed.

"Scroll!" The nearby drained souls chanted. The word spread up the cylindrical chamber like waves.

I shoved the scroll into the inside pocket of my jacket.

"Climb to God." She interlocked her fingers, making a cup for my foot.

I stepped onto her hands, and a man reached out and grabbed my arm from above. As the chill from his cold hand spread to my arm, I felt sadness creeping through me.

"Scroll. I will hold it for you," said the man.

I didn't like the sensation, so I yanked my arm from his grip. I shoved the top of the scroll back into my jacket and reached for his shoulder to ascend. The moment my hand touched him, I understood the sadness I felt—an image of his past life flashed before me.

—He is held in a chokehold by a bearded man.

His mother, wife, son, and daughters are all in tears with knives held against their throats by a group of men.

"This land is ours now," says one of the men.

"Let my family go," he stammers.

"They are ours, too," says the bearded man. "Kill the old woman and the boy. We'll keep his wife and daughters."

"No," he squeezes a plea through the chokehold.

His son cries as the old woman's throat is slit, and she hits the floor. He flaps his arms and legs, but his frail neck snaps in the captor's arm—his limbs dangle like a marionette without strings.

His wife and daughters are kicking and screaming, but they can't escape the men.

"Don't worry. We'll take care of your girls." The bearded man slices the throat of the man sharing his memory with me.

Drowning in his blood, he watches the girls' clothes being ripped from their bodies.

I took my hand off the man's shoulder, and the vision disappeared, but the feeling of his loss lingered as if it were my own. I reached and grabbed onto another soul, a boy.

—He is standing with a wooden figurine in his hand and a noose around his neck. A man in full body armor checks the rope around his neck. Next to him, a little girl dangles with a snapped neck. He screams, and the wooden plank under him opens. His body bounces once.

I retracted my hand from the boy, and my mind was back in the well of Drained Souls. My hand was shaking. The woman who provided my footing hoisted me up. "Climb," she said. I didn't know what else to do, so I did.

But every soul my hands touched forced me to relive a fragment of their memories.

—There is a grass field, more red than green. He cries out as a spear pierces his heart. The soldier with the spear in hand wears a cracked helmet; a trail of blood drips from where his ear used to be. He shouts, "You brought filth to this holy land. Die for your sins."

"My God will come for you," the man sharing his memory says before his head sank to his chest.

—A woman is looking into a mirror, trying to hide her bruises with her clothes. On the counter is a pregnancy test stick showing a plus sign. She applies powder on her cheekbone, but no amount of makeup will conceal the darkening bruise. The wound on her lip reopens as she cries. She puts on a pair of sunglasses to cover her swollen eye as teardrops cut through the makeup.

—An adolescent girl wearing a blindfold stands in the middle of a dirt road. She trembles in fear as she uses her bound hands to remove the cloth covering her eyes. A large crowd stands before her, twenty yards out, with rocks in their hands. She wails as her lover turns away and disappears behind the crowd. A stone strikes her forehead, turning her tears red. The rocks hail down on her, smashing every square inch of her body.

The images from those I touched were relentless, wrenching my heart without mercy. I stopped. Standing on the heads of two souls, I leaned with my back against the wall of souls. I didn't want to see any more, so I tucked my hands under my armpits. I looked up towards the light. I wasn't even halfway to the top.

Abby—I have to get to her. I can't let her end up here.

I looked at my hands. I didn't want to touch another soul but knew I had no choice but to go up. I lunged to the other side of the well of Drained Souls.

—A girl is running barefoot through a scorched city with a half-burnt doll in her hand. She keeps wiping tears from her eyes as she calls for her daddy. She sees an airplane and screams. A line of bullets rips through her. Left to die, she keeps calling for her daddy who would never come.

—The blue sky turns red in an instant, and the earth shakes. A man is thrown across the street as the houses are blown away like dust in the wind. A mushroom cloud rises in the sky as he gets up. His melted skin flaps against his bones like a flag of surrender. Gasping for air with extreme thirst, he drags his feet through the rubble to his home. He sees his son motionless with flames on his back. Unable to cry or scream, the man heaves and collapses.

—He is among dozens of people—all naked and covering their genitals with their hands. They huddle close in the middle of a chamber, shivering on the cold concrete floor. They hear what sounds like a gas leak, and some start to cough and gag. They erupt in panic and trample over him as they run to the exit. On the floor, he claws at his throat and watches others pound on the door and plead to the guard on the other side. They all begin to roll on the floor, foaming at their mouths.

—A gathering around a smiling couple, their hands bound by white lace—gone with a flash in the sky.

—A girl is getting shoved into a van. She glances back and sees her mother counting money. In the back of the van, she plants her face against the back window and sees her younger sister waving as the van drives away.

My will to go on was waning. I could barely feel my footing. I lunged left and right, hoping I wouldn't fall. Countless tragedies in the hands of man—stories I have read in books and seen on TV. But I was born with a privilege to ignore them—until now. With their memories as vivid as my own, I wanted to curse at Lucifer, but I realized I didn't see his presence in any of them. He was right: we were born into the cycle of suffering already in motion, and we don't know how to stop it.

"Damn you!" I cursed at him with tears in my eyes and my back against the drained souls.

When I opened my eyes, the top edge of the well was within reach with white mist above it. I jumped, and my fingertips found the top surface. I lost my footing and dangled on edge. *Abby!* I got my elbow up on the edge and pulled myself up.

The Path of the Drained Souls was finally behind me, and I was bathed in white light. I sat by the hole, hugging my legs, and wailed. I cringed as the soulless groans from the dark well rang into the tranquil white space around me. I plugged my ears with the palms of my hands, but the cries did not go silent.

I don't know how long I sat there like that, but at some point, a grunt broke the moans from the well, and I opened my eyes. A hand appeared at the rim of the hole, then an elbow. A woman climbed out, and color returned to her ghost-white skin, a spark returning to her eyes. Her singed hair grew, straightened, and shined against her body. The white mist around us swirled and wrapped her pear-shaped body, morphing into a white robe. She slowly lifted her hands to her face and twisted her wrists to examine them like she was seeing herself for the first time. She glanced back at the hole behind her and gasped.

"Is it really over?" she murmured.

"I think so," I said to her.

She covered her mouth with her hands and wept.

I got up and approached her. "What happened to you?"

She wiped her tears and looked past me. "My anger and hatred trapped my soul for longer than it could bear. I want to be alone now."

She walked away from me, and a golden gate with a semi-circle arch top appeared in the mist.

I followed her to the gate, and it opened. On the other side was a man in a white robe sitting at a desk.

"Come in, child." He cocked his head and saw me behind her. "And you, too." He waved me in.

As I followed her through the gate, three doors rose behind his desk.

"Place your hand here," he pushed a thick book with a wood plank cover towards the woman. He waited for her to touch it, and then pulled the book away. He flipped the cover open. "Andrea Watson."

"I don't need my name anymore," she replied.

"Good." He closed the book. "To the base level of Heaven or the pilgrimage?"

"I desire an end to it all, my good angel. Grant me this wish."

"You forfeited that option when you entered Heaven long ago, my child."

"Solace then. The middle of the pilgrimage, a place where I'll feel no passage of time or space."

"Follow me, child." He took her hand in royal style and walked her to the middle door.

The door had a long horizontal slit with the left end having a dial that read zero and the right end a dial with an infinity sign. A wooden sliding mechanism marked with a downward arrow rested next to the left dial. He turned the left dial until it read negative infinity and moved the slider to the middle of the scale.

Is that zero? I squinted my eyes at the idea. *No. $(\infty-\infty)/2$ is undefined.*

"Find eternal peace, my child." He opened the door for her.

"That is not what you offer, my good angel." She walked through the door.

He shut the door and toggled the left dial back to zero. "And you?" he said to me as he walked back to his desk.

"I have—"

"Place your hand on the book." He pushed it toward me, so I did.

He opened it. "Hershel Byne." He skimmed the page with his finger. "How interesting."

"I have this—"

"Scroll. How fortunate that you didn't drop it."

"Yes, I suppose so." I handed it to him. "I need to see God. I need to save my daughter. Last I saw her, she was unconscious."

"Yes, I see that here." He rested his finger at the bottom of the page.

I leaned forward to see what he was pointing at, but the page was blank.

He laughed. "You are not allowed to read it, my child."

"First of all, I'm not your child. And…" I stopped. My sense of urgency had returned and got the best of me. "I'm so very sorry. Can you please tell me if she is okay?"

"That is where the entry ends. The rest is up to you and the gods. But let me give you a piece of advice." He leaned closer. "Lower your expectations."

"What does that mean?"

"You'll see." He closed the book and turned around. "Third door. Come with me."

He rolled the scroll tight and approached the door. It had a circular metal flap where a door knock would be. He pushed the flap to the side and inserted one end of the scroll into the hole.

"Good luck, Mr. Byne."

As the door swallowed the scroll, the frame of the door shone bright—so bright that I covered my eyes. When I reopened them, the simple wooden door had been replaced with a familiar one.

I looked up at the enormous golden door, still locked by a pair of steel swords crossing in the middle and guarded by four fire-breathing dragons at the corners.

Back where I started?

"Yes and no." The angel who inserted the scroll was no longer there, but Lucifer had taken his place.

"It's you." I took a step back.

"Oh, you don't trust me?"

"Is this another trick of yours? I will not be fooled twice."

"Oh, I could if I wanted to." He walked around me and then leaned in. "But I won't try this time."

"There won't be a next time."

"There will always be a next time, my child. Everyone will fall to Hell eventually…again and again, in fact."

"What are you talking about?"

"There's always a chance that a soul will fall from Heaven. Even for an angel like myself." He smiled devilishly. "What do you think the odds of anyone falling from Heaven is in any given second? One in a million? One in a—?" He paused as if he wanted me to give him a number.

One in a billion? One in a googolplex? One in a Graham's number?

Then I realized.

"Eternity…" I said under my breath. Whatever the number I would have said, the result would've been the same when multiplied by infinity: everyone will go to Hell—infinitely many times.

"Eternity is a bitch, isn't it?" He sneered. "But, I will open the door for you this time."

"But this is the same door. You said there was a shortcut to the Gods' Realm through Hell."

"Yes, indeed. Look on the other side."

I walked around to the other side of the free-floating door, and it looked the same as the front.

"This side used to be nothing but a black abyss," he said. "Your journey through Hell now grants you access to this portal."

I completed circling the door and looked at Lucifer.

"It's time," he said. He breathed heavily, inhaling more

than exhaling. With each breath, he grew bigger. I stepped aside to make room for his growth. When his height matched the size of the door, the dragons stopped scorching the swords and looked away. Lucifer grabbed the swords, removed them in a single swoop, and tossed them aside.

"The Realm of Gods." He pulled the double door open, revealing the marble steps behind it. "I wish you all the best in finding what you are looking for, my child."

I looked up at the giant. He looked gentle and kind like the first time I saw him.

"Thank you," I said. "You are letting me go?"

"Letting a couple of souls go from time to time is part of the business. Some call it redemption. I call it recruitment. Keeping hope alive is part of the game."

I stepped into the doorway and looked back at him. "Will *you* be saved someday?" I asked him.

The Angel of Light lifted a corner of his mouth. "Eternity, my child." He gently closed the door behind me.

Realm of Gods

THE MARBLE STAIRS with gold trim led me to a grand hall with many rows of stone columns that pierced the amorphous white mist above. I walked among a series of pedestals that displayed archaeological artifacts from all over the world. After a short stroll, the grand hall branched out into separate rooms: each one seemed to feature various cultures from different time periods in more depth. I set my eyes on the gallery ahead of me, determined not to stray. I didn't stop to hold the fist-sized jewels in my hand, place a star-studded crown on my head, or yank at the Excalibur lodged in stone. I marched on.

I need to get to Abby.

The gallery narrowed into a corridor, and the white mist engulfed me. It felt like I was back on the pilgrimage, except the light at the end was close. I ran toward it, and the passage opened to an amphitheater-sized space that was carved into the side of a mountain. I peered down at the lush green valley from the edge, being careful not to lose my balance. Winding rivers cut through the carpet of green trees that was flanked by an endless ocean on the left and mountains with cascading waterfalls on the right. A flock of birds flew in a V formation, and the patch of forest under them turned bright pink as flowers replaced leaves. The picturesque valley was what I imagined Heaven to be.

"Welcome, Hershel." There was a flutter by my ear.

"Thank you," I said instinctively and turned my head toward the voice.

She was no bigger than the length of my forearm and flew with gentle flaps of the four wings on her back. Her wings weren't the feathery kind typically associated with flying angels or unicorns, but transparent like those of a dragonfly.

"Who are you?"

"A creature of the Realm." Her hair was a soft, gentle green, and she displayed a cartoonish smile with a mesmerizing pair of huge eyes—Tinker Bell came to mind.

"This is the Realm of the gods?" I looked down at the valley below again. It was a magical sight, and a small flying fairy fit quite well with the view. "No rainbow over the waterfall?" I said.

"Light is everywhere, don't you see?" she said as she moved like a hummingbird. "I don't know why people like rainbows so much."

"Why not? They are pretty to look at."

"Yes, but for a rainbow to appear, light must come from behind you and hit the sky where someone else is being rained upon. The beauty comes at the cost of someone else's misery," she said. "I don't know," she added playfully. "Is finding beauty in misery a virtue or a fault of man?"

I thought about it for a second, but I didn't know the answer. Then I remembered why I was there. "Where is God?"

"There are many. Come." She flew to my right, and I followed. She flew up, and I noticed a cliff jutting out of the mountain range. It was so tall that I could not see its summit.

She reached out her tiny hand. "Everyone wants to see them first."

I took her hand between my thumb and my index finger. "I don't have time for a tour. I'm here to—"

"Time, oh time. Time will wait for you." She giggled with her other hand over her mouth.

I looked down and gasped—I was already off the marble floor and quite high in the air.

"Don't worry. I won't let you fall." She turned her gaze to the mountainside.

We flew above the line where vegetation no longer grew. The surface of the mountain was like a quartz crystal, reflective and transparent. Just when I thought we would crash into it, she pulled me straight up. We broke through the clouds and landed on a platform sticking out from the summit of the crystal mountain. Massive stone columns lined the circular edge of the platform. Statues of goddesses stared at us from atop the columns.

"Welcome to Mount Olympus." She let go of me and proceeded to the interior.

Inside the Great Hall, twelve Greek gods sat in a circle. I guessed that the one sitting on the throne was Zeus. I tried to recall the names of the others. *The beautiful woman next to Zeus—Aphrodite? No, Hera was the queen, right?*

"We have a visitor," said the one I was certain to be Zeus.

"You are Zeus. The god of thunder?"

"That is correct."

I sighed in relief. *Aphrodite, Ares, Apollo, Artemis, Athena, a lot of names with A. Hermes, the one with wings, and…* I was stuck. I hoped he wouldn't demand me to name all the others.

"What brings you here?"

"I'm in search of God… my God. I need to save my daughter in the world of the living."

"God? We are all gods here."

"Can you help me save my daughter?"

"We do no such things."

"What is your sect?" said the one with heavy armor and a sword—I assumed it was Ares.

"Sect?"

"Your religion."

"Christianity…I think." I didn't want to offend the god of war.

Zeus pounded on the armrest. "A damn tourist. You"— he pointed at the fairy—"it's you again. You brought him here. We are not an attraction."

She flew close to me. "I'm sorry, Mighty Zeus. But everyone loves you; everyone wants to see you." She pulled her arms together, hands under her chin, and batted her eyes.

He stood up, and I retreated a step.

I looked to the fairy flying next to me and whispered, "What did you get me into?" She was all smiles.

Zeus' voice was loud. "Loves me? We once ruled the minds of the world. Our tales were of great importance, bringing love and peace, breathing courage in men, hopes to those who worshiped. But now we have been reduced to childhood fantasy and scripts for theater."

The fairy flew backward a little, and whispered in my ear, "We should probably get going."

"Unless you came here to worship, to kneel before us…" Electricity sparked all around him and the air thickened.

"My mistake, Mighty Zeus." The fairy yanked my ear and pulled me toward the exit.

"LEAVE." A gust of wind blew as he yelled, and the fairy and I were blown out of the Great Hall and off of the mountain.

I screamed as I went into a free fall, flapping my arms and legs.

"Well, that was fun, wasn't it?" She flew beside me without a shred of concern. "He gets mad sometimes, but I think he secretly likes getting visitors."

She grabbed my jacket at the shoulder and saved me from the free fall. We glided over a cascading waterfall and away from the mountain. She laughed and flew me toward the ocean on the other side of the Realm.

She dropped me, and I landed on my knees on the white sand beach. "I don't have time for this." I got back on my feet and patted the sand off my knees.

"Oh, relax. Besides, you don't know where to go without me, do you?"

"No. But please, take me to him."

"You mean Jesus?"

"Yes. He is the one who can help me, right?"

"I don't know the answer to that, but I can take you to him. Let's see." She looked around to position herself. "Oh, look behind you."

There was a moment of hope as I turned around, but God was not there. It was just a giant clam at the edge of the ocean, waves ebbing around it.

"That is not him."

"I know, but it is THE Giant Clam." She looked more excited than she should've been.

I followed her to the giant clam.

"It comes from somewhere in the South Pacific, I think." She flew in circles over it.

"A tale of a black spider and a snail…" I vaguely recalled a lecture in college, some sort of creation myth.

"Smaller than you thought, isn't it? For the earth and sky to come from it," she said.

"Great. Interesting. But can we go now?" I couldn't contain my frustration.

"You are no fun. Come this way." She flew along the coast.

She didn't stop talking. She pointed to the distant sea and talked about the gods who gave birth to a chain of islands in a literal sense. "Can you imagine pushing those out," she said as she held her stomach.

"That does sound silly."

"And you think your god did a better job?"

I twisted the corner of my mouth.

She went into a rant. "Your guy made day and night without the Sun. Also plants before the Sun, which makes no sense." She wagged her finger. "A man out of clay and a woman out of a rib? A rib! I never understood why people make fun of other religions, but never their own. Personally, I think your god is pretty boring. Is that why you are too?"

The coastline ended, and we ventured into the forest. She was so keen on going off course. She tried to tempt me to take a path that led to the realm of the Hindu gods. I said *no* and kept walking. She threw her hands in the air and started to talk about the epic tale of Kali and Raktabija. It was interesting, but I kept my mouth shut. If she saw any sign of interest from me, she would have persuaded me to go back. "Yes, I'm no fun," I said repeatedly before she had the chance to tell me herself.

We traversed rivers, deserts, mountains, and jungles. We didn't stay long in any one spot, but it was enough to see all kinds of gods. At one point I asked her how many there were, but she didn't know.

There were some absurd looking gods. One was a woman holding open a vulva bigger than her belly, which I assumed to be Sheela-na-gigs. There was also a rooster walking with a pair of snake-like legs, a monkey god, and a man with the body of a winged horse. They each glanced at us but went back to their own business, whatever it was.

I even met the Flying Spaghetti Monster. "I thought you were a parody," I said to him—it?

It swayed its pasta as thick as my arms. "Not after I gained real followers," it said. "My meatballs are the biggest of all, even bigger than those of Zeus," it proclaimed and flew away.

"Are we there yet? I said to the fairy, like a child in the backseat of a car.

"Oh, look. It's Baron Samedi." She veered toward a skeleton guy donning a black tuxedo and a pair of sunglasses.

"Hey, whatcha doin' ma little fairy? And who's this shit you got wi'ju?"

"You are a god?" I said, not even bothered by being called "shit."

"Ya, ma man. I'm a loa of the dead. You wanna smoke? A drink?" He handed me a bottle of dark rum.

I put my hand up to block him from shoving a cigar in my mouth. "I don't smoke."

"Whatever, ma man. You keep the bottle; I've got plenty."

I turned to the little fairy flying next to me. "Really, he's a god? I literally had to go through Hell to get here. What has he done?"

"But he's fun, and you are…you know." She rolled her eyes at me.

Baron took another bottle of rum from the inside of his tuxedo, banged it against the one in my hand. "Cheers." He took a big gulp. The liquor went through his mouth, down along his neckbones, and soaked right through the tuxedo. "Shit, how will I ever get drunk like this? Now you try."

"No, thanks. I'm in a bit of hurry."

He grabbed my shoulders and turned me around. "Nonsense, ma man. You are here for a tour right? See the couple over there? That, ma man, is Osiris, and the woman is his sister turned his wife." He put his arm over my shoulder like a drunk.

"The Egyptian gods? Isis, right?"

"Yep. His brother chopped him into bits, and Isis put him back together. Except, she couldn't find his dick. A goddamn fish ate it. Instead of a man eating a fish stick, a fish ate a man stick." Baron slapped his thigh hard and had a circus laugh. "So get this, she made a golden dick for him. If your erection lasts more than 4,000 years, you should call your doctor."

"Ha, ha, funny," I said sarcastically and pushed him off me. "But I really have to get going."

"Oh, she's right. You're a bore. A buzzkill. Where'ju find this guy?"

"Sorry, Baron. I'm stuck with him until I get him to you know who."

"What, another Jesus fan?" said Baron.

"Maybe there's a reason He has more followers than you," I said in a spiteful way.

"Not the quantity, ma man. Your guy doesn't even know if he's the Father or the Son. Who knocked up Mary, huh? That's some weird shit, man." He chugged the rum, which ran down his pants.

"Good thing you're wearing black, you don't wanna brown yourself," I said.

"Hey, was that your shot at a joke? You know, you should stay awhile. I can loosen your stiff ass up a bit."

I returned the bottle to him and walked away. "Fairy, can you please take me to *my* God? Now?"

"Fine, fine. Sooner you get there, sooner I can meet someone more fun. I'll catch up with you later, Baron." She flew past me and headed toward the mountain in front of us.

At the foot of the mountain was an opening, just big enough for a man to pass.

"Through this cave, you'll reach the realm of Yahweh, Jesus, Allah, or whatever you want to call him."

"So how do I find Jesus?"

"It's a little confusing, but they are all God, one in the same, only different in how the stories are told."

"So how?"

"Just follow the cave to the other side and whoever you find there is who you want to see."

"That's it?"

"Yep. Goodbye, Hershel. I'm going to go find somebody more fun."

A and Ω

AT THE CAVE opening, I let out a big sigh. *This is it. Finally, the One for me, the One for a Christian.* I stepped in, and the torches that lined the passageway lit up one by one. *Jesus, Jesus,* I kept thinking as I walked—I didn't want to end up with Yahweh or Allah.

The passageway opened to a bright courtyard with a circular patio. Birds splashed in the water fountain at the center of the patio and then flew to the fruit trees planted along a hedge. The trees and bushes blocked the view of what lay beyond, but I spotted a break in the hedge on the far side of the fountain where a school of fish swam in circles. There was a cobblestone path that cut through the hedge like an English maze garden, and it stepped down to a field of green grass and wildflowers. The meadow was filled with thousands, if not millions, of souls, all settled into rows like farmland. They wore identical white robes with a sash around their waists and sat on their knees with their hands clasped at their chest. They looked up at the sky, but their eyes were closed. Nobody moved—except one. A man walked between the rows, gently touching the forehead of each man, woman, and child.

"Hello there," I called.

The man glanced up. He adjusted his sash and hoisted his long robe to clear his feet for a faster stride.

When he reached the bottom of the stone steps, he looked up at me. The dark-skinned man with a round face removed the hood covering his short curly hair. There was an aura of lights behind him.

"Hershel Byne," he said.

"I'm looking for—"

"I am He."

"You are Jesus?"

He raised a corner of his mouth. "Yeshua, Iēsous, IESVS," he spoke in different accents, "I am the Alpha and the Omega, only because a Greek wrote about me. If you had written it, I would be the *A* and the *Z*." He came up the steps and looked into my eyes. "You were given the name Hershel. Now imagine people insist on calling you by a different name." He passed me and proceeded through the hedge and toward the fountain. "Jesus Christ," he cursed short.

"Did you just curse your own name?"

"It's not really my name." He pointed one finger up and glanced back at me. "Besides, imagine everyone in the world of the living constantly yelling this name. Jesus this, Jesus that, Jesus Christ for spilling a cup of coffee, and Jesus F-ing Christ for banging their heads. Day in and day out. Billions of times a day, it'll get to you."

"So you are Him? Je— I mean God."

"Why? Do I not look like the pictures painted all over the world?" He turned to me when he reached the fountain.

No, you don't.

"How's this?" His face slimmed and elongated. The pigments in his skin faded, and his hair straightened and grew longer, turning a lighter shade of brown. As he posed with his hands raised a bit, a gentle white glow surrounded him.

Yes, that's him.

"Not a bad looking fella," he said to himself, looking at his reflection in the fountain.

"But you don't like it."

He gave me a stern look that said: "Are you serious?" So I didn't pursue the issue.

"People call me Jesus Christ, but the name is more of an idea than who I am. They celebrate Christmas as if it's my birthday. They wear necklaces with the torture device that ended my life and say 'Pray the Lord.' Would they wear an electric chair or a syringe around their neck if that's what killed me?" He huffed. "Some celebrate my death more than my life, and wait for the Rapture, as they call it."

He sat on the edge of the fountain, and his previous look returned.

"Just as my name evolved, so did what I taught. I preached to help the poor, and now some think it's a good idea to hang them out to dry. Others think that I would vouch for the tools of destruction. Why would I do that?"

I sat on my knees before him. "You once said, 'I did not come to bring peace, but a sword.' You vouched for violence, did you not?"

"I meant it as a metaphor for separation. To divide those who follow me from those who do not."

"But division creates conflict. Wars!" It just came out of my mouth. *Shit, I just attacked God,* I thought, but it was too late.

He laughed. "Interesting one, aren't you. It's not often that I get a visitor like you. Usually, they are just soulless followers, happy to plant themselves in the field. This monotheistic business is a lonely affair. Zeus and his company; Brahma, Shiva, and the rest of the Hindu deities; the Egyptian pantheon...all a bunch of bickering gods, but they have the company of each other. I tried to morph myself into another being, calling myself the Trinity."

"The Father, the Son—"

"And the Holy Spirit. Yes, yes, I know," he said. "A head scratcher isn't it?"

Indeed, I did scratch my head.

"But, in the end, it's still just me. I have no one to play with but myself."

He shifted his gaze toward the cobblestone path that led to the field and became silent. It was a little awkward. Then I remembered I was there for a purpose. I stood up. "I'm here because—"

"I know why you are here."

I forgot He's omniscient. "My daughter Abby, Abigail Byne, is in the world of the living. She needs your help..." I didn't know what to call him, so I added, "My Lord."

He looked at me and raised an eyebrow.

"It's been...I don't know how long. The last time I saw her, she was—"

"Time hasn't lapsed since you last saw her. Relax," said God. "Why don't you join the others down there? It makes my life a lot easier." He pointed in the direction of the worshipers in the field.

Somehow the gentle look on his face eased my anxiety over Abby. "Who are they? How did they get here?" I asked him.

"Mostly from the path of the pilgrimage."

"So they finally achieved their dream."

"I suppose you can say that. Did you ever ask people while you were alive what they thought of Heaven, Hershel? Have them describe it to you?"

"They usually said that it's a peaceful place with no more suffering…where they will be bathed in white light and be with God."

He looked to the cobblestone path and swiped his hands at the hedges; they moved apart like curtains, and I could see the field of believers. "Well, there they are, sitting like a potato plant in a field, having what they thought they wanted. You would think they are happy, but only a select few chose to stay."

"Where do the rest go?"

"They came with the same simple wish…to be with me." He pointed at himself and smiled. "But when they arrive, they quickly realize how boring it is just to sit and hear my words over and over. Most make it a couple of hours, then look around, and think 'Is this it?' After a couple of days, they are itching to be somewhere else. Let me remind you, these are the same people who used to look at a clock or check their phones nowadays while sitting on a church pew.

"Eight thousand seven hundred sixty hours in a year. Tick tock, tick tock. Then they try to imagine sitting there for a decade, a century, a millennium, millions, and billions of years. Little by little, most of them politely ask to return to the base level. Of course, I smile upon them and grant their wish. 'Thank you, my Lord,' they say. 'I wish to come again,' they all say before leaving."

Through the parted hedge, I stared at the rows of people praying, motionless and emotionless. "This is not what I wanted."

"What did you want, Hershel?" He ran his hand through the pool, and ripples moved toward the middle of the fountain.

I watched my reflection in the water as the gentle waves distorted my face. "I...I just wished that I wouldn't die. I wished that I would live to see my daughters get married and hold my grandchildren in my arms. I had no wish for an afterlife."

"Then you should have said no to the angel at the Gate."

"But I wanted to see my family again."

"And when you did, it only brought suffering to your heart, didn't it? Seeing your daughter in danger, standing there helpless."

"That's why I'm here."

"You went through quite a lot to make it here. That I know."

"So I beg you. Please help her."

"It won't change a thing, whether you try to save her or not."

"Of course it will," I raised my voice at God. At God!

"Things are just the way they are, son. It is the curse of mortals to have a sense of free will."

"Are you saying we don't have free will?"

"Maybe you do. Or maybe it's an illusion so good that you believe it to be real."

"I don't understand."

"The ultimate question is whether the world is deterministic or inherently uncertain?"

"Like quantum mechanics?"

"Well, yes," he replied. "You have learned many things since my death." He smiled.

"You know quantum theories?"

"I AM God. I know what you know and more. I simply converse in a language you understand."

"So, do we have free will? You are God, why don't you tell me?"

"I'm the man you call 'God,' but I'm not the creator of this world." He winked. "The universe is made of matter, a collection of particles zipping through space without thoughts or a soul, their motion governed by the laws of nature. Do you remember playhouses where a blower on the floor would move colored balls in its turbulence?"

I nodded. He swirled his hand. The view of the fountain disappeared, and we found ourselves inside of one.

"Each ball is following the laws of nature. If you had a powerful enough computer, you could calculate where each one would be in the next five minutes. But now imagine you are a two-dimensional creature, living on a plane in the middle of this box." The three-dimensional ball pit vanished, leaving only a square plane with no thickness before us.

"Every time a ball passes, you will see a colored circle grow bigger and bigger until it reaches its maximum size, then shrink and disappear. Over and over, you will observe this."

Although I was looking at the colored circles appear and disappear over the two-dimensional plane, I knew that they were the same balls in the three-dimensional playhouse passing through my flat world.

"By counting the occurrence of red, blue, yellow, green, and orange, you could determine the composition of this flat-world. But in order to explain the way in which they appear in your flat-world, you would need to introduce the idea of randomness—a stochastic process that you do not fully understand. You could try to model the behavior of the balls. You might find that you can predict their behaviors with 90% accuracy for 30 seconds and think you understand the world."

"What does all this have to do with free will?"

"A man's free will resides in his brain, which is made of cells, which are made of molecules, which are made of atoms, which are made of what you call elementary particles. Those particles are like the balls in this play box. You still do not understand their true nature. But what if there is a hidden variable that could explain it all? No more randomness, no more uncertainty. Then you'll have a deterministic world, a divine creation set in stone with no free will at all."

"So in theory, we can predict the future. The future is determined."

"Not so fast." The plane with the color circles disappeared, and we were back in front of the fountain again. He raised his finger. "But who's going to calculate it? And how? How fast does a computer have to be in order to calculate the behavior of every particle in a cell, a whole brain, a whole person?"

"That won't be enough. I mean, we interact with things around us, other people."

"Why not calculate every elementary particle in a city then? How about the entire Earth? Solar system? The rest of the cosmos?"

"We may not have to calculate every particle's behavior; we can use approximations." The mathematician in me was doing the talking.

"If you introduce randomness, statistics, or approximation in your calculation, it defeats the purpose of our exercise. So in practice, is there a difference between being unknowable and undetermined?"

He let me contemplate this for a little while.

"The best you can ever do is draw an imaginary boundary and say 'if nothing gets in or out of this box, we can predict with such and such accuracy for some arbitrary length of time.' So I ask you, do you have a true free will or just an illusion of it?"

"But having the thought of free will changes how I feel. I need to save Abby. I have to try."

"It seems there is nothing I can say to change your mind. So do what you must. But remember, if she were to live, does it mean she was always meant to live, or does it mean that your act of free will saved her? And if she were to die, does it mean she was always meant to die, or does it mean that your intervention changed the world in such a way that she died. It seems it is not the outcome that drives you, but how you want to perceive it."

I understood what he said. But this was about Abby, my daughter.

He gave me a quick glance, then stood up and faced the fountain. He raised and lowered his hands. The fountain that had been spewing water receded into the pool, and the surface of the water became perfectly still.

I leaned over and gazed into the pool. I saw an aerial view of a tree with half a car sticking out from under its canopy. I tried to look for Abby, and I felt drawn into it. Through the portal, I was back in the world of the living, diving feet first through the night sky with God beside me. Our bodies went through the tree branches like wind through a screen. Our descent decelerated rapidly, and we gently touched down on the ground.

Abby!

It felt like eons since I left her, but she was still lying there, just as I remembered. The car that smashed into the tree was still venting steam from its cracked radiator. God stood beside her in silence as I checked on Robert in the car. His head was resting on the white airbag, but his fingers on the steering wheel twitched.

I looked back at Abby and screamed, "Abby, GET UP." Robert groaned, and I rushed to her side.

"Do something. Please!" I pleaded to God, whose white robe seemed out of place among the junk of the twenty-first century.

"She will awake," he said—unconcerned.

Kneeling beside Abby, I clenched my hands together and tried to pound on her chest, but my hands went through her body and hit the ground. Her pulse ran up my arm—at least I thought it did. Her jaw dropped halfway, and a puff of warm air escaped from her mouth.

"Wake up."

Her eyes twitched several times and then opened.

I heard the sound of the airbag being collapsed. Abby rose up on her elbows and looked in the direction of the car—right through my body.

"Oh, no. Robert, please stop," she said.

Robert banged his body against the car door, but the

car frame was bent, jamming the door. "Look at my fucking car!" He banged on the door a few more times, the window fogging up with his breath. He shoved the airbag against the steering wheel and moved toward the passenger seat.

She tried to stand up, but in her panic, her foot slid on the wet grass. "Help…Dad." She kept slipping on the slick grass.

"I'm here, Abby. You need to calm down."

She did not respond to my voice; instead, her eyes were fixated on the car that was subtly rocking.

I looked to God, but he did not say a word. Instead, he looked up at the tree.

Directly above the car was a large broken branch teetering on a thin leafless limb in the shifting wind. I left Abby and ran right under it.

If it fell, it would land right on top of the car.

"Make it fall," I said to God. "Please."

"You want me to harm the boy?"

"Yes! No…just stop him."

God stood still.

"If you won't do it, give me the power." I reached out my hand to God as if his divine power would transfer like a lightning bolt between us.

"So you wouldn't put a knife through Robert's eye, but you are willing to crush him with a branch?"

"It's different."

"Is it? In the beginning, taking the life of another was face-to-face, whether it was fist against fist or sword against sword. But then came arrows and guns. They could kill without a pair of eyes looking directly back at them—no faces, just bodies hitting the ground. Killing became even easier with bombs—no bodies, just numbers. Isn't that the real difference?"

But it's my baby girl.

The collapsed dashboard restricted Robert's movement; he banged on it in frustration. He wriggled to get his legs freed and reached for the seat lever of the passenger seat. He managed to lay the seat down.

"Just leave her alone," I shouted at him.

A strong gust of wind swept in and gave the branch a wild push. It teetered like a seesaw. I held my breath and watched, wishing for it to fall.

Robert pulled himself onto the passenger seat, his feet still over the middle.

Come on! My gaze darted between him and the branch. He sat up on the passenger seat and unlocked the door.

A second gust came and sent the branch barreling down at the car. The heavy end of the branch hit the hood first and jolted the entire car. It fell lengthwise on the passenger side of the car, and the roof caved in by a foot.

"Oh my god," I said with God standing beside me.

Abby got up, ran to the car, and gave a quick look inside. She held her hand over her mouth and walked backward a few steps.

"Did I do that?" I looked to God.

"Does it make a difference? Maybe it was meant to fall whether you were here or not."

"But did I? Am I going back to Hell?"

He pointed at the car with his chin.

I dashed over, stepping around Abby to look inside. He was lying flat on his back with the roof of the car just inches above his face.

"Fu-u-ck!" Robert shouted. He noticed Abby outside the car. "Abby, wait. I just want to talk."

Abby shook her head and ran away.

I chased after her.

She passed the gate of the junkyard and stopped. She stuck her hand in the pocket where she always kept her phone.

"Abby, you dropped your phone," I said to her.

She looked around as if she heard my voice.

"The corner of…forty-eighth and two seventy-fifth."

She pivoted on the ball of her foot and ran toward the residential area.

God was standing by the entrance to the junkyard. "Looks like you got your wish, Hershel."

"My wish…" I watched her run. *She is safe,* I thought. Relieved, but I felt empty. *She didn't see me.*

"You always want more," God said. "But we are done here."

I watched Abby run until I couldn't see her anymore.

"You'll see her again."

"Thank you." I reached for his hand and bowed at the same time.

"What makes you think I did anything, son?" He smiled.

White vertical lights streaked around us. We ascended from the world of the living. Through the clouds, the circular pool of God's fountain lay above us. I closed my eyes before hitting the water, and when I re-opened them, we were back in the garden of God.

"You didn't cause the branch to fall?"

"Have you heard of true miracles, Hershel?"

"I've heard there are things that people can't explain."

"There are lots of things that humans can't explain. Are they under the delusion that they know everything?"

"But some appear to be beyond the ordinary," I said.

He sat down at the edge of the fountain, and fish resumed circling in it. He scratched his beard in contemplation for a moment. "Hershel, you were a mathematician, so you know everything has a distribution. What is the height of an average man?"

"I don't know, about five-ten?"

"And what about the standard deviations?"

"About 68% of people fall within one standard deviation, 95% within two standard deviations, and so on."

"By the time you get to five deviations, only one in 1.7 million falls outside," he said. "People exclaim, 'That is extraordinary.' But with billions of people, isn't it expected? You have also heard about a person winning the lottery multiple times. Now what is the chance that the tallest man in your country winning the lottery more than once? Miracles are such things. One unlikely event on top of another, on top of another, makes it seem impossible to occur in your daily lives."

"So what you did for Abby. That wasn't a miracle?"

"I never said I did that, did I?"

"Did I do it?"

"You? You are as common as they come. Did you think you are so special among the billions of people in the world and the billions who lived before you that you could change the world as you wished?"

I felt embarrassed for thinking that even for a split second.

"If everyone who came and pleaded for me to do this or that got their wish, the world of the living would be in chaos. Miracles would be expected and no longer miracles. Look at hospitals around the world. To the people who lived a century ago, what doctors do routinely now would've been considered miracles. But nobody in present time thinks that; it's just how it is. Miracles are holes in the knowledge of man, and the holes are shrinking."

I felt sick, like all hope had been drained from me. *No miracles. I have no power even here in God's realm. I'm sorry, Bella. I can't help your dad. I thought I could, I really did.*

"Isabel was a strong girl. So is her father," said God. "People in dire grief consider lots of things. But you must have faith that her father will do the right thing."

"Faith? You said everything's the way it is and there's nothing we can do about changing the future."

"No, that is not what I said. I said the future is simply unknowable to man. Things you do may or may not make a difference, but you do them anyway. You keep making an effort to do the right thing."

"What's faith then?"

"It is a temporary state of mind, an aid to overcome the weight of uncertainty until things work out for themselves."

"And what if it doesn't work out?"

"You keep the faith that it will work out in the end. It's just that you haven't found the end yet. Faith keeps your life in a positive light. That's the benefit of having faith, nothing more. Why live a life of pessimism? Life is more joyful when you strive to find something good in even the most unfortunate things. The world is so hopeful and perfect under the guise of faith."

I looked into the pool of water where a school of fish swam clockwise. I wished I could peer down at Bella's father. *I'm sorry, Bella.*

"Don't be. Have some faith."

How do you stay in business?

"I heard that." He made a wry smile. "In the eyes of my followers, I can do no wrong. Every good thing that happens gets credited to me, and most bad things are blamed on Satan and the sins of man. Anything else gets put under the umbrella of 'God works in mysterious ways.' How isn't that perfect for me?"

"Was it not your intention to create a more perfect world?"

"More perfect?" he repeated mockingly. "It is either perfect or imperfect, nothing in-between. What is perfect in the absence of imperfection?"

"It could've been better than this. You could've made the world less evil." The moans of the drained souls returned to my thoughts.

"Good and evil are the result of perception, son. If a bear mauls a child to death, you would ask why God would allow such thing. But what is the difference between that and a praying mantis mauling a bee? You feel nothing about the tragic death of the bee, working selflessly for the good of its hive. Do you think the feeble brain of the bee perceives being eaten alive as an act of evil? Does the bee even perceive it as an unfortunate event? The bee may feel pain, but does it feel injustice? Now a mother elephant losing her cub to a poacher feels the heartache of losing her baby, even anger toward the man. But does she contemplate the balance of good and evil like you do?"

"But why—" I raised my voice at God. I paused and calmed myself. "Why did you create a world of eat-or-be-eaten? Kill-or-be-killed? Why not create a world where everything feeds off the rays of the Sun? Instead, you made Adam and Eve…and the talking snake. You built a world destined to fail."

He howled in laughter. "The tales of *Genesis* credit me for Creation, and people like you blame me for the failures of the world. You might ask, 'Why would a perfect being create men with a curved back, a blind spot in their vision, or genitals so close to their anuses?' Humans are quick to admit they don't know anything before God. Yet, they act all knowing about the nature of God."

"Are you implying that you did not create this world?"

"I'm said to have created the world as you know it. But so are many of the gods you met back there." He pointed to the mountain through which I found him. "What was in the universe before *Creation*?"

"Nothing. Emptiness."

"But *we* must have been here to create your world. I'm not nothing, so where did I come from? Where did Zeus and his company come from?"

"You simply existed for all eternity."

"You mean someone as complex and powerful as I could just exist? Without a maker? If you can believe that, then why can you not accept that the universe simply existed for all eternity? There would be no need to imagine my existence. Whoever made me must be an intelligent being. Isn't that the logic of all creations?"

"If there is a creator who made you, who made him?"

"There is always a sensible answer to that sort of thing."

"Lucifer said the same."

"Yes, he did. There is a sensible explanation for that as well."

He stood up and gestured me to get back on my feet. "You have come this far. You should meet the Creator of my world, the Realm of Gods."

The ultimate maker of Heaven and Earth?

"No, just Heaven," he said. He pointed to the sky.

While it seemed bright as day in the garden of God, the sky was dark. Billions of lights twinkled above us.

"Beyond the stars that you can see, billions more shine. Beyond that are billions more. Fly through them and reach the very edge of existence."

"The edge of the universe?"

"There you will find what you seek—the answer to it all."

"How?"

"Believe you can fly. Believe you will find the answer. Have faith."

"Have you seen him?"

"Of course, I have."

All at once, I found myself floating above the white patio that surrounded the fountain. When my waist was just above his face, I looked to him; he was smiling.

"Goodbye, Hershel Byne," he said.

The garden shrunk to a small circle of light under my feet, and as I looked up at the sky, the darkness engulfed me.

Prime Mover

I FLOATED INTO the night sky, and the fabric of spacetime rippled around me as if I traversed through a dimensional barrier. The garden of God was below me no more, and in its place was Earth with the Moon passing on my far left. As a child, I dreamt of being an astronaut just as Abby did, wondering what it would be like to wear a space suit outside the pull of Earth's gravity. The view was just as I imagined—a bright sphere of blue and white in the background of the dark abyss. I felt no sense of zero gravity or the fear of floating into the void.

Under my feet, the North Pole of Earth was covered in the swirl of an aurora. In my fifty years, I never encountered one. Its aqua green hue wasn't accompanied by red or yellow like in a rainbow. I remembered watching a university lecturer on TV who said: "Everyone has *looked* at a rainbow, but not many have *seen* a rainbow"—its true awe comes from knowing that it is created by two refractions and one internal reflection within each and every raindrop. I was *seeing* the aurora below me—charged particles of solar wind slamming into atoms within Earth's atmosphere and stripping off their electrons.

I watched the Moon waned and waxed as I moved away from our planet. I was too young to remember the Apollo missions firsthand but grew up in the lingering enthusiasm of space exploration—when the future looked bright. Our passion for exploration had waned since then, but as I traveled to Mars, I became hopeful that a new age is upon us. New heroes will rise and set their feet on this red planet, and restore our awe for the universe. Back toward the Sun, there was a dot that I assumed to be Venus. Cities in the clouds may be in our future as well.

Next up were the gas giant Jupiter and its many orbiting moons, named after Zeus and his share of lovers. My favorite Jovian moon is Europa, named after a goddess who was abducted by Zeus. With an ocean deeper than that of Earth, I hoped the moon to harbor life under its thick ice. A water geyser erupted just as I flew past it.

I arrived at Saturn with its famous rings made of rocks and ice, named after Cronus, who wanted to eat his baby son Zeus. The average distance of six hundred million kilometers should be far enough to keep the Titan and the god of thunder apart from each other.

I zipped by Uranus, Neptune, and Pluto—the gods of the sky, sea, and underworld— just like the Voyagers and the New Horizon probes did. We still know so little of these icy planets, but they are sure to hold secrets far more interesting than what we know about the bickering gods.

I wasn't even close to getting out of our solar system, let alone reaching the edge of the universe, so I sped up. Breaking through the termination shock, where the solar wind slams against the interstellar medium, I exited the heliopause into interstellar space. I saw a parabolic dish pointed in the Earth's direction. It was Voyager 1, flying at 55,000 kilometers per hour beside me. Launched in 1977, it has endured a lonely journey through our solar system, carrying a message from Earth to anyone or anything that might find it among the specs of dust in the Milky Way galaxy. One of its messages reads, "We are attempting to survive our time so we may live into yours." In three hundred years, it will reach the Oort cloud, and another thirty thousand years to go through it; even then, it will be far from reaching the closest star to the Sun.

I don't have time to be chugging along with Voyager 1. Fifteen kilometers per second was too slow.

I sped up to the speed of light and the flow of time ceased…except when I stopped now and then to look around.

I reached the triple star system of Alpha Centauri, part of a constellation that resembles a mythical creature, which at 4.4 light years away is still our closest neighbor. I remembered looking up at Alpha Centauri as a child in the southern sky, fantasizing about seeing a ball of fire like our sun with Earth-like planets harboring mountains and oceans. But when I finally got to see the star through my first telescope, it was only slightly bigger—still a dot of light with no sign of planets around it. I didn't use my telescope much after that. But now I realize that I merely *looked* at it that day. I didn't *see* the fact that the image was formed by photons, which came into existence through nuclear fusion, bounced around inside the star for a million years before breaking free, made a lonely journey of trillions of kilometers through the vast expanse of the universe, escaped the scattering by the Earth's atmosphere, went through the lens of my telescope, became captured by the photoreceptors at the back of my own very eye, and transformed into a memory that survives to this day—a romance of the cosmos.

Next up was Vega, the fifth brightest star in the Earth's sky, at twenty-five light years out. It reminded me of a novel by Carl Sagan, where aliens made contact through radio signals that were relayed through Vega, inviting us to travel through wormholes to meet them. Supernal sentient beings disguised as humans in order to ease the shock of talking directly to an alien being. I wondered if the Creator would do the same for me.

I can't make small stops like this. I need to get to the edge of the universe.

I resumed my journey, leaving behind the three hundred billion stars of the Milky Way galaxy. As I moved forward, I looked back. The Milky Way's spiral arms that stretched one hundred and fifty thousand light years across were now smaller than my hand. Two and a half million light years later, I encountered another galaxy. Several million light years after that, I found another; but they were just three of a hundred billion galaxies in our known universe.

To the edge.

As I darted across the universe, the galactic lights before me disappeared as their wavelength shifted. Now only the blurry halo of background radiation filled my vision. In the complete silence of this endless expanse of space came a voice that rang softly in my ears. Incomprehensible at first, the pitch became clearer as I slowed. Visible light returned before my eyes. The sight of a space indistinguishable from where I left—stars and galaxies, pinpoints of light against the pure black—filled my view.

"Hershel," a voice called.

"Who's there?" I spun with no sense of direction.

"It is I. The one you seek."

"Where are you?"

"Do you not see me? I'm right in front of you."

I looked left to right and up to down, but I could not see him. I let my sight go, like trying to see an image in one of those Magic Eye 3D pictures. The lights of the stars began to merge. I followed the blurry lines that formed, being mindful not to focus on any one individual star. The lines became an outline of a man, a dark silhouette backlit by the billions of stars and galaxies behind him. I could not see his face clearly, but he was not featureless, just dark. I could see the outline of his nose as he moved his head subtly from right to left, and the outline of his lips rose and fell as he spoke, "Can you can see me now?" He pried his arms off the star-studded canvas.

As I focused on the giant figure, the blurred light of the stars became pinpoint illuminations again, and the fuzzy outline of the Creator became sharp.

"I've been waiting for you." He was larger than the stars, larger than a galaxy; he spanned all the space I could see.

I felt like an insignificant speck of dust floating in the vast emptiness of space before him.

"You are the Creator of the gods? You look like a man."

"You feel at ease seeing me in this form," he replied.

I didn't disagree.

"This is the edge of the universe? It looks the same as

the night sky on Earth." I searched for familiar constellations, like Orion, the Big Dipper, and Cassiopeia.

"Not quite. You are searching for the belt of Orion and the nebula under its sword, but you won't find them here. This is the edge of *your* visible universe if you were to see it from Earth. The small corner of the cosmos that you used to call home is behind you now."

I looked at the same star-studded space behind me. "How can this be the edge of the universe?"

"The universe has no true end. It is only bound by your ability to see. You are always at the center of your limited world."

"And all this time, I tried not to act like I was the center of the universe."

"There is a difference between your universe and *the* universe, Hershel."

"So you are the one who created the universe and the gods."

"No. The very question of *who* created the universe has no meaning. You could ask, 'What is the smell of red?' and waste your whole life trying to make sense of it."

"But you created the gods?"

"Yes. Thousands of them, and a thousand more if you wish."

"So who created you? Are there more of you?"

"Yes, there are many more like me."

He didn't answer my first question, but I asked, "How about Heaven and Hell?"

"Those are my constructs, indeed."

"But not the Earth, the Moon, the Sun, or man?"

"Man repeats questions that are not relevant to what

they need to know. Have you ever wondered why the gods made people in their image?"

"Why not? Because they think they look great?"

"Do you think your dog Lyla thought you looked great?"

Lyla cared about her meals, being walked, and how the butts of other dog smelled.

"No, I don't think she cared how I looked," I replied.

"If she believed in a god, what do you think it would've looked like?" He paused for me to contemplate. "The question is not why people look like the gods, but—"

"Why the gods look like us," I said.

"Precisely. Have you ever wondered why God needs ears when the thoughts of man stream straight into his mind? Why does God need hands when he moves the entire universe with his thoughts? Why does God need feet when he is already everywhere? Why does God need eyes that can only look in one direction when he sees everything there is to see? Does he eat and defecate? Why would he need a mouth and anus then? And why, for heaven's sake, does he need a penis?"

"You look human, too. Is this your true form?"

He didn't answer, and no matter how much I squinted or widened my eyes, I could not make out his face.

"Do you have a name?"

"Yes, I do. Everyone has seen me, but not many realize."

I shook my head at his answer. "What is it?"

"Only the truly enlightened ones know my name."

"I don't know your name."

"Then perhaps, you are not ready for this place." The shoulders of the great silhouette moved up and down as if he was laughing.

"Have you been watching me since the beginning?"

"Yes, your first wobbly step, falling off your bike on the grass hill, meeting Faye for the first time, Abby, Nina, the car crash that sent you here. Bella, James, Duncan, Lucifer, Eleanor, Jesus. All of it."

"Is this part of Heaven?"

"This is the highest level of enlightenment. The answer to all your questions lies right in front of you. There is nothing more."

I stared at the silhouette of the Creator but saw no answers. I had come this far, but I didn't feel enlightened. It was the end of my journey, yet I felt trapped in a lucid dream that refuses to advance its plot. *What if this isn't real?*

"Am I dreaming?" I muttered.

"What if you are? Does this feel real to you?"

It did.

"Sometimes things that aren't real feel more genuine than those that are. To true believers, the distinction has no value. People once believed the location of the stars in the sky governed their lives. They had no doubts in this idea. For millennia, they passed this belief onto their children even though the location of the stars changed as the Earth sailed through the spiral of the Milky Way galaxy."

He spread his arms across the universe. "Look around you. How large is your visible universe?"

Ninety-something billion light years across," I answered.

"At ten raised to the power of twenty-three miles across, it is the biggest thing you know. But,"—he held a finger in front of his chest—"you can imagine something bigger, endlessly bigger. Likewise, the smallest distance that can exist is the Planck's length: ten raised to the power of negative thirty-six, which is a billion-billion-billionth the size of an atom. Yet, your mind can imagine something smaller, even if it cannot exist in the real world."

My mind drew thirty-six zeros, then added a few hundred more after that. It was easy.

"Humans have the gift of imagination," he said. "Think of a purely fictional person."

And I did. *Fred*.

"What is he like?"

I never did well being on the spot, but I tried. "He is a tall guy with a pair of glasses…a generic looking man."

"If you try, you will be able to construct his life story, from his birth to his death from memories of countless people you have ever met, however fragmented or insignificant, all residing in the back of your mind. You can mix them, combine them, and construct one person after another. For every one of them, there is a story; and there are so many souls," he said.

That's what Kristen said.

"The human mind is a peculiar thing. It keeps chugging along, even when there's no need. With every sight, sound, touch, smell, and taste that streams to the brain, it tries to assign meaning. When you hear the vibration of air around you, the mind doesn't assign it a number or an equation; instead, it would say, 'It sounds like a truck crushing a violin.' No matter how ridiculous the assignment is, it tries. What is red plus the number π?"

Cherry pie.

"My point exactly."

"So this place isn't real? This is just my imagination?"

He didn't answer directly. "You live on a small piece of

rock, nothing special from anything else in the universe, except for the fact that you live there. Looking at the horizon as the sun sets, you spot a red dot with your naked eye and dream of walking on its red soil. You find the rings of Saturn, the hydrocarbon lakes of Titan, and the giant storm on Jupiter all fascinating. Even on Earth, just a couple of miles below the surface of your ocean lies a world filled with unknowns. A drop of your blood contains molecular machines that keep on ticking without your knowledge of how they work. You do not know the answer to simple math problems, like 'Are there infinitely many perfect numbers?' The greatest mysteries are still not solved, and you are not even aware of the questions you should be asking. Yet, as death creeps around the corner, your mind cannot let go of the thought of an afterlife. You stop thinking about the things between the Planck's length and the size of your universe. Instead, you focus on things beyond the natural world. I cannot tell you if our encounter here is real, but I have faith that you will figure it out someday."

Faith...the word had a different meaning now. I looked at my hands, as real as I remembered. My feet, too. *If this isn't real, what is?*

"Sometimes, there is value in trying to figure things out on your own, rather than having someone tell you what the answer is," he said.

Leaving the vast expanse of the universe behind him, he stepped closer to me, getting smaller with each step. His silhouette began gaining definition. He reached out his left hand, and I extended my right. He reached out his right hand, and I extended my left. Palms against palms, I faced the Creator.

Who is he?

The shadow cast by the bright starlight robbed my view.

"It is time, Hershel."

"Time for what?"

"Live out the rest of your life. You do not belong here." He gave my palms a gentle push.

I drifted away, spinning in the black space.

Is this the end?

"No. A new beginning," his voice echoed.

The galactic lights behind the Creator pierced through his body, making the outline of his body fuzzy. I covered my eyes with my hands, but the lights were so bright, it was like looking at an x-ray scan. The skin and bones of my fingers began to disintegrate and disperse like grains of sand blown by the wind. The last remnant of my hands and the rest of my body disappeared, and my mind became one with the stream of light. Scenes from my time in Heaven flashed in my mind—God, Lucifer, Colin, Matt, Zoe, Eleanor, Mary, Joshua, Kristen, Connor, Paul, and…Bella.

She lingered, smiling and hugging Tessa in her arms.

"Bye, Mr. Byne," she said. With every wave of her hand, she faded.

I was all alone in the white light again, drifting with no end in sight. The complete absence of sensory references was disorienting; I wasn't even sure if time was ticking forward, backward, or sitting still. My past memories felt like future events: suddenly coming to me as if new, then fleeing from me like photographs tossed into the ocean. I thought about the family picture with tilted horizon hanging on the wall in my house. I fought hard to hold onto that memory, but it disappeared.

I want to go home.

The stream of light started to flicker like pixie dust, and outlines of my body emerged from it. I watched my hands turn opaque as the twinkling stardust coalesced to become part of me. The ubiquitous white light dissipated, and the view of the star-studded universe was restored. The familiar blue planet with its swirling white clouds was underneath my feet.

"Time to go home." I heard the voice of the Creator.

I broke through the clouds and glided over the Pacific Ocean toward the Olympic Mountains of the Pacific Northwest. Against the backdrop of the Cascades to the east, a concrete jungle came into view. I could see individual buildings, even cars, but I wasn't slowing down. My senses returned. I felt my gut ram against my lungs like I was on a rollercoaster. The ground was in sight, and I clenched my sweaty hands tight. My heart skipped, and I shut my eyes.

My back hit something and stopped. Warmth spread along my spin, and I felt a smooth surface under my fingers. Cool air brushed against my face, and I felt the air fill my lungs.

"Hershel?" A hand touched my face.

Born Again

A FAMILIAR KISS on my cheek, warm wet tears smeared on my face…my vision was still blurry, but it was unmistakably Faye.

"Dad."

"Dad."

Abby held my hand, and Nina grabbed my leg through the bed sheet.

The white light above me was no longer the soft, gentle glow of Heaven, but the harsh flicker of fluorescent bulbs from behind a plastic diffuser.

I am back!

Three faces looked at me—the women of my life.

"I thought we lost you," said Faye.

"I'm sorry," I said. My jaw felt sore, but I never felt happier to feel pain.

They cried and laughed. Faye parted her peppered hair and tucked it behind her ear, the sexy pose she always makes to get my attention. Nina squeezed in between Faye and Abby and kissed me on my cheek.

"Abby, are you alright?"

She leaned and kissed me too. A small bandage crossed diagonally over her right temple. "I'm fine, Dad."

It turns out that I flat-lined a couple of times and remained unconscious in intensive care for two days. After I woke up, the doctors kept me at the hospital for a few more days and then let me go. My left leg didn't work so well, but I had no broken bones. I was lucky, considering.

My dear friend Duncan really did die from a heart attack while I was at the hospital. The service was held at Faye's church a few days after I returned home. Clean-shaven and tubes removed, Duncan rested in a casket with flowers all around. Reverend Reed gave a very nice speech. He choked up a couple of times, so did everyone in the room.

I looked up at the ceiling, but I couldn't keep the tears in my eyes. I knew he wasn't there watching me, but I talked to him anyway as if he was.

Reverend Reed stopped me on my way out. "How are you doing, Hershel?"

"My leg bothers me a bit,"—I tapped my left leg—"but fine otherwise. The things you said about Duncan…it was nice. I'm sure he would've appreciated that."

"He's with God now, smiling upon us from a perfect world with eternal happiness."

I left it at that.

"Thanks for the thing you did for me at the hospital. Faye told me about it."

"Of course. Who would I be, if I couldn't do that for you?" His smile was genuine.

"Right." I nodded and smiled back. I reached out my

hand and thanked him again. He was a good man doing what he thought was right.

"So are you going to join us this weekend?"

"I don't know, Reverend."

"After all you have been through?"

I looked over his shoulder. There was a framed painting of Jesus in a white robe, extending his arms to the men below him.

Reverend Reed joined me in looking at the picture. "In his eyes, you weren't ready to part with this world, Hershel."

I stared at Jesus's pale face and long hair.

"I prayed for you. Thank the Lord, you are still here," said the Reverend.

In my thoughts, I thanked Bella.

"I need some time to think, Reverend."

"Of course. Come back when you are ready." He placed his hand on my shoulder.

That was the last time I went to church.

Promise

NEWS OF ISABEL Remming had disappeared from the TV. Around the clock, the news coverage was now on yet another mass shooting in Texas. It seemed like the media had reached a consensus formula on how to cover such events. They knew whom to invite for interviews and analysis. Their words of outcry and manner in which they conveyed despair became refined and polished through unending rounds of practice. I had become desensitized to the cycle of violence on the news as well—the names of victims and killers from several events all jumbled up in my head.

But not Bella.

Her website hadn't been updated for several days now, but still hosted pictures of her life, including the one where she sat on her bed smiling with her chin against the top of Tessa. It wasn't trivial to find where Bella had been laid to rest, but after a day of searching online and making a couple of calls, I succeeded.

I drove through the iron gate of the cemetery with a stuffed animal in the passenger seat—a shabby dog just like

Bella's Tessa. I parked in the gravel lot under the cloudless summer blue sky and asked the caretaker for Bella's location.

I walked across the field with a bottle of water and Tessa in hand, counting rows and searching for obscured markings under the blistering sun. I turned onto the row that matched the number on the small piece of paper in my hand. Her grave was just past a tree and a shrub, a small rectangular stone on the ground. Flowers in small vases that flanked the gravestone were wilted in the bright daylight. Paper cards left on the stone were warped from cycles of morning dew and afternoon sun, and the words written on them had bled.

I filled the vases halfway with water I had brought and wiped the water spots from the stone with my handkerchief. After bundling the desiccated bouquets of flowers that littered the area into a single heap, I straightened the cards as best I could, rearranging them neatly around the stone.

Isabel Mae Remming
2007—2018
An angel who left too soon

Kneeling on the ground, I placed the shabby pooch next to Isabel's name.

Rest in peace, Bella. Thank you.

I heard footsteps stop behind me.

"People have stopped coming here."

I got up and faced him. It was Bella's father.

"It lasted a good three days, but that was it."

"Mr. Remming." I lowered my head slightly. "I'm very sorry for your loss."

"I'm Ned. And you are?"

"Hershel." I reached out and shook his hand.

"What brings you here? Did you know my daughter?"

"Ah, yes. Actually…not really. It's just that—"

"Are you a reporter or something? If you are, I'm done talking to you."

"No, I'm…just a math teacher. I live not too far from here, and…I just felt like I knew her. Her story saddened me, and I wanted to come."

He glanced at the stuffed animal I had placed on her gravestone. "Bella had a dog just like that, except it had a purple ribbon rather than pink. Where did you get it?"

"Oh, just an online store. I don't remember the name. I thought it was cute, so I bought it."

Actually, that was a lie. It took me a while to find it, especially when all the search terms I could come up with were "dog," "stuffed animal," and "brown." I paid good money for it at an online auction site.

"Of all the animals she had on her dresser, that was one of her favorites. I think I bought it for her on Valentine's Day when she was seven or eight." He pinched his nose between the eyes.

"She was such a strong girl," I said. "She saved my life." I muted the last word, but it was too late.

Shit, why did I say that?

He sniffled and looked me in the eyes. "What do you mean?"

I can't tell him that! He'll think I'm a complete nut. Or worse, if he did believe me, I'll end up causing more pain than necessary.

I had to come up with something. I turned toward the gravestone to buy a little more time.

"Recently, I was diagnosed with cancer." After that, words rolled out without a hitch. "I thought this is it, you know. I'm done. It was hard to get off the couch. That's when I heard Bella's story on TV. I believed she hadn't lost the will to survive—to see the next day. I thought if an eleven-year-old girl can be strong, I should be too. So that was the end of my moping."

"I can't go half a minute without thinking about her." Ned covered his eyes and wept.

He looked just as I remembered from the basement.

"It's not fair," I said.

"That monster," he said, "Death is too kind."

"He can't hurt her anymore, Ned."

"I want to dig him out of his grave and feed him to the pigs…after I smash him to bits."

"I know how you feel, Ned, but—"

"I don't think you do." His stare was sharp and threatening.

"You are right. I'm sorry, that was insensitive."

"You know what his father said about that monster of his?"

"Yes, I heard."

"He raised him like that. He knew…and helped him keep my Bella. He deserves to be in the same hole as that piece of shit. I wanna kill that son-of-a-bitch."

"Ned, it won't help Bella."

"How would you know?" He spat out the mucus that had built up in his mouth.

"She'd be sad to see you get into trouble."

"She'd be happy to see him punished. She would be proud to know that I did it for her."

I looked to her grave and the shabby dog. I could picture her holding Tessa tight in her arms and looking back at me. I wondered if I really knew Bella or it was just a dream.

What am I doing here? I thought. But Bella's image inside my head didn't disappear.

"Don't do anything stupid," I said to Ned.

"I've gone stupid." He banged his head with his knuckles. "There is nothing up here anymore."

"What if Bella was here...with you right now. Are you going to take the law into your own hands and risk going to jail for the rest of your life? She'll have to watch you every day until your last, wearing the same prison clothes, eating food off a metal tray. She'll have to watch her brother grow up without his father and her mother scrape by to keep the roof over her head. She doesn't want you to anything stupid, Ned."

He stood there with both hands over his face. I didn't know what else to say, so I just lay my hand on his shoulder. He lost the strength to stand, and sank to the ground. He put his hands on the gravestone.

"I'm...I'm sorry, my princess. I can't do it. Your mom and Nicky...they need me. You'll have to wait a little while to see us again, Bella."

I knew the dog on the gravestone wasn't Tessa and Bella wasn't there watching us from above, but I hoped she would've approved of the outcome.

"Do you think she's in a happy place now?" he asked.

The images of Joshua on his baseball-themed bed and Bella crying in the basement filled my thoughts, but I couldn't answer *no*. If the thought of a reunion—call it faith—could keep him sane until the next day, I couldn't take that away from him. People often say, "She is in a better place," but what would they say if there was no heaven? *Recycling-In-Progress* just doesn't convey the same sense of comfort as *Rest-In-Peace*, even though the former is verifiably true and the latter is purely on faith. Maybe it is a reflection of our emotional response to our language, which had evolved alongside the idea of an afterlife. I wondered if we would invent a new way to communicate our thoughts on this matter someday—but not now.

"No one can ever hurt her again, Ned." That was the best I could say. I added, "For that, I think she's in a better place."

That was the last time I saw him, and the last time I visited Bella's grave. I haven't heard anything about the Remming family since then. I didn't pray for them, but I wished their memory of Bella's tragic death would fade like a decaying math function—never reaching the asymptotic zero, but fainter each day—so that their happy memories of Bella would outlive her tragic death.

Heaven

MY LIFE WAS still hanging in the balance. The weeklong hospital stay after the car crash didn't miraculously fix my cancer. I wished they would have opened me up and took out the tumors when I was unconscious, but apparently, they don't do that sort of thing—legality often trumps efficiency. After talking to a neurosurgeon, we decided to remove the tumor in my head. Mapping out its location from the 3-D scans, the doctor thought it should be a pretty routine procedure.

For my previous surgeries—wisdom teeth removal in college and appendectomy in my thirties—I was under full anesthesia with no recollection of what happened after the doctors told me to count backward from ten. But brain surgery was something else. I was awake the whole time, answering questions as the scalpel, forceps, and god knows what else hit the metal tray behind the blue curtain glued to my forehead. Before the operation, the neurosurgeon said he didn't anticipate any problems. But, of course, tinkering with the brain isn't an exact science; my whole left side was numb for a good six months after the surgery.

My oncologist didn't want to wait for me to fully recover from the surgery before starting chemotherapy. As soon as I was judged to be stable, the sessions began. I was pretty miserable for about three months. As much as I hated the fact that Abby decided to postpone college, I appreciated her being home.

Even though there were days when I didn't feel like doing anything but lie in bed, I wasn't going to dedicate the rest of my life to merely beating this cancer—I wanted to focus on living a life, so I forced myself to get up. A second of this imperfect world was more important to me than the prospect of eternal white. Even being bound to a wheelchair, I asked my girls to take me to the shore of Puget Sound. It was freaking cold as hell to just sit, but I enjoyed the view of the ferries against the backdrop of the mountains and the sound of the freight trains that ran along the coast. I opened a can of beer every night, sometimes only having a couple of sips. It didn't taste good, but it was a reminder to live. In the matter of a month, I looked like I aged ten years. I was on the most effective weight loss program too—and that's not counting the weight of hair that I lost. I counted the days to the end of my treatment and wished for my taste buds to fully return. I wanted to enjoy Faye's lamb chops with a glass of red and eat more than anybody else on taco night.

Being out on medical leave, I had a lot of time on my hands when I wasn't in bed. I got out the old keyboard that Nina used when she took piano lessons at the age of eight. I figured learning to play the piano was something I could do while sitting down. Nina showed me where middle C was, and I spent the better part of a day memorizing the notes to

Mary Had a Little Lamb. The numbness on my left side was still there, but I hoped that someday I'd be able to add the left-hand accompaniment to all the melodies that I'd learn.

A full year after the car accident, I got to send both Abby and Nina to college—two daughters, two colleges. Leaving them in their dorm rooms was a lot harder than I thought. But they were both excited about their five-by-eight-foot cells, which at their age are sanctuaries away from parents. I looked at their hands—the same size as mine, not the baby hands that barely wrapped around my finger. Eighteen years seemed far too short. I didn't want to let go of their hands, but I knew it was their time to leave the nest, and we said our goodbyes. They both promised to come home for the holidays, and they did.

It took Faye and I a month or so to get used to the empty house. We thought of getting a dog but instead decided on traveling. We made it all the way to India and ate nothing but vegetables for a whole week. I found a street just like the one I walked with James and Duncan, except it was like a festival that went on year around. It was visually overwhelming, the city noise deafening, and our nostrils were saturated with every imaginable scent, good and bad.

I got to see Abby and Nina metamorphose from being kids to somehow adult-like in just a couple of years. There were hiccups and emotional bruises along the way, but they made it to graduation. Abby continued onto graduate school, and Nina had a job lined up. Seeing them in their graduation gowns was well worth the misery of chemotherapy.

But, shortly after their graduation, my remission was over—just shy of the magic five. Cancer came back with a vengeance—somehow I always knew it would.

The chance of beating it again was not realistic—ten to fifteen percent, and that was probably on the optimistic side. With the first round of treatment, I sacrificed six months of chemo for four years of good life. But the second round of treatment would've been a lot harsher. I'm all for living, but not like that. I wasn't going to trade several more good, pain-free months for a slim chance of living six extra months in misery.

With death just around the corner, the vision of the eternal white of Heaven and the darkness of Hell returned to my dreams. But when I woke up in sweat, I remembered the words of the Creator: *Stay between the size of the Planck's length and our universe.*

I do not know for absolute certainty whether the things that I experienced were true or mere constructs of my unconscious self. But maybe a conclusion isn't as important as the process of thinking about it on our own. White light allows us to see the world in full color, but the beauty of white light rests on the premise that there are obstructions that absorb and refract some of its essence. What I know for certain is that the moment I awoke from that experience and felt Faye's hand on my face, it was heaven itself. The eye rolling laughs that Abby and Nina make at my unfunny jokes, ice cream that we share on a park bench, huddling together on a couch watching a movie that should have never been made, those little things are what I cherish the most. Heaven is when I close my eyes but know my family will still be there when I open them again.

But the time to leave my heaven was fast approaching. Faye resisted the idea of assisted suicide—death with dignity sounds a little better. I shared a small part of my experience with her, telling it as a dream—nothing about Heaven or Hell, nothing about Bella, and nothing about Abby. I told her about Mary, and about Kristen and Ben. She kept saying, "It's not fair" and "I love you." I knew it wasn't fair, and my love for her goes without saying. In the end, she agreed, and we gathered all the paperwork, a lot of hoops to go through just to have the right to decide how to end my own life.

There was so much I wanted to say to my family, but when I tried to make a list, my pen wouldn't move. I wasted a lot of paper with just a couple of words written on them, but I kept at it.

1

Dear Faye, Abigail, and Nina,

Faye, I know this wasn't part of our grand plan when we got married. I'm sorry that I fell thirty years too short. I have nothing clever to say, but I know in my heart that the last twenty some years we had together were the best years of my life. You are beautiful, smart, and funny. I love you now more than I loved you when we got married—and I was crazy about you then. Gray hair looks good on you by the way. Don't let Abby, Nina, or anybody else tell you different.

You know I was never a believer in finding THE one. How can we? With billions of people in the world, what are the odds? But we found each other, and over the years, we made ourselves the best for each other. I'm sorry for the heartache I will cause upon my departure, but focus on the future. Life is full of surprises, so let it surprise you. My only wish is for you to find happiness again. You will find someone who already knows where a dirty sock should go or how to cut a cucumber without slicing his finger. I know it's hard to think about the future now, but it will get easier. You have my full blessing on whoever comes your way.

Abby and Nina, you were beyond what I could ever have hoped for. I still remember the day each of you were born. You were the most precious, most fragile things that I had ever held in my arms. Looking back at your newborn photos, you did look funny, with your cone-shaped heads and the scant amount of hair. But from the moment you were born and every day since, you continued to be the most beautiful things in my eyes. You both got sick many times, snot coming out of your nose, wheezing. I don't even want to describe what came out the other end. To anyone else, you were the most disgusting creatures that ever roamed the earth. But all you wanted to do was to snuggle, finding comfort in my arms—my insignificant arms. Sleep deprived and miserable, those are still the happiest moments of my life. "You'll be alright," I said as I rocked you for hours in the darkest of the night, imagining the day when you grew up to be something great. I'm so lucky to have you two, and you are lucky to have each other. I had a list of things that I wanted to teach you, but I realized you already know everything you need to know.

I do hope that you will have children of your own someday. Not because it's something people do, but because I want you to experience the joy that you have given to me all these years. There is nothing in life that can compare. You were always my first thought in the morning and my last at night. I love you.

Without the three of you, the world would have meant very little to me. When I leave this place and return to the soil, I will not be able to feel the sadness of never seeing you again. You will have a hole in your heart where I once lived, and I know that's not fair. But a hole is meant to be filled.

Find someone or something to fill it, let it be flooded with joy and laughter.

Embrace the preciousness of every moment you are alive. Don't rely on the camera to record those moments. Burn them into your memory through your own lens. Feel the world through the touch of your own skin. Let the sound of joy echo and linger in your ears—your laughs still do in mine. There is no eternal happiness in this world… or the next. I know that now. I'm truly grateful for the time I had with you. I do not resent the fact that I have to leave a little early. Do I think it sucks? Of course. But I would rather focus on the wonderful years, days, minutes, and seconds I got to spend with each of you.

I'm not going to a magical place, and I will not be watching you from above. Believe me, it's better that way. I have already experienced both heaven and hell while I was alive. Heaven was all the years I had on this earth, and hell is the very thought of leaving you. It is how our lives are constructed, and there's no escape from it. I lost my father as he did his. I lost my mother as she did hers. I know this pain very well, and unfortunately, it is upon you now. But I promise you, it will ease in time, as it did for me.

I'm with you in your memories—that is my home now. As you move on with your lives, you will think less and less of me, and that's okay. Don't feel guilty for the fading memories. But when you are least expecting it, something will remind you of me. You will remember that I loved you more than anything in this world. Knowing that is all I need on my last day on earth.

Love,

It took me fifteen minutes to sign my name after that last comma. My heart ached with every word as I read it over. Death with dignity, knowing the end, turns out not to be as comforting as I had hoped. It's what separates us from the rest. Intelligence comes with a price, and it's my time to pay the debt. But for all the joy that I was privileged to have, it is a small price to pay. I sealed the envelope and wrote "To Faye, Abigail, and Nina" on the front. I tried not to imagine their faces when they read the letter, but I'm only human. My gut wrenched and my strangled heart pushed up into my throat. Faye's name on the envelope bled with a teardrop, but that's how I left it.

Ever since my trip to Heaven and Hell, I dreamt of the Creator every now and then. He didn't talk, and I couldn't see his face. We just pressed our palms together and stared at each other. Last night, the darkness that shrouded his face finally cleared. It was the face I've seen all my life. He was there when I looked at the hole in my gum after losing my first tooth, when I fixed my hair with tingling nerves before my first date, when I tied a bowtie on my wedding day, and every day of my life with a toothbrush in my mouth.

This morning, I combed my hair for the very last time. I played Für Elise with both hands on the piano. It was still a little choppy, but I did alright. Like Lyla on her last day with no desire to eat the juicy steak, I had no appetite. I was due for my last sleep.

I said goodbye to every room in the house; even the small marker lines we couldn't scrub off the walls had stories to tell. I checked the drawer in my desk to make sure the letter was still there. On the shelf above the desk were two books lying side by side. One was the Bible, and the other was Euclid's *Elements*. Both are over two thousand years old and never out of print. One is to be taken solely on faith, and the other is a collection of truths, no matter who reads it. I have faith that one will outlive the other.

The sadness is overwhelming, not for death itself, but knowing that this is the last day to see my family. Life's endless possibilities always count down to one for everyone, but today it is my choice. I hope when I close my eyes for the last time on this imperfect yet beautiful world, it will be the end with nothing more—like the time before I was born. But, if I must see the angel at the Gate again, I need the courage to say *No* to the temptation of eternal white.

Wish me luck.

0

Acknowledgment

First, I thank my wife, Suzanne. She always has the tough job of reading through my first draft. It is hard to imagine completing a book without her help. I also thank Yamini Dalal for reading and commenting on the book. We used to share a bay in a laboratory when I was still working as a scientist, arguing almost daily over anything from the nature of centromeric chromatin to whether her dinosaur joke was funny…or not. We disagreed often, but I always valued her opinions.

The inspiration for the mathematical theme of this book came to me as I watched *Numberphile* on YouTube. If you enjoyed this book, you should definitely check out that channel.

I'd like to thank Suzanne again. Yes, I already did that, but considering she read several versions of this book while still having her full-time job, I can't thank her enough. She makes writing novels possible and worthwhile.

About the Author

T. Furuyama has degrees in genetics and mathematics but left the life in academic research to write stories. He is the author of Vaus Chronicles. He lives in Washington State with his wife and two children.

Note from the author

Thanks so much for reading this book. Reviews from readers like you are what sell books, so if you've had enjoyed this book, please consider rating and reviewing it on Amazon. com. Thank you.

For more, visit:
http://www.tfuruyamabooks.com

More by T. Furuyama:

Terra-transformation of the planet Vaus is nearly complete. Yet, humans choose to live as gods in the space colonies, enslaving Vausians to do the grunt work below. But a fateful encounter between Alethia (human) and Zade (Vausian) sparks hope for Vausian freedom.

Rebels rise against the humans, but General Lander unleashes an army of bioengineered soldiers to obliterate the resistance. Only the legendary sword *Divinity*, constructed by a mysterious man known as the Architect, can lead the Vausians to victory — if it is found in time. Alethia believes Zade is the one to wield it; but born a cripple, he does not share her confidence. Now, Zade must conquer his doubts and claim the sword. But General Lander will stop at nothing until the power of *Divinity* is in his hand.

Humans and Vausians. Peace or annihilation. The Architect's true intent and *Divinity*'s real purpose. The fight for Vausian independence has just begun.